AND DON'T LOOK BACK

ALSO BY REBECCA BARROW

BAD THINGS HAPPEN HERE

AND

DON'T

LOOK

BACK

REBECCA

BARROW

MARGARET K. McELDERRY
OOKS

NEW YORK   LONDON   TORONTO   SYDNEY   NEW DELHI

MARGARET K. McELDERRY BOOKS ◄ An imprint of Simon & Schuster Children's Publishing Division ◄ 1230 Avenue of the Americas, New York, New York 10020 ◄ This book is a work of fiction. Any references to historical events, real people, or real places are used fictitiously. Other names, characters, places, and events are products of the author's imagination, and any resemblance to actual events or places or persons, living or dead, is entirely coincidental. ◄ Text © 2023 by Rebecca Barrow ◄ Jacket illustration © 2023 by Elena Garnu ◄ Jacket design © 2023 by Simon & Schuster, Inc. ◄ All rights reserved, including the right of reproduction in whole or in part in any form. ◄ MARGARET K. McELDERRY BOOKS is a trademark of Simon & Schuster, Inc. ◄ For information about special discounts for bulk purchases, please contact Simon & Schuster Special Sales at 1-866-506-1949 or business@simonandschuster.com. ◄ The Simon & Schuster Speakers Bureau can bring authors to your live event. For more information or to book an event, contact the Simon & Schuster Speakers Bureau at 1-866-248-3049 or visit our website at www.simonspeakers.com. ◄ The text for this book was set in Calluna. ◄ Manufactured in the United States of America ◄ First Edition ◄ 10 9 8 7 6 5 4 3 2 1 ◄ Library of Congress Cataloging-in-Publication Data ◄ Names: Barrow, Rebecca, author. ◄ Title: And don't look back / Rebecca Barrow. ◄ Other titles: And do not look back ◄ Description: First edition. | New York : Margaret K. McElderry Books, 2023. | Audience: Ages 14 up. | Audience: Grades 10-12. | Summary: After her mother's death, teen Harlow pieces together the truth of her family's past and what her mom was hiding from. ◄ Identifiers: LCCN 2023019950 (print) | LCC 2023019951 (ebook) | ISBN 9781665932271 (hardcover) | ISBN 9781665932295 (ebook) ◄ Subjects: CYAC: Secrets—Fiction. | Families—Fiction. | Identity—Fiction. | Mystery and detective stories. | LCGFT: Detective and mystery fiction. | Thrillers (Fiction) | Novels. ◄ Classification: LCC PZ7.1.B3727 An 2023 (print) | LCC PZ7.1.B3727 (ebook) | DDC [Fic]—dc23 ◄ LC record available at https://lccn.loc.gov/2023019950 ◄ LC ebook record available at https://lccn.loc.gov/2023019951

PROLOGUE

She's standing in the silence of the woods, in the milky night with the moon obscured behind dark clouds.

Go back and get your things and leave, *now,* the voice says, words ricocheting around her, whipping up through the air.

And then she hears something break the silence of the night—something real, not in her head, for as much as she can tell the two apart: the snap of wood, as if beneath a foot.

She whips in the direction of the noise, to the west of the house, somewhere within the trees. "Who's out there?" she calls, a yell into the absorbing wall of green. "I'm coming after you. I'm not afraid of you!"

There is no mistaking it then, the sound that follows—definite footsteps, disappearing deep into the woods.

She takes one last look back at the house, full dark.

Then she turns in the direction of the noise and takes off at a run, into the depths.

1

"Meredith. Meredith. *Miss Bloom.* Are we boring you, Miss Bloom?"

Harlow stays slumped over her desk, chin propped up on one hand, eyes glazed.

Somewhere beneath the hum of her brain she registers words, noise, but she doesn't actually hear anything. Not until the girl next to her kicks her worn-down Docs against the leg of the desk and Harlow's hand slips from beneath her, jolting her awake. Only then does she become aware of Mr. Thompson at the front of the class, staring at her expectantly.

"Well, Miss Bloom?"

The girl to her left hides behind her hand and mouths something. *Just say no.*

Harlow reaches to tug at hair that is no longer there. She keeps forgetting about the clippers she took to it almost a month ago now, her soft dark curls falling around her, drifting through the bathroom air like dandelion seeds. "No," she says, like her accomplice told her to. And then, because she has learned that men like Mr. Thompson, with their power trips and overinflated egos, really only want one thing, she makes her voice small and adds, "Sorry, Mr. Thompson."

The teacher raises one eyebrow, a look Harlow imagines he's practiced in the mirror of his studio apartment a thousand times, modeling it with his carefully rumpled shirts and skinny ties. He probably tells women in bars that he teaches high school English and waits for them to sigh. *Teachers are so amazing. You're, like, so important to those kids.* He probably saves the other part for later, when they're all three pretentious cocktails deep: *I teach, but I'm a writer, too. A poet, really.* He probably takes those women home and pretends not to notice their college IDs in their tiny bags.

Up front now Mr. Thompson still watches her like he's so disappointed. "Try to stay awake in my class, Miss Bloom."

Harlow nods, keeps nodding as he goes back to the board, starts running through whatever chapter they were supposed to read this week. It's been a long time since she forgot her name.

She can't do that. She has to remember that here, in this classroom, in this town, in this particular time, she is Meredith Bloom, new girl, quiet girl, inconspicuous girl. She is not Harlow Ford, whoever that really is.

When class ends, she packs up fast, senses the girl with the beat-up Docs hovering. Really Harlow should say thanks, but she doesn't have the energy. She picked out the kids she would target on her first day here, and this girl wasn't one of them. No: Harlow had seen three girls laughing at something on a phone as they sat on the wall by the parking lot, all wearing short skirts in some kind of pastel, but with tights that meant they weren't technically breaking dress code, and decided she could be one of them. It's important, she's learned, to ingratiate yourself with somebody. Give yourself a layer of protection. Most people would think the way to stay unnoticed, out of trouble, would be to keep your head down and not talk to anyone. But people notice a loner way more than they notice a girl who quickly becomes just another body in the halls, another clone.

As soon as the bell rings, Harlow is out and weaving through the crowded hallway, heading in the opposite direction of her math class. Her powder-blue Mary Janes pinch as she takes the stairs toward the drama department, and she shouldn't be skipping class, not really, it goes against her rules, but she also can't have another moment like the one she just had. *I need a minute,* she tells herself as she pushes through the heavy door that marks the shift between the new part of the school building and the old, the air instantly cooler as she turns left toward the music rooms. *Get it together, Meredith, Meredith, Meredith.*

Harlow slips inside the last practice room and turns the lock behind her. All the practice rooms lock from the inside, sealing to keep them as soundproof as possible, to mask the noise of a dozen different instruments being played simultaneously. She crouches to unbuckle her shoes and kicks them off, standing in knee-high socks.

That's the kind of girl Meredith Bloom is. She wears kitschy, shiny shoes, pleated skirts, plastic pieces of fruit as earrings. She waits for her friends—Sam and Elle and June—outside the cafeteria at lunch. She laughs at her friends' stories, takes selfies with them in the mint-green bathrooms, listens to them talk about the boys they want to kiss but don't want to sleep with. She tells them about the boys she wants to kiss, the boyfriend she left behind at her old school in her old town. Meredith Bloom is definitely not a lesbian. Meredith Bloom is not on the run. Meredith Bloom is a nice, normal girl, with a nice, normal family, a mom and a dad who goes on a lot of business trips and an older sister away at college.

Harlow smiles to herself. Nice, normal girl. Nice, normal life.

As fucking if.

She sits at the piano, pressing her socked feet on the pedals. She took lessons once, for three months when she was eleven. The lessons had to stop, though, like everything Harlow does stops, comes to an abrupt end when it's time to run again.

Harlow plays fragments of the elementary pieces she learned back then, all that she can remember, and picks out the melodies of songs by sad girl singers who she likes to listen to when she falls asleep. She should be learning about parabolas right now, but this slow, aimless exploration is way more soothing than the drone of yet another teacher's voice.

By the time the period ends and she has put her Mary Janes back on, Harlow is more awake, the dust of a chain of sleepless nights falling off her. When the bell rings, Meredith Bloom heads to the cafeteria to resume her life.

"Mom?"

Harlow closes the door to their latest apartment behind her, listening for movement. Habit.

Her mom appears out of the bathroom, wrapped in a towel,

her dark curls hanging loose and heavy with water. "Hi. How was school?"

"Boring. Fine. Whatever." Harlow drops her bag by the door and crosses into what they call the living room but is really just the half of the apartment where the kitchen isn't. This isn't one of the worse places they've lived, but it's far from Harlow's favorite, with its gray walls and faded rose-print carpet in the bedroom. The landlord didn't ask for references, though, and accepts the rent in cash, which is all her mom really looks for.

Harlow throws herself onto the couch and closes her eyes. "What's for dinner?"

"Hold on," her mom says, her voice fading as Harlow hears her walking. She pictures her mom back in the bathroom, raking leave-in conditioner through her hair, and then moving into the smaller bedroom, picking out her favorite Friday-bar-shift outfit, sitting down at the tiny vanity to paint on smudged black eyeliner and three coats of mascara and scarlet lipstick. Cora Ford doesn't have to change the way Harlow does, to fit in every new place. She finds a bar, a pub, a grimy club, and shows off how running the bar is nothing to her, how she can pour a perfect measure without looking and handle belligerent drunks without sacrificing her tip, and that's it. Here in—where are they now? *Oh yeah,* Harlow thinks, *Madigan*—she's assistant manager at a club that has fading grunge bands almost every night, where her silver jewelry and nose ring make her look like everybody else.

By the time Harlow hears her mom's footsteps come near, she's almost asleep. Only almost, though, and she opens her eyes to see her mom looking down at her. "Hi."

"You look tired," her mom says.

"I am tired," Harlow says. "I feel sick."

"Sick like what?" Her mom perches on the arm of the sofa. "Like you might throw up or like your bones ache?"

"I have a headache," Harlow says, aware of the whiny tone of her voice. "And my throat hurts."

Her mom lays a cool hand across Harlow's forehead, a rare move. "Hmm," she says. "You don't feel warm. But maybe we should order pizza just in case. There's ice cream in the freezer already. Mint chocolate chip," she says before Harlow can even ask, laughing. "Would that fix you?"

"Maybe," Harlow says, and sinks deeper into the couch cushions. Pizza and ice cream might be, like, *the* most basic comfort food choices, but it's what her mom always gets for her when she says she feels sick.

She closes her eyes, and maybe it's because she's so tired, exhausted really, or maybe it's the feel of her mom's hand on her head, but she lets herself ask a question she wouldn't usually dare. "What did your mom do for you when you got sick?"

Then her mom's hand is no longer on her, and Harlow opens her eyes in time to see her mom jump up from the couch and move toward the door. "Actually, I really need to get going," she says, making a show of checking her phone. "How about I leave you the money and you can order the pizza yourself?"

She grabs her bag and takes her wallet out, digging out enough bills for Harlow to pay and tossing them on the table. "I'll be back later," she says without looking at Harlow. "Make sure you lock the door. And save me a slice, okay?"

Then she's gone, the door slamming behind her before Harlow can even process what just happened.

Harlow stays frozen, lying there on the couch, her cheeks burning with the embarrassment of thinking she could ask a question like that and get any kind of answer. *Stupid, stupid, stupid,* she thinks. She should know—no, she *does* know better than that. What did she think, that just because her mom put her hand on her forehead that meant she had suddenly become an entirely different person? That suddenly the parts of her mom that she keeps hidden, the pieces of her that Harlow can't—has never been able to—reach would be right there for her to take?

"Stupid," she says aloud this time, the word small in the emptiness of the apartment. There has always been this divide. Up on the surface her mom can be good—the kind who takes their kid's temperature and makes sure there's always the specific kind of ice cream they like in the freezer, just in case. But it's what's beneath that haunts Harlow. The way that Harlow doesn't know what it is they're running from, because her mom refuses to tell her, so Harlow long ago stopped asking. The way her mom shies away from Harlow's touch, has never liked to be hugged or hold Harlow's hand and jumps about a thousand feet if she's surprised by a squeeze of her arm or something. How sometimes her mom can be sweet—a hand on the forehead, despite her discomfort— but sometimes she's so far away, retreating to her bedroom, talking to herself in whispers that stop as soon as Harlow enters the room. Retreating as soon as Harlow asks a question she doesn't want to touch.

Like she was ever going to answer.

Harlow sits up and orders the pizza anyway, because even if the moment is gone, she's still starving. She waits for it to arrive, shoving the bills her mom left into the delivery guy's hand, and then leaves the box on the table while she goes to her room. In there she strips out of Meredith Bloom and back to herself, scrubbing off her makeup and putting on black boxers and a black sweatshirt that used to belong to her mom, with some band Harlow doesn't know on the front. She takes a Diet Coke and a Gatorade from the fridge, puts them on the low coffee table next to the food, and pulls the big forest-green blanket off the couch. Then she wraps herself up, sits on the floor, and eats a weed gummy she got in their last town as she puts on her favorite doctors-fucking-and-crying show. When the edible hits and the pizza is still warm and she feels relaxed for the first time since they got here, Harlow thinks she might actually cry.

But she doesn't, only eats enough pizza until her teeth hurt from chewing and bats texts back and forth with Sam-Elle-June and even remembers to put the remains of the pizza on a plate for her mom, in the microwave with a note on the door that says *I'm the best daughter ever, I know* in her messy writing.

Then, mind blurry, Harlow crawls into bed and plummets into deep sleep.

2

"Harlow. *Harlow.* Come on, wake up."

One minute she is deep in a dream about headless carousel horses, and then Harlow snaps violently awake, clawing at the sheets as her heart thrums like a hummingbird. "What the fuck—"

Eyes gleam in the dark, and Harlow throws herself backward before she puts the face and the voice together, before she understands it's her mom shaking her awake. "It's okay," Cora says, but the urgency in her voice tells Harlow it is anything but okay. "Come on. We have to go."

"Go?" *Go.* Harlow wipes the back of her hand across her mouth, her lips dry and sticky, the inside of her mouth sour. Oh. Go.

There isn't time for her to think. There never is. It doesn't matter: they've done this so many times now that Harlow is an expert at packing without thinking too much.

"Ten minutes," her mom says, still in the dark, and disappears down the hall.

Harlow slips out of bed, her feet landing soft on the old carpet, adrenaline pushing her to start moving and put on real clothes and begin packing her familiar black duffel bag. She has no idea what time it is, only that it must still be night because the light around the curtains is that Mars-dust shade of black sky and orange streetlights, and she can't hear anything coming from the apartment on the other side of her bedroom wall.

She is used to this, so practiced in quickly dismantling what passes for a life. She collects everything important—birth control, old busted-but-usable laptop, the photo of her five-year-old self held in her mom's arms, the last time she can remember being held—without even having to think about it. Throws it in the bag and piles her clothes on top, leaving behind the parts of her Meredith costume that she knows she'll never wear again—those painful blue Mary Janes, the white tights. Goes to the bathroom and tosses in her makeup bag, her period cup, her toothbrush.

In seven minutes Harlow is standing by the door, ready to go, leather backpack over her shoulder and duffel bag gripped with both hands. She watches as her mom finishes a final sweep of the apartment, ensuring no identifying fragments remain. They don't own much beyond their clothes and a few personal things each. It is easy for them to do this. That's the entire point, the thing around which they frame their entire lives. They must be able to pick up and leave at a moment's notice, and they must not leave anything of themselves behind.

Her phone buzzes in her back pocket, and Harlow takes it out like a reflex, like she's forgetting for a second that there are more important things happening than whatever Sam-Elle-June is texting her at three a.m. But they don't usually text at three a.m., and Harlow opens the message to see it's a link to a local news site, and beneath it June has sent a string of comments:

oh my god jack was there
he just called me
he said they barely made it out without getting caught ha
omg can u imagine?
his dad would have locked him up for the next year
and then how would i get those coachella tickets???

Eight minutes.

Harlow clicks the link. It takes her to a bare-bones story about a disturbance at a local club, a fight of some kind, police on scene. There's a picture to go with it, a slightly blurry image clearly taken by a bystander, a raft of police vehicles with their lights on outside the club, a club that Harlow knows. The club where her mom works.

Cora picks up the keys and pulls the one for the apartment off the ring. "Ready?"

Harlow looks at her mom, still dressed in what she wore to work. Her makeup a little more smudged than before, her hair a little wilder. The questions hover on the tip of her tongue: *What exactly happened, Mom? Was it the cops being there that scared you? Was it somebody in the club? What did you see, hear, remember in the time since you left the apartment and now that scared you so much? Who is it that we're running from?*

But Harlow stopped asking years ago. She never got an answer, not one that made sense, not one that felt like the truth. The truth is somewhere deep down, hidden in the abyss that Harlow can't reach. All her mom would ever say was *I'm doing this to keep us safe. If we stop moving, we'll be found. I can't let that happen.*

Nine minutes, and her mom is looking at her expectantly. "Ready, kid?" she says again, and this time Harlow answers.

"Yeah," she says. "Let's go."

They pack their bags into the trunk of their old dark car, both shivering in the night cold. The car doors sound loud, but it's okay: once they are in they are gone, rolling out of the parking lot, leaving the sleeping apartment complex behind as they head out onto the road.

3

Harlow watches the town she barely knows roll past the window as she tucks herself down into her wool-lined denim jacket, the heater barely kicking in. Despite the adrenaline and the rush, the nervous energy she can feel radiating off her mom, these are the moments Harlow feels most at home in. When it is just her and her mom in the car, wherever they've been in the rearview mirror, whoever they've been fading away like a half-remembered dream. This is the only life she knows, a life spent in perpetual motion since before she can even remember. Always outrunning something. Someone.

"You want music?"

Harlow glances over at her mom behind the wheel, her fingers drumming like always. "Sure," Harlow says. "But no Cure."

"You used to love the Cure," Cora says with a shake of her head. "When you were tiny. Sometimes it was the only thing to put you to sleep. Getting into *Disintegration* is, like, a rite, you know? I still remember when someone first played it for me when I was your age, how I got *chills* right away."

Harlow stays quiet, waiting for her mom to continue, to tell Harlow all about whoever it was who played her an album from the eighties when she was in high school. Was it a friend, a lover? Were they in Cora's teen bedroom, where the walls were painted green or white or navy blue, where she had pages ripped out of *Vogue* or reproduction van Gogh prints or a hundred overexposed instant camera pictures stuck on her walls? After the album was done, did she talk about her deepest secrets, her biggest fears, where she wanted to go to college?

But her mom says nothing more, only fiddles with the stereo until crackly jazz comes out of the speakers, and Harlow wonders why she ever thinks things are going to change. Again—this has been her life since before she can remember. Always the two of them, and nobody else. And always the threat following them. Someone—something?—on their heels who poses great danger if they catch up to them. That is really as much as Harlow has ever gotten from her mom. When she was little, it didn't register as strange to her; it was just a fact of life, a thing she thought everybody else experienced too, to the point where when in second grade a girl named Olive said her family was moving, Harlow said, "Oh no, did the chaser catch you?" And then she learned that other kids moved because their parents got new jobs, or to be closer to family. Not because some monster was after them.

It was only then that she started asking questions, and started learning that there were things she wasn't allowed to know. It was only then that she started wondering about their life—no family to speak of, no history beyond the ones they would build and dismantle every time they started fresh. And it has only been in the last couple of years that she has stopped asking, tired of never getting any kind of truth.

Well. No, that's not quite it. If pressed, Harlow might admit that the reason she stopped asking is because there is a part of her that no longer even wonders. A part of her grows bigger every day that thinks—*hush, say it quietly*—that they're running from nothing. No one. That the only thing snapping at their heels is her mom's paranoia. Take tonight: it would be simple enough to infer from tonight's events that it's the cops her mom fears, that she once did something and never got caught and so now they run. Right? But that doesn't explain the other times they've taken off. Once there was an argument in the apartment next door; the couple who lived there screamed at each other until the door slammed and they heard footsteps walking away, and then a minute later there came a knock at their door, and five minutes later Harlow watched as her mom held ice to the woman's bleeding eye socket. They left town that night, the next-door woman left with a fake number that Harlow's mom told her to call any-time. Another time they left because the neighbors were *too* quiet, her mom said. *Makes me nervous.* And another time, Harlow came home from school with a letter about an overnight field trip, and before she could tell her mom she didn't even want to go, their belongings were packed into the trunk of the car and they were on the road. It doesn't take much to trigger her mom's defense mechanism. It doesn't make much sense, what causes them to have to run.

This is what hurts, Harlow thinks, curling toward the door. This is the part of her mom that makes Harlow want to scream—and sometimes she does, face pressed hard into a pillow at another new apartment, sweatshirt mashed into her mouth as they change clothes in a gas station bathroom as the sound comes out of her, stripping her throat raw. Sure, her mom buys her small, pretty things, is always there at breakfast—but what about *anything* fucking *else? Like, what about a stable fucking life, Mom? What about a world in which we're not always escaping some ghost that I'm not even sure exists? What about me knowing where I come from, who made me, who made you, us? What if you would tell me anything real and I could quiet the voice in the back of my head that says you have no idea what you're doing, that you're not keeping us safe at all?*

She hears her mom fiddling with the heat, the *click-click-click* of the dial. "Try to sleep," her mom says. "I'll wake you up when we get to—"

And then the truck smashes into them.

4

Harlow's head snaps into the door, and there is no sound but the screeching grind of metal on metal, the splintering of glass, so loud Harlow can't think. They're still in motion but going the wrong way, sliding sideways across the intersection instead of forward, and it's as if they've become unstuck from time and space, glitching.

It lasts for a minute or an hour, Harlow can't tell, and then suddenly there is silence. Or near silence: a faint hiss of steam from the crumpled hood of their car, the occasional noise of still-falling glass like the wind chime that swung on the balcony of an old apartment.

There is a second before Harlow feels back in her body, and then the searing pain in her head kicks in, and there's a dull ache across her torso as if her ribs might snap if she breathes too hard.

"Mom?" It comes out too quiet. Or is it the ringing in her ears that is too loud, drowning everything else out? "Mom. Mom, talk to me."

No response comes, and Harlow tries to turn but she is pinned close to the door by something.

Harlow looks around as much as she can: the window is shattered, and she can see the torn-up front end of the car out of the corner of her eye. She flexes her fingers, her toes, relieved to feel her feet are not trapped, that she can move her legs freely. They are flat on the road, at least: didn't roll, aren't hanging upside down facing a drop. For a moment Harlow wonders what she's supposed to do: Sit and wait for someone to come, for the truck driver to get out of their cab and help them? "Shit," she says. "The truck driver."

A cough. "Shitty truck driver." Her mom's voice is soft, shocked, but Harlow could cry.

"Mom," she says again, half a breath away from a sob. "Mom, I'm going to try to get out. Are you okay?"

"I'm okay," Cora says. "Are you okay?"

Harlow struggles with the door handle and thinks for a second that she might be stuck for real, but then it pops and the door swings open. "I hit my head," she says. "My ribs hurt."

"Seat belt," her mom says shortly, and Harlow realizes she's right, that it's the seat belt still tight around her that is responsible for that tender feeling across her chest. Something to be thankful for, really.

She undoes the belt and eases out of the car, until she is standing in the middle of the night road so quiet that she again feels like she has glitched out of existence, passed into some alternate dimension where there are no people anywhere for miles. Then she turns, finally, and all the breath goes out of her as she surveys the aftermath of the accident.

There is the truck, towering above their small car, lights still beaming bright. There is their car, smoldering in the center of the intersection. And there is no way, Harlow realizes as she stares at the concertina remains of the car, at the exploded driver's side that was so clearly the impact point, that took the entire force of the eighteen-wheeler—there is no way that her mom is okay.

"*Mom!*"

She ignores any pain as she runs to the other side of the car, squeezing into the gap between the truck and where her mom is. "Mom, I'm here, I—"

Harlow freezes. Her mom is pinned in too small a space. There is a violent gash across her forehead, and a bright red bloom on her cheek, and a thin line of blood running from her mouth. Her skin is pale, her eyes closed, chest rising and falling too rapidly. But it is the shaft of twisted, snarled metal disappearing into her chest that is the worst.

Somewhere in the distance sirens sound.

"Oh my god." Harlow sinks to her knees, reaching through the mess of broken glass and metal to lay her hands on her mom, just to feel her still breathing, heart still beating. "Oh my god, Mom— I'm here. It's going to be okay. Mom? Can you hear me?"

Her mom's eyes flicker open. "I didn't see it," she says. "It came out of nowhere. I didn't think . . ."

Her lips keep moving but her voice is a whisper, and Harlow leans as close as she can, catching the murmur of her mom's words but unable to decipher them. "Don't try to talk," Harlow says. "Hold on, okay? I think an ambulance is coming. Or I'll call—" She pats herself down, trying to remember if she shoved her phone in her bag or in her back pocket. "Shit. It's all right, it's all right, I can still hear the ambulance—"

Her mom shakes her head, the movement making the wound on her head flex and gape, torn skin and muscle gleaming wet and red under the truck's headlights. "No," she says, the word half a gasp, urgency making her voice loud again. "No ambulance. No one."

"You're hurt, Mom. You need help."

"Can't help me," her mom says, her gaze drifting down to the metal erupting so incongruously from her body. "But I—I can help you."

Harlow's fingers clutch at her mom's shoulder. "*They* can help *you*," she says, even though she knows it's not true. It's not only the injuries that Harlow can see: What about her bones, broken by the initial hit? What about her organs, crushed by the weight of the semi and probably bleeding now, slowly filling up her mom's insides with blood?

Look at her face, Harlow thinks. So pale, all the warmth leached out of her brown skin. Her eyes focus, unfocus, roam around with no aim.

The knowledge comes without warning.

Without pause.

She is dying.

Harlow feels it sure as anything, a cold fact rolling around her head. But she also feels how important it is not to acknowledge that. Harlow can't acknowledge it, because then that would mean her mom is dying and she will be alone and that is not a future she can accept happening. "They'll help you," she says again, and is the siren getting louder or fading away? "Hold on."

"Listen," her mom says, and it is evident in every word how hard she is struggling for breath. "There's a safety-deposit box. In the bank. North Langston. Not far from here. Go there. It's in my name but you. You're on it too. The key—in my bag."

"What?" Harlow says. "Why do you have—"

"Just go," her mom rasps. "It has. Everything you need. You have to go now. Listen to me. *Go.* Keep running. Don't ever stop. And don't look back. Just go." Her eyes search for Harlow's and lock on, the desperation easy to read. "Tell me. What are you going to do?"

"Mom—"

"*Tell me.*"

Harlow swallows. "Go to North Langston. Open the safety-deposit box. Keep running, and don't stop."

"Good." Her mom closes her eyes, her chest sinking.

Her breath rattles. Harlow can hear the liquid in it, as if her mom is drowning from the inside out. She hears sirens for certain now, getting closer, except this time it scares her rather than reassures. Her mom scared her, the urgency in those clipped, breathless words. *Keep running. Don't ever stop. And don't look back.*

Her mom's eyes stay closed, each breath a challenge, and then she moves, only a little, a pained noise as she lifts the hand closest to Harlow and holds it there.

It takes a second for Harlow to understand. To see that her mom is reaching out, her fingers stretching and searching for Harlow's.

She swallows as she takes her mom's hand and laces their fingers together. Her mom's skin is cold, sticky with blood, but Harlow leans in and presses her cheek against their joined hands.

It's been so long. She's thought about it, before, when the last time she held her mom's hand was, because she often thinks that if she had known it was going to be the last time, her little-kid self would have held on forever.

And now here they are and Harlow is going to have to let go, she knows, and this is going to be it, the real last time.

She holds on tight as the sirens grow nearer, a quick flash forward of the options in front of her. One: stay here until the ambulance arrives, and maybe they'll be able to keep her mom alive, maybe they'll be able to come through this to the other side together, except that will mean hospitals and surgeries and insurance, and that means people will have to know their real names, that they'll be registered in so many systems, and all those years drifting beneath the surface will be for shit.

But then there is option two: do as her mom says and run. Disappear from here while she still can, and get whatever is in that safety-deposit box, and find a new place to become yet another new girl. Running from something she's not sure she even believes in.

Her mom exhales, a sudden rush of air, and then she does not breathe in again.

Harlow shakes their joined hands. "Mom. Mom, come on, please—"

She slaps her other hand over her mouth, holding an anguished sob in. In front of her, Cora Ford lies still, bloodied and bruised and most of all so quiet.

Harlow does not have time to feel this moment, to register that her mom just died in front of her, that what began as an escape earlier tonight turned into an end as soon as the eighteen-wheeler had them in its sights.

Salt tears slip down her cheeks as Harlow brings her mom's hand to her lips and kisses her knuckles, desperate, over and over until she knows she has to stop. She unlaces their fingers, lays her mom's hand carefully onto her damaged chest. Then she is up on her feet as if on autopilot, doing the only thing she's ever known how to do.

The crunch of glass beneath her boots barely registers as she rounds the car, praying that the trunk will open. It's not as bent as the front of the car, and when she presses, it springs halfway open—all she needs, room enough for Harlow to reach in and tug her bag free. She is about to turn to leave when she thinks better, twists back and reaches inside again, tugging her mom's duffel free this time. With the bags weighing her down, she breaks into the best run she can and crosses the intersection, trips up onto the curb and toward the building closest to her.

Harlow slips into the shadowed alley right in time as two ambulances and an accompanying fire truck come screaming to the spot where the vehicles still smolder. Where her dead mother waits.

She allows herself to watch for a minute as the EMTs and firefighters swarm the scene, as they wrench open the door to the truck's cab, as they pull out medical instruments and heavy equipment like any of it is going to help.

Before it is too late, before someone spots her, Harlow picks up the bags again and, with quiet, careful footsteps, she vanishes into the night.

BEFORE

The night is thick with ice rain, fog swirling eddies in the air, and it is just like that night two years ago, before everything changed.

That's all Cora can think about as she leans out the car window, shimmying as much of her upper body out as she can before Ruby reaches over and grabs at her shirt, a handful of material to keep her anchored. "Jesus, do you have a death wish?" Ruby says, but she's laughing, her other hand on the steering wheel keeping them locked in a fishtail spin.

They can do what they want out here; there's no one around to care, not this late, not on these streets of another abandoned half-built housing complex on the outskirts of town. Ruby knows all the best places, where they can scream at the top of their lungs and light firecrackers and, like tonight, drive way too fast. Cora, on the other hand, knows almost nothing. But that isn't her fault. She has to remind herself of that so often. Not her fault that she doesn't have a history in town like Ruby does, like all Ruby's friends do. Not her fault that she's still learning what it is to be reckless like this.

Cora closes her eyes and smiles as wind rushes over her body, the rain stinging as it smacks her skin. "Faster," she calls, the word almost snatched right out of her mouth. Always wants more, faster, farther, *yes.*

Yes, she said on that first day a few months ago, when Ruby asked, "Hey, you need a ride?" And Cora had noticed her before in their GED class, Ruby the only one there with a bleached-blond ponytail and black lipstick. Cora had noticed her from her seat at the very back and wondered who this girl was, and then this same girl had appeared in front of her where Cora was waiting at the bus stop, and so she said yes.

She says yes to whatever Ruby asks. *Do you want to hear my favorite album? Do you want to go skinny-dipping? Do you want to kiss me, Cora?*

"Faster!" Cora says again, a yell this time, and then a giddy howl of delight as Ruby gives her what she wants and Cora's whole body vibrates with the speed of the car, the metal frame cutting into the soft flesh of her back.

She has to get it all out tonight, in preparation for tomorrow, the part she has to play. Two years exactly, and she's still good at the act.

They drive through the empty streets, past skeleton buildings, homes that hang suspended like maybe one day a beating heart will move in and bring them to life. *Or maybe they'll rot forever,* Cora thinks.

When she can't bear the cold anymore, she slides back inside the car, rolls the window up tight, and puts the heat on full blast. "Will you teach me?" Cora says, a sudden inspiration.

"Teach you what?"

"To drive stick. I feel like it's the kind of shit I should know, you know?"

Ruby's black-painted lips curl into a smile. "Sure. Why not."

Cora drums on the dash before leaning back, chill rainwater snaking down inside her shirt. She's never sure if Ruby knows about her, about what happened, that other Kennedy curse, but Cora figures she must. Neither of them have ever brought it up, though, and that's the way Cora wants it to stay. It's better if they don't poison what they have with all of that. She likes to keep things separate: there is home, and what happened, and who she is. And then there is Ruby, and the eighties goth music she likes, and the way she always smiles when she is finished kissing Cora.

If Cora had it her way they'd never go home, but that's not how the world works; she's learned that lesson the hard way several times over. So when Ruby clicks her tongue against her teeth and says, "Shit, I'm almost out of gas," Cora knows that means time's up.

Cora has Ruby stop at the usual place, right on the side of the winding road that cuts through the woods, a snake-slick scar through the trees. The first time, Ruby raised her plucked-skinny eyebrows and said, "Are you for real?"

There's a turn not much farther along, and then another, onto a worn track. It would be easy enough for Cora to show Ruby where to go, because follow that track all the way and it ends deep in the woods, at Cora's front door. But she can't let Ruby follow that path. Ruby belongs out here, away from all of that.

Cora steps out of the car, dragging her jacket behind her. "Later," she says to Ruby.

"That's it?" Ruby says. "That's all the goodbye I get?"

She laughs as Cora gets back in the car and leans over to kiss her, a move that still makes Cora nervous. When they separate, Ruby laughs again. "Lipstick," she says, and reaches out to run her thumb across Cora's chin. But Cora ducks her touch and slides back out of the car, using the sleeve of her jacket to wipe at her face instead. "Good night," she says, pretending not to notice the small hurt look on Ruby's face, and turns toward the trees.

She knows Ruby is still there, waiting, the headlights throwing Cora's shadow long and lean. But eventually the lights dip and disappear, leaving Cora in the ink-black night.

She slips her jacket, cracked fake leather and once-white wool, over her shoulders.

Then Cora makes her way into the forest.

5

Harlow enters the first open-all-night place she sees, a too-bright diner where the few other people inside look exactly as exhausted as she feels. She spends an hour or two there, drinking coffee black and bitter enough to keep her awake.

She tries not to think of her mom left behind.

She keeps on drinking coffee until she's the only person in the place and starts to feel like the white guy with a wispy mustache behind the counter is paying too close attention to her. That's when she goes into the small bathroom and looks at her own damage for the first time.

No wonder he was staring. There's an angry red bloom on her forehead that will soon become bruised, Harlow knows. When she lifts her shirt, she can see the impression the seat belt left in her skin. She has a couple scrapes on her arms, and her neck is stiff and sore, but other than that, she is fine.

Harlow drops her shirt, meeting her black-eyed gaze in the

mirror. Still not used to her short hair, but shockingly used to the speed at which everything is going. A few hours ago she had a mother. Now she doesn't. It feels both real and not, and maybe if she were the kind of person to stay still, she would feel the wave of grief rush over her, knock her down and drag her out to the open ocean of loss.

But she is already putting the feelings away, shoving them into the box inside her chest where everything else lives—the questions she can't get answered, the half memories she clings on to, all of it. She pushes the memory of her mom's blank face into it and locks the box tight shut. No room for that. Don't think about it, *don't think about her face, don't think about holding her hand, don't think about her voice—*

Her whispered words that come back, Harlow's brain suddenly knowing what the end of her mom's unfinished sentence was: *It came out of nowhere. I didn't think this is how we would get caught.*

Harlow watches herself have the realization that her mom's most immediate thought was that the accident was *not* an accident. That the force chasing them was behind it, that she thought they had been found, caught, finally.

But it can't be, Harlow thinks. Her mom was hurt, scared, not thinking straight. What better time for the paranoia to kick in, full effect? *It doesn't even make sense,* Harlow thinks. *Not logically. Who would do that? Better question—why?*

She splashes icy water on her face and scrubs it off with rough paper towels. Then Harlow leans in and rests her forehead against the mirror, wincing as her still-forming bruise presses against the glass. "You are in shock," she says, watching her reflection's mouth move, distorted from this angle. "You might even have a concussion, you stupid bitch. Come on. Time to make a plan."

She's never had to make a plan on her own before. She's not even sure why she ran from the scene of the accident other than her mom told her to. That's all she knows how to do—run, like her mom taught her. Hide, like her mom taught her.

Harlow's mind flicks back to the road, the second before the hit, the coldness after. And as much as she has grown to not believe that anyone is looking for them—standing here in the bathroom of a diner, washing her mom's blood from her hands, while blocks away paramedics are loading her mom's body into an ambulance with no lights, she can't help but let a little of her mom's fear find its way back inside. Because as much as she doesn't believe, it's also all she's ever known. And if there is any small, so small, chance that her mom was right and it wasn't an accident, then Harlow isn't safe.

If she isn't safe here, and her mom told her to run, and all Harlow knows how to do is exactly that, then—

Running it is.

She takes as deep a breath as her ribs will allow. North Langston, her mom said. Harlow has not been to North Langston and does not even recognize the name. Her mom never mentioned it before tonight, and Harlow has to wonder what made her pick that place, what it was about some nearby town that she deemed important enough to leave whatever she left there. *Or maybe this isn't new,* Harlow thinks as she crouches to rifle through her bag, finally finding her phone in the inside pocket she slipped it in. *Maybe she does this in every place.*

Yes: that is something Harlow can see her mom doing. In every new place they arrived, finding somewhere close enough to feel in reach, but not so close that it might be obvious, to place her important things. *Everything you need,* she told Harlow. She can imagine her mom driving out in the daytime while Harlow was at school becoming Kristen or Nora or Jill, walking into the bank and arranging it all, and then driving back to be home in time for Harlow to return without knowing anything had happened. Speeding there whenever she decided it was time to run, if she had the time, so she could collect whatever it was she'd hidden, or maybe even returning once they'd already fled. *Who the fuck knows?* Harlow thinks, and isn't that always the question?

She looks up the town and sees it is not that far, maybe a couple of hours by car, slower by the bus she'll have to take. According to the schedule, the first bus is still five hours away. "Shit," Harlow says, and stands. She pulls up her maps and traces the route from the diner to the bus station, then puts her jacket on and lifts the bags.

As she leaves the bathroom and walks through the diner, she has the burning sensation of someone's eyes on her. At the door she pauses and looks back, expecting to see the reedy kid with the mustache watching her go. But he is not there: there is no one at the counter, no one seated slumped over a tuna melt, nobody else at all.

Harlow steps outside and tries to tell herself that now *she* is the one paranoid. Nobody is watching. Nobody at all.

After waiting out the night on an unforgiving bench at the bus station, and then a slow bus ride made slower by construction, Harlow steps off the bus into North Langston.

The morning is cold and wet, winter making itself known. Two weeks ago Harlow stared out the window as snow clouds gathered, the colored lights on their tiny Christmas tree flashing. Now the snow is gone, and Harlow blows on her hands as she takes in her first impression of the town.

(She kept her eyes closed the entire ride in, her whole body held rigid, pulse racing as she couldn't stop her body's ingrained reaction to being back in a moving vehicle, recalling the last time.) It looks like the town she just left, or as much as she can tell from the station and the slice of small office buildings and car dealerships that she can see from it.

She uses the little charge left on her phone to look up the nearest and cheapest hotel, finding a Days Inn only a few blocks away. There's a convenience store on the way where Harlow buys a bottle of water and a SIM card with a generous data plan. She drops her old SIM card in the trash can outside the store—how many times did she watch her mom execute this same dance?—and heads to the hotel. It's easy enough to get a room, with Harlow willing to pay a little extra so she can check in immediately. She looked up the bank while she was on the bus, but she can't go there looking like she does.

When she gets to her room on the third floor, she puts her bag and her mom's bag at the foot of the bed. Turns the TV on and finds some old sitcom for background noise, as if that will make her feel less alone. She strips out of her clothes and steps into the shower, where the lukewarm water rinses the small flakes of dried blood that she missed in the diner earlier off her arms, spiraling down the drain.

When she's done, she wraps the scratchy hotel towel around her body and sits on the edge of the bed. She only means to stay there for a few minutes, but the curtains make the room so dark and her head is so sore and the bed so much more comfortable than the bus station bench that before she knows it, she's asleep.

When Harlow comes to, she's sprawled across the bed, half-covered in a tangle of towel and sheets. The laughter from the TV slices through her headache and she winces. "Fuck," she says under her breath. "What time is it?"

Her phone—at least she'd managed to plug her charger in before she passed out—says four, and Harlow scrambles out of the bed. She imagines the texts from Sam-Elle-June that would probably be flooding her phone if she hadn't ditched the old number, the ones asking why Meredith isn't in school, why Meredith won't respond, if Meredith is okay. Soon they won't be asking if she's okay, Harlow knows, but who the fuck she really is, and where the hell she's gone. It doesn't matter; they don't matter anymore. What matters right now is that the bank closes in an hour.

She pulls black jeans and a plain black sweatshirt from her bag and dresses in a rush. Then she kneels, her hands resting on her mom's bag, fingers toying at the zip. She needs to open it, to search through the contents in order to find the key that she needs to gain access to the safety-deposit box, but she also knows if she opens it she'll see all her mom's clothes and be hit with their smell, the citrus perfume her mom always wore saturating the fibers, and then she might start sobbing and never stop.

Beneath her fingers it almost feels as if the bag has a heartbeat of its own, blood thumping under her hands.

Harlow snatches her hands back and takes a breath. She does not have time for this. *Keep the box of emotions closed. Open the bag, find the key, and go.*

She rips the zip back before she can think about it too much more and begins pulling out everything her mom packed. It makes sense that she would put it somewhere safe, an inner pocket or maybe in one of the little bags her mom always kept her silver rings inside.

Harlow feels the pressure building in her chest as she searches and then, at the bottom of the bag, a small white envelope with something solid inside. Harlow opens it and pulls a key out, curling her fingers closed around it.

Then she gets to her feet without looking back at the mess in front of her, the pressure inside so tight now she feels like her chest could burst open at the slightest touch.

"It's okay," she tells herself. "It's okay, you're okay, it's all going to be okay."

She'll go to the bank and get what she needs, whatever her mom put in there that will help her stay in motion, the only way Harlow knows how to be, and then she'll be out of this hotel and this town.

She checks her reflection before she leaves. The spot where her head hit the car door is tender, and a redness radiates outward from it, the flush ending halfway across her eyelid. She tries to arrange her hair to cover it as much as she can, wishing as she pulls the longer soft curls left on top across her forehead that she hadn't been quite so brutal with the clippers and shears. When it's as hidden as it can ever be, Harlow pulls on her jacket and boots and throws her phone into her leather backpack, where her wallet and real ID already are. *Not too bad,* she thinks, turning in the mirror, pushing her sleeves up. *I don't look like I just got in a car wreck. I look like a normal girl coming to the bank to do normal things. Absolutely no reason to be concerned.*

"Be normal," Harlow says to her reflection, and then: "Jesus Christ, I have got to stop talking to myself."

Downstairs at the front desk she gets a number for a local cab company and waits outside for the car. When it arrives, she slips in with only a small nod to the driver and closes her eyes like she had on the bus as the car takes her downtown to the bank. Soon the car stops, and she steps out onto a small thoroughfare lined with a mixture of chain clothing stores, cheap restaurants, and coffee shops. The bank looks out of place, an obvious fake aged facade slapped onto a new building.

Harlow leans back through the cab window and hands cash to the driver, straightening as the cab takes off. It's been less than twenty-four hours, and she's already itchy, uncomfortable with the amount of public transportation she's had to use. It goes against everything her mom ever taught her—trains are acceptable, if in a big enough place, if it's easy to slip on and off along with a crush of other passengers and hopping from platform to platform won't get you noticed. Buses less so—there's more chance of the vehicle being stopped and you not being able to get off, being trapped in place as the threat makes its way down the aisle to you. Cabs are an *absolute* no, unless *absolutely* necessary:

it's only you and the driver, them knowing exactly where it is you wanted to go, so easy for them to let slip to someone who wants to know after. They've always had a car, something that belonged only to them so they could go wherever they wanted, whenever. Her mom taught Harlow to drive when she was twelve. She remembers the nervous energy when she put her hands on the wheel for the first time, her feet straining to reach the pedals.

I could have been driving last night, she thinks. *I could have been the one behind the wheel, and then the truck would have smashed into me, not her, and then she'd still be alive and I'd be dead, sure, but Mom would still be alive, she'd still be alive—*

Harlow takes a deep, shuddering breath and then exhales slowly, trying to calm herself. Don't think about that. Can't think about that.

Keep moving. Keep running. Don't stop. Don't ever look back.

She slides her shoulders back and down, standing tall, and strides into the bank.

6

It's quietly busy inside the bank. Not a lot of people, but the steady hum of their chatter with the tellers and the whir of the heat and the general electric buzz of the place are enough to fill the space.

Harlow waits for the person ahead of her to finish counting out their quarters, as if they think the bank has shortchanged them. When they're satisfied and walk away jingling a handful of coins, Harlow moves to the counter and smiles. "Hi," she says. "I'd like to access my safety-deposit box."

Clean, quick, confident. That's what Harlow knows will work. Don't let the teller or anyone else hear any kind of inflection in the statement—and make sure it's a statement, not a request, that her voice didn't go up at the end to make her sound as nervous as she actually is: *I'd like to access my safety-deposit box?* Let there be no question—it is *hers* to see, and it is their job to allow her in there.

The woman behind the counter—twenty-two, maybe twenty-three, Harlow guesses—has red hair with dark roots, blush that sparkles coral against her white skin, lash extensions long and delicate. She's the kind of pretty Harlow covets. When she was younger Harlow thought she wanted that pretty for herself, to be able to glow like girls who looked that way did. She'd paint her lips pink while her mom was at work and roll her skirts higher the way she saw high school girls in every town do. Then she figured out she didn't want to look like those girls; she wanted *them,* to kiss and hold and touch. But she doesn't, can't. It never feels safe, because how can she trust herself not to whisper her secrets into a pretty girl's ear as soon as she looked at Harlow with the kind of pretty doe eyes they always have?

So Harlow does nothing. Just watches and remembers and files hands brushing in the hall or borrowed lip gloss in the bathrooms or lingering eye contact over coffee cups away in a closed-off part of her mind.

When the redhead smiles, Harlow realizes she's been staring and goes warm all over. "No problem," the redhead—Nasrin, her name tag reads—says. "What was the name?"

This, Harlow knows, is where she might lose it. She has no idea what name her mom would have given, which of her IDs she might have pulled out to show whoever at the bank had been the one to see her. If Harlow gives the wrong name, though, it's all over.

She licks her lips quickly. There's only one option really. Her mom said Harlow's name was on it. She didn't say anything about an alias. And maybe this is something so important that her mom was willing to break all their usual rules. Maybe she needed this to be connected to their real identities. In case anything ever happened.

"Harlow Ford," she says to the teller, and god, it's been so long since those words have come out of her mouth. Her fingertips prickle and she shifts her weight, the toes of her boots so worn she can feel the floor through them. "Actually, it should be under my mom's name. Cora Ford. But she said it's set up so I can access it, too."

"Oh yeah," Nasrin says, her neat, nude nails flying over the keys. "That should be fine, as long as you . . ." She frowns, her arched eyebrows pulling together and her nose wrinkling.

Harlow holds her breath. *Fuck.*

In a second she tries to calculate how much trouble a person can get in for trying to access a box with the wrong name, and if it'll call more attention to her if she stays and attempts to play this off as a silly little mistake, or if she makes a run for it right now.

But then Nasrin's face clears, and she looks up at Harlow, bright smile back in place. "As long as you have your key," she says. "And some ID."

Harlow's entire body goes loose, and she swings her bag off one shoulder. "Yeah," she says. "Of course."

After Nasrin gives Harlow's ID the most cursory of glances, she beckons her back behind the counter and leads her through a short corridor into a room filled with identical boxes. The teller finds the right box—number 307—and slots the master key into the lock. Then she turns to Harlow. "I'll leave you to it," she says. "But I'll be right out front if you need anything. Oh, and we close in twenty-five minutes, in case you weren't aware."

"Thank you," Harlow says, and then Nasrin is gone, and Harlow is alone in the room.

She palms the small key and waits for a minute before she slides it into the lock. Imagines her mom coming here and locking something precious away, things that Harlow would need if she was gone. Her mom thought about the reality of Harlow being on her own, made sure to prepare in case of the worst.

Harlow wipes roughly at her eyes and opens the box.

The first thing Harlow pulls out is a thick wad of cash.

She presses her tongue against the back of her teeth, turning the rubber-band-tied bundle over and back again. "Holy shit," she breathes. At her most conservative guess, she's holding at least five grand. It could be a lot more, though. A lot more.

Harlow can't help the slight curl of her lips as she places the cash on the table in the center of the room and pulls out the next item: another bundle tied with rubber bands, but not money this time. Instead it's shiny, credit-card-size things that Harlow turns over, to see her face staring up. She snaps the bands off and shuffles through them: seven replicas of her looking out, with different names on each one. A selection of new versions of herself, ready to be used in whichever place the money will help get her to.

"Like a fucking Boy Scout," Harlow says to the empty room. Always—albeit illegally—prepared.

She reaches inside again and brings out something bigger. It's a sheaf of documents, and Harlow scans the front page quickly, taking in what sounds like a law firm name. A will, and behind that, life insurance papers.

She tosses all of it onto the table and it's this, finally, that breaks her, putting an end to the bravado and adrenaline she's been running on since last night.

In the quiet of that closed room Harlow bursts into panicked, dizzying sobs, sliding down the wall of locked boxes until she's on the floor. She grinds the heels of her hands into her eyes and hears herself coughing, the heave of her chest sending piercing pain through her bruised ribs.

You're gone, she thinks. *You're gone and I'm alone and you knew that this might happen one day, you knew it so much that you made plans for me. Plans for what I would do without you.*

And Harlow can't push down the anger it brings out in her, even when she shouldn't be *angry,* how can she be angry at her mom in a moment like this? But she is. For doing all of this, for going to such extremes to keep them agile, always ready to run, always prepared for the worst—but never telling Harlow what the worst actually was. If it even existed—exists—at all. And she's angry at herself, too, for going along with her mom's plan despite the not knowing, because that's what she does, isn't it? She follows the route her mom leads. She's here because her mom told her to come. Wherever she goes next, she'll be going there because it's what her mom wants her to do.

Wanted.

She stays on the floor until her tears subside, until she can breathe in a regular in-and-out fashion again. Then she gets to her feet and looks at the survival kit her mom left for her here. The things she's left for her in every place they've ever been, Harlow knows.

Keep running. Don't look back.

The clock on the wall says there are only ten minutes until the bank closes. Harlow wipes her face again and starts to make a plan. She'll put this stuff in her bag, go back to the hotel, and get a real night of sleep, or as much as she can. In the morning she'll use some of the cash to buy herself a car, and then she'll be gone. Exactly like her mom wanted. Like she taught Harlow to do.

Harlow picks up the life insurance papers to fold them into her bag, but a page falls loose, fluttering back to the table. She sighs and reaches for it. Then stops. Looks closer.

"What?" Harlow leans over, scanning the page. The language is different, the subject—Harlow's lips move as she scans the document. "Wait," she breathes. "What?"

It's not a loose page from the life insurance, but something entirely different. Something that seems like, as best as Harlow can tell, the deed to a house. The name on the deed: Cora Kennedy.

Cora *Kennedy*?

Harlow touches her fingers to the name. Their last name is Ford. That's the name that they never give, their real, government name—the one her mom gave to get this safety-deposit box. Harlow has never heard her mom use the name Kennedy for anything.

And a house? For all of Harlow's life, they've lived in rentals, mostly apartments, and her mom has never—*had* never—mentioned anything about a house that she owned.

Harlow looks back at the open safety-deposit box. She thought she'd taken everything out, but perhaps—

She turns her phone's flashlight on and shines it into the box. It illuminates something else, tucked right at the very back of the box, and Harlow reaches in. She struggles to get a grip on it; it feels as if something is caught, whatever it is slipping between the joints of the metal box. Harlow digs her teeth into her lip and yanks and something tears as the hidden thing comes free in her hands.

Harlow turns over another rubber-banded bundle, but it's not money or IDs this time. No: it's something wrapped in newspaper, and Harlow is about to peel the paper off when a rapping on the door makes her jump.

"You doing okay in there?" The teller's voice carries through the door. "We're going to be closing in five minutes, so if you want to wrap up . . ."

"I'm almost done," Harlow calls back, and then waits for the sound of the teller's heels to fade.

Her fingers fumble at the paper, rushing now. Inside the wrapping is a stack of photos, a postcard laid on top of them. Harlow takes in the faded image printed on the card, the letters coming into focus: *Visit Crescent Ridge!* in gently curving font, over a watercolor painting of a town-hall-like building surrounded by lush foliage. She flips the postcard over and finds the other side is covered in black ink far less faded than the front: tiny drawings of flowers and leaves and slivers of moons. Where the address should be, there is a black lipstick print.

She can't make sense of it at all, but the photos are easier. Harlow recognizes her mom in the first one instantly—she's never seen her mom as a teenager, but it's unmistakably her in the cut-offs and bikini top, head thrown back in joy, a lake behind her.

Harlow wants to linger on this, touch her thumb to her mom's image in front of her, but the clock says she has four minutes until closing and so she flips to the next photo. It's her mom again, the same outfit, same setting, except this time she isn't alone. There are two other girls with her—one taller and curvier, a short white dress clinging to her body, and one smaller and younger-looking, a chain of small purple flowers adorning her hair. They are all different, but they are also all so alike: black curls and coils, light brown skin gleaming under the sun, matching wide smiles.

They look like—

Sisters.

Harlow glances at the clock. Three minutes.

She doesn't have time to process this, or to look through the rest of the photos. Instead she slides them back into a neat pile with the postcard on top again and picks up the sheet of newspaper they were wrapped in, meaning to cover them again before she slips them into her bag along with everything else.

But as she folds the paper over the photos, her eyes catch on a slice of the print: . . . *missing for two years now. Eve's three daughters remain hopeful . . .*

Harlow's breath stalls in her chest as she unfolds the paper again and smooths it out on the table so she can see the entire spread. So she can see the headline:

WHERE IS EVE KENNEDY?

Beneath, a photo of a white woman, her eyes dark and piercing even in faded newsprint, long light hair spilling over her shoulder.

Eve Kennedy. *And Cora Kennedy,* Harlow thinks, her mind already racing.

But another knock on the door, sharper this time, cuts her off. "Hello," the voice comes. "We're—"

"I know, I know," Harlow says, and she shoves everything from the safety-deposit box into her own bag. She locks the box and opens the door, revealing Nasrin still smiling pleasantly on the other side, the twitch in her cheek muscles barely noticeable. "Sorry. Thank you for all your help."

"Oh, no problem at all," Nasrin says, and she gestures to the front. "Would you like me to—"

Before she can finish, Harlow is past her, heading toward the exit, with her new possessions burning a hole in her bag.

7

Back in her hotel room, Harlow locks the door and pulls the curtains tightly shut. In the dim light of the small table lamp, she sits on the bed, pulls out the contents of the safety-deposit box and lays it all out in front of her.

The money. The life insurance papers. The will. The IDs.

And the deed to the house. The postcard. The photographs. The newspaper article about the disappearance of a woman named Eve Kennedy.

Harlow reaches for a curl to pull on, the old nervous tic she hasn't managed to shake yet. All of this was important. Important enough to her mom to move with them from place to place, and to go somewhere in each new town to find a safe spot to keep it securely hidden.

The cash, insurance, IDs—those all make sense to Harlow. They were a safety net for her, things her mom made sure would be there if she ever wasn't, so that Harlow would have some kind of cushion and way to keep on living. That's what her mom had said, using her shallow, pained breaths to get the words out: *It has everything you need. Keep running.*

But the rest of it—

Harlow rubs her hands together, trying to get some warmth into her cold fingers. Her mom kept these things because they were important to her. The question Harlow has—okay, one question of so many—is whether she ever meant for Harlow to see them. She had to have known, in her last moments as she told Harlow where to go, that opening up the box would mean opening up these secrets to her daughter.

Because that's what they are, Harlow knows. Her mom's secrets. Three girls in the photos, the missing woman, the house—things her mom kept to herself for years.

Things Harlow has to understand, now.

Her stomach growls, but Harlow ignores her hunger as she reaches for the article first.

It's brief, not a front-page piece or anything; more likely buried farther back, relegated to running alongside the report on a new pizza place opening and the number of potholes repaired by the county.

Two Years Gone: Where Is Eve Kennedy?

Police are once again appealing for information in the continuing disappearance of local woman Eve Kennedy. After last being seen buying groceries, Ms. Kennedy has been missing for two years now. Eve's three daughters remain hopeful that their mother will return home alive and well. They, along with the police, hope that new information may come to light that will both shine a light on the reasons behind her disappearance and enable them to locate her and bring her home. If you have any information, call or email the Crescent Ridge Police Department."

"'Crescent Ridge,'" Harlow reads aloud. Yes, the words on the postcard, but also—

She reaches for the deed to the mystery house. There it is, on the address line: Severn House, Crescent Ridge, Washington. This must have been their house, their home. Where Eve lived with her three daughters.

She picks up that photo from before, the three girls posing in front of the lake. Eve Kennedy and her three daughters. Cora Kennedy's name on the deed. It's both obvious and not, if only because Harlow can't quite believe that in one strange day she has gone from knowing nothing about her mom's past to discovering that she didn't spring from the earth or some secondary plane fully formed, as Harlow sometimes bitterly joked, but that she had a mother, after all. A mother, and sisters. A mother who had gone missing.

My grandmother, Harlow realizes suddenly, and there's an itch of resentment beneath that realization. *My aunts.* A family, like she has always wondered about. A family that her mother has denied her.

Harlow leans off the side of the bed and pulls her laptop from her duffel bag. She opens it up and connects to the hotel Wi-Fi before typing Eve's name and the town into the search bar, then hits enter. She's not sure what exactly she expects to find, but she is disappointed when the results load. It looks as if all that's really out there are a handful of articles from the same paper, ranging from twenty years ago to the last one she can see, posted around eight years ago. There's a singular reddit thread with only three comments, and she finds Eve's name in a registry of missing people, but that's it. No deep-diving internet sleuths working hard to uncover this mystery, no one with a complicated theory of how a mother could up and vanish never to be seen again.

Because that's exactly what happened, according to each of the articles. The earliest, from when Eve first disappeared, says that she was reported missing to the police by her eldest daughter after she didn't return home and couldn't be reached by phone, text, or email. The last recorded sighting of her was at a local grocery store, where she was captured on CCTV leaving with a single shopping bag. (She had purchased a bottle of wine, a bag of oranges, and a loaf of bread, the article reports breathlessly, as if that's the most important thing.)

After that the articles become a rehash of the same thing every time, with minor updates about how long Eve has been gone: three months, then six; a year, then two, then ten.

Harlow sits back, illuminated by the light of her laptop screen. She imagines the woman from the picture in the paper walking through a store on a weekday night, grabbing a few extras while her teenage daughters wait for her at home. Or maybe they were at school, or driving around blasting music too loud, or not even thinking about where their mom was because why would they?

Their lives were normal and boring: they'd see her at home, where she'd make spaghetti for dinner, and the four of them would eat while they watched terrible-good reality TV. Eve would open that bottle of wine, Harlow imagines, pouring herself a glass to wind down from the day. The girls would go to bed and tell their mom that they loved her, that they'd see her in the morning, and she'd tell them not to stay up too late, and then, when they were tucked away in their rooms, another glass of wine, some of the fancy gelato she kept hidden away in the back of the freezer.

Except she never came home.

The cold spreads from Harlow's fingers throughout her whole body. Is this it, then? This is why her mom has always been so afraid?

But afraid of what, exactly? That the same thing would happen to her? Of the memories? Or was there something more—something her mom had known, had maybe seen, that set her running?

Harlow presses her fist into her mouth and allows herself a short, sharp scream of frustration, muted against her knuckles. *Jesus* Christ, *she kept this hidden my whole life? Why did she have to keep everything so fucking close to the chest, like she couldn't rely on her own* daughter *to keep her secrets? I did everything else she ever told me.* Giving fake names, not talking to strangers, looking both ways when she crossed the street, always observing everyone around her for someone acting a little too interested. Packing up her life the second her mom told her to and playing along even after she stopped believing in any real threat, still doing what she had been taught because it was the only way she knew. And now Harlow has to find out that perhaps it wasn't all in her mom's head, there was some real kind of history lost in her wake, but it's too late to talk to her mom about it.

Harlow picks up the photo of her mom again and marvels at how similar they look, all the years wiped off her mom's face to leave her baby-faced and fresh, just a girl having a good time. Before her life changed, before her mother disappeared, before Harlow was even around.

People don't just vanish, Harlow thinks as she stares at the picture. *How is that even possible? To not come home, and never be seen again. To not be caught in a photo or spotted in a laundromat, to not have your credit card register somewhere?* After all, that's what she and her mom have spent years trying to do, trying to disappear. But it takes work, and that's for two people who no one has written articles about, or called the police about. For two people who no one is really looking for.

Two people who no one is really looking for. She's thought it so many times before, her doubts of her mom and the ghosts chasing them. But now.

Now there is a missing mother, and two sisters whose existence her mom never even hinted at, and a place that it seems her mom set off from first, so many years ago. It's the most she's ever had to go on. And yet—what does it tell her? Those girls in the photo are strangers to her, along with their mother, who is trapped in time, on the day she disappeared.

She presses her thumb into the photo, leaving a smeared fingerprint where her mom's face used to be. *I'm trapped, too,* she thinks—in a loop of new identities, new places, and the same old fear she doesn't know how to escape.

8

She wakes up again like she did before, disoriented and in a tangle of sheets, from a sleep she didn't intend to take. She pretends it's fine, definitely not an aftereffect of the accident, a sign that she should really see a doctor, and gets out of bed.

When Harlow opens the curtains to peek outside, it's fully dark, winter night closing in. She's ravenous now, her stomach so gnawingly empty that she feels sick, and decides to venture out in search of food.

She finds a pizza place with a few small tables in the corner a few blocks down from the hotel and busies herself eating two slices. In another world, she and her mom would be settling into their next destination right now. Usually they'd do a couple nights in a motel, until her mom found them a place to live. Then they'd move their bags in and begin getting used to somebody else's furniture, somebody else's life. The longest they'd ever stayed in one place was six months, when Harlow was around eleven. She always remembers that place—a tiny one-story house with pretty rugs covering the cold floorboards, in a tiny town with pretty blossoms littering the streets for a solid three months—because she got her first period there and learned to put a tampon in while her mom waited outside the bathroom door.

Harlow wipes grease from her fingers and takes out her phone, tapping her short nails on the screen as she tries to resist what she wants to do. To type in *accident* and *eighteen-wheeler* and *Miller Street,* to see what comes up.

I just left her, Harlow thinks, the fact she has been pushing down for the last eighteen hours, keeping herself busy enough with her mission and her travels and her collecting of old secrets. *I just left her there, dead. My mom, in the street, like I was never even there, like I didn't care at all.*

She turns her phone over, facedown on the pepper-flecked tabletop, so she's not too tempted. They would have taken her to the hospital, right? Or did they even bother when somebody was dead like that, no hope of saving them.

A drop of water lands on the table where Harlow is looking, and she blinks, tipping her head back to see where it came from, a leak in the stained ceiling. Nothing there. She looks back, and another drop falls, matching the first, and then Harlow understands they're coming from her and she flushes, feels embarrassed to be the cliché girl crying in a pizza place without even realizing it.

She flips her phone back over and types in the search before she can stop herself again. She has to, doesn't she? Has to see whether they've identified her mom yet. Gotten her real name to put in their reports, so that the article in the local paper will tomorrow include the line *the victim has been identified as 39-year-old Cora Ford, of Hickling Avenue.*

When the results fill in, they show a few preliminary reports of the accident. The death toll standing at one—the truck driver walked away with a shattered collarbone and not much else, Harlow reads. There is no mention of her, no suspicion yet of another occupant in the car. But once her mom's name is out there, Harlow will be connected. Their landlord will see, or the neighbor next door who liked to smoke in the parking lot at the same time every day and saw Harlow and her mom coming into the building together, or the delivery person from the Thai place they liked. And then her picture will be out, the shot from her school ID she was required to get, except the name on that will be Meredith Bloom, and someone from school—maybe Sam-Elle-June, irritated by her sudden silence—will say *Hey, I know that girl, but what do you mean her name is Harlow Ford?* and then it will all start to unravel.

Harlow scrolls slowly through the grainy pictures of the accident's aftermath, captured by someone's surreptitious phone, it seems. That's why her mom made her go. That's why Harlow did it without a second thought. Wanted to stay and say a proper goodbye, but those are the kinds of things you don't get to do when you're running. Ceremonies that belong to the kind of girl Harlow is not.

Back at the hotel Harlow takes a shower in water hot enough to peel her skin away from her bones. Her ribs ache, the impression of the seat belt turning red and raised in a diagonal stripe across her chest, and she still feels grimy, as if there's a layer of dirt and blood from the accident that will never leave her, even though the water runs crystal clear.

Afterward she pulls on cleanish sweatpants and the same sweatshirt of her mom's that she had put on yesterday evening. Then she climbs on the bed and surveys her spoils again. She starts with the pictures this time, staring intently at the image of her mom and these two girls who she knows now are her mom's sisters. They look happy, a day at the lake, where Harlow can imagine they ate hot dogs and drank sweating sodas and pushed each other into the water as they squealed at the feel of slippery plants beneath and promised to get revenge on each other.

She allows herself a smile too, to match theirs, before she shuffles to the next photo. It's the three sisters again, but they are much younger in this one, dressed in matching itchy-looking dresses and sitting on the floor in front of a sparse Christmas tree. Harlow brings the photo close to her face, examining every detail of the house that she can make out, but it's not much. Only patterned carpet, the beginning of a staircase, and the tree blocking most of the frame. The girls look more serious in this one, their smiles more subdued. Coming down off a holiday candy rush, maybe, or tired from the family expectations of the day.

She turns it over and her breath catches. There, on the back, in faded blue ink: *Cora, Christina, and Clementine. Christmas Day.*

The names seem to correspond in order to each girl, because her mom is on the left in the photo, and the one who Harlow has deduced from the lake picture is the oldest is sitting in the middle. So that's Christina, and the smallest on the end must be Clementine. "Christina and Clementine," she says, trying the names out in her mouth. The three sisters, the alliteration of those delicate names. Suddenly they seem more real, three-dimensional girls who are somewhere out there in the world now, far from this place, probably.

Who are out there not knowing that their sister is dead and gone.

Harlow flicks through the rest of the photos, seven in total, and they are all of the girls at various ages, in various combinations and sometimes smiling, sometimes not, sometimes obviously irritated at the presence of the camera, sometimes preening for it. There is no sign of their mom, of Eve. No sign of a father, either, although Harlow thinks less about that. She has no dad; it's always been her and her mom, her own father a mythical waste of a figure left in some town her mom ran through so many years ago. Wasn't interested in being Daddy, her mom has always told her, which Harlow should maybe have been hurt by, but by the time she was old enough to understand the rejection, she didn't care. By that time, it had been her and her mom against the world for so long that the mere idea of somebody else in their lives felt laughable. So Harlow never dreamed of her father showing up one day, had no fantasy or idea of who that man could even be.

Maybe that's how it was with them, Harlow thinks, arranging the photos back into a neat pile. Their dad must have stuck around for longer, to have the three of them—she is sure they all share the same parents, because what else could have produced the same face three times over?—but maybe he left after that. Maybe it was just them, Eve and Cora, Christina, Clementine, tucked up in Severn House, in the town named Crescent Ridge. Four women and no need for a man, because what did they bring except trouble?

The four of them, happy in their home, until something or someone came and took Eve away. Spirited her into the ether and started the running, the path that Harlow is still on.

Out in the hallway, beyond the locked hotel room door, Harlow hears the murmur of voices—other people leaving their rooms for the night, to go wherever qualifies for thrills on a Saturday in this town, or maybe a couple members of the housekeeping team carrying out some mundane task.

Harlow breathes out noisily and sinks back into the surprisingly soft pillows piled up against the headboard. Like before, she has the photos, postcard, and article on one side, the money and insurance papers on the other. She picks up the roll of bills now and weighs it in her hand, trying to guess again. Then she changes her mind and decides to count it out.

It takes longer than Harlow thought, including the couple times she slips and has to go back, but when she lays the last bill on top of the final pile, she's pretty sure she has it right:

Fifteen thousand, seven hundred, and twenty-nine dollars.

"Holy fuck," Harlow says, eyeing the bills spread out before her. "That's a lot of fucking money."

Enough for her to get set up in a new place and stay safe. Harlow fingers the money.

She knows that's what it is meant for, that this is why her mom directed her to the safety-deposit box. She's supposed to take this money and use it to get far, far away and then keep on going like they always have.

Except now—

Harlow looks from the money to the photos. Her mom and these brand-new sisters, and a house somewhere in a town that Harlow has never heard of, a town that meant enough for her mom to carry a postcard bearing its likeness around for years. After all this time, she has a hint of what her mom's life used to be like. And yet—she's supposed to ignore all that. File it away as more things she'll never have real answers to and pack it up to carry to the next place. Allow her mom's refusal to let her in persist, keep on running along the surface.

Harlow closes her eyes and, beneath the covers, claws at her aching muscles. *I'm so tired,* she thinks. Tired tonight, and exhausted by the constant movement, the perpetual motion that has been her entire childhood, her entire *life.* Tired and fucking *angry* because—what, is it supposed to be like this for the rest of her life too? *Am I supposed to keep on running forever, by myself?*

Before was one thing. When it was her and her mom, the two of them. But now Harlow is alone, and if she keeps on going like this, she'll be alone forever. No friends, no family, no pretty girls who she might actually one day let herself do more than fantasize about. She'll be keeping a secret that she only knows half of. Hiding from a ghost she's never even seen.

But on the other hand, there is this house in this town. The root of all of this. Harlow can feel it without knowing anything more; it seeps out of those photographs, out of Eve Kennedy's face in the newspaper article and the words that frame her face: *still missing.*

Before she can fall asleep again, Harlow forces herself out of the bed and begins walking an arc around it, past the windows, and back again. "She had to know," she says to herself, twisting her fingers together as she paces. "Mom had to know what I would see when I opened that box. She had to know there was a chance I would want to go back."

Harlow shakes her head. If her mom really wanted to keep the past hidden from Harlow, she could have done it. Could have rented two separate boxes and made sure Harlow never saw the other parts, only what she needed for the future. On some level, Harlow thinks, her mom must have felt like Harlow was entitled to know.

She stops pacing and picks up the photos again, shuffling through until she finds the second to last shot. It's her mom and the older girl, standing ankle-deep in snow and wrapped up in coats, scarves, hats. It's not them Harlow is focused on, though: at the very right edge of the frame, there is the beginning of a dark brick wall, something green wrapping around the sharp corner. Severn House, Harlow knows.

I don't want to run anymore. I'm so sick of running, and the secrets, and the lies.

She wants answers.

She wants to know about her family, about Eve and what happened to her and what all of it means.

And along the way maybe she'll prove to herself, once and for all, that there's nothing to be afraid of. And then she can stop being scared like her mom told her to be, and she can stop being all those girls her mom always made her be, and she can live a life without that fear, out of the shadow of her mom's paranoia.

Harlow rubs her thumb over the glimpse of the house. *I want to be there.* In Crescent Ridge, where her mom ran from. Where her grandmother vanished. Where her aunts may still be.

Where the truth lives.

I'm going. Harlow swallows hard. *Not running forward, but back. Where it all started.*

9

First Harlow buys a car. Something cheap but reliable, with only thirty thousand miles on it, and when she hands the entire payment over in cash, the owner of the dealership raises his eyebrows but asks no questions.

Then she sets off on the drive that the internet says will take thirty-something hours, which Harlow knows means more like three or four days, depending on traffic and weather and how tired she'll find herself once she's seven hours in. It's a long way from Pennsylvania to the Pacific Northwest, and Harlow feels every mile as she drives. The landscape changes, but to Harlow it barely registers, hour after hour after hour. There is only the endless unspooling of road ahead of her, the cars and trucks and occasional bikes that she is hyperaware of, all her energy going toward making sure nothing and no one comes near her, that she is in control all the time. Stopping at gas stations that feel like they exist outside of time, filled with an odd buzzing quiet and always a couple arguing over a bag of chips. At one rest stop she is startled by the blare of a passing truck horn and tries to leap to her feet, only to realize she is still sitting in the car and had fallen asleep, been lying with her cheek pressed against the steering wheel.

On the first night she stops at a motel where no one says anything about the bruise on her face—it is purple at the edges now and still tender to the touch, and her hair doesn't really hide it well, but the woman at the desk looks like she's seen things a hundred times worse than Harlow. The next day she drives through rain, everything stormy gray, and she flicks through radio stations as she drifts in and out of contact. Turns them up loud to try to convince her body that this car ride is vastly different from the fateful one before. No accidents here, Harlow tells herself somewhere around North Dakota, the roads lonelier now. Once, when her eyes are stinging, she pulls over to the side of the road and forces herself to get out and walk in circles, stamping her feet as if it will wake her up. The last thing she wants is to fall asleep behind the wheel, her eyes drifting shut peacefully right before she smacks into the median.

In the second motel Harlow collapses onto the worn-looking bed. Her entire body feels ragged, tired beyond words, and the pain in her ribs has localized on the left side, turning into a sharp stab that comes any time she moves too fast or reaches too far. In the bathroom she peels her clothes off and turns to examine the redness marking her brown skin.

There is another day, another endless navigation of road, more pauses in liminal spaces and supplies bought from people who look through Harlow like she isn't even there. As the sun begins to set on her third day of driving, Harlow wonders if she has taken a wrong turn somewhere. Driven out of her world and into some other place where time has no meaning and the roads are only a never-ending loop designed to trap you and drive you mad.

But then she makes it out of the loop, back into reality. When she finally reaches the third motel in as many days, Harlow checks in on the news back in Madigan. Her mom's name appears in the local reports, just like Harlow had known it would. It is only then, sitting in an uncomfortable wooden chair with her feet propped up on the desk in the room, that Harlow realizes she hadn't got it all right. Cora Ford is the name on the report. But Cora Kennedy is the name written on the deed; Cora Kennedy is the girl in the photographs. The first layer of her mom that Harlow has peeled back.

She looks out the window to the night sky and misses, for a moment, that other world she had found herself driving through only a few hours ago.

In the morning she packs her things back into the car and sets off on the last leg of the journey, the roads before her now carrying her closer and closer to Crescent Ridge.

Her hands are steady on the wheel as she thinks about how wrong what she is doing feels, in one way: undoing all the work her mom put in over the years. Retracing a path they so carefully forged, away from the place that her mom was so afraid of. Like she's driving right back into the eye of the storm, Harlow finds herself thinking, among other clichés. Back into the spider's web. Into shark-infested waters. All that.

But the closer she gets, the more of her old life recedes, and the more it solidifies in Harlow's mind, exactly what is drawing her back to Crescent Ridge. She and her mom have been running for years—maybe away from whatever force vanished Eve. But where has it gotten them?

Her mom would have claimed safety, Harlow knows. Her choices kept them safe from the thing behind them. *But did they?* Harlow is bitter. *Is it safety, a life alone like this? No connections, no roots, nowhere to retreat to?* Always on edge and wondering whether that shadow is something sinister, or just the light falling the wrong way? Is it safety, when your seventeen-year-old daughter is so conditioned not to give out her real name that she panics any time she hears a similar sound called out in the melee of a school hallway? Harper or Hannah or Hargreaves, all enough to make Harlow's heart skip several beats, enough to make her entire body tense like a sprinter in the blocks.

This is what Harlow thinks about during the long, slow hours of driving, as a curiosity gnaws the closer she gets to Washington.

She has tried doing things her mom's way for as long as she's been alive. And now her mom is *not* alive, and Harlow has to make her own choices. She does not want to spend the rest of her life on the run, with no one to confide in, no one who even knows that her name is Harlow Ford. And she can't stop thinking about Eve's eyes staring out from that newspaper. Somebody in Crescent Ridge must know what happened to her. Where she is— or was. How hard did people really look for Eve? How seriously did the police take her disappearance? Did they file her under *single mother who liked wine a little too much, probably fell into a bad situation, probably doesn't even matter?*

Did they listen to my mom when she told them how afraid she was? Or did they dismiss her, too, leave her with no choice but to leave, to get away from the place that didn't care? She tries not to think about that too much—the police not believing her mom, and then Harlow herself continuing the trend years later, turning her fears into baseless panic.

Now Harlow tightens her grip on the wheel as she reads the sign ahead of her: VANCOUVER and an arrow pointed straight ahead, keep on driving. Beneath, in smaller lettering, the less important places: KELLER 35 MILES. PORT BRAYTON 20 MILES. CRESCENT RIDGE—NEXT EXIT.

Harlow drifts across the empty highway and peels off where the road splits in two. She can fix it now. *I know you weren't making everything up now, Mom.*

Almost there.

10

Harlow arrives in Crescent Ridge without even noticing.

It's not a place like so many Harlow has lived in, towns that were constructed whole and entire, carved out of the land and slotted in neatly with their identical houses and strip malls.

No: Crescent Ridge more rises piece by piece, limb by limb, as Harlow navigates the twisting road that should deliver her in town. It's only when she glances out the window again and sees the fifth set-back house nestled among the trees, cars parked neatly outside, and signs at the entrance to the driveway alerting people to its existence, that Harlow realizes she's passing the residents of this place. That she's already there.

She stays on the road, though, because it keeps promising her the heart of the town and also because there's nowhere else to go. Eventually, the forest falls back, and solid structures take over— houses, a school, redbrick bed-and-breakfasts offering local produce, a run of small restaurants with similar handwritten signs and insides glowing warm orange.

Harlow follows the signs that direct her toward the center until she catches sight of an imposing building, not redbrick like so many others she's passed but sandy stone, pillars out front like the whole thing was cut out of Grecian rock and airlifted to be dropped right into the heart of this town. The recognition is instant: it's the building from the postcard, come to life right in front of her eyes.

At least I know I'm in the right place, she thinks.

The building crowns what she assumes is the main drag, the road wider than usual and stores up and down either side. There's parking right on the road, and Harlow pulls over into one of the many open spaces, then turns the engine off and picks up her phone.

She takes a minute to scan up and down the street, the people walking through the rain that's starting, some of them ducking into stores to keep dry. With the car off and the heat gone, Harlow feels how cold it is, a winter chill blowing in with the rain.

She looks away and taps *Severn House* into her maps, and then frowns when nothing comes up. "Come on," she mutters, hitting search again. Still nothing.

Harlow sighs and squints through the window at the places right ahead of her: a hair salon, a book store, a coffee shop. Okay.

She can't just go in and start asking questions. Her mom did teach her well, after all; Harlow is not so cavalier or desperate enough to walk into these places, a stranger from out of town, and start up with a story about a missing woman. No—she needs a cover story, and she needs to be smart. She scans the storefronts, pressing her palms together. *Which one, which one—*

The salon. It's where people go to talk all kinds of shit, where bonds are formed and broken, where gossip seeps from glossed mouths under the guise of concern.

She prepares herself before she walks over: black denim jacket brushed free of the last few days' crumbs, her short curls covering as much of that bruise as possible, a series of deep breaths, in and out, to relax her bones. So she might appear to the salon staff as a girl without a care in the world, instead of bearing the whole weight of it on her shoulders.

Harlow glances back at the car before crossing the street. When she pushes the door to the salon open, a warm rush of bleach-tinged air and chatter greets her. She steps in and is about to open her mouth when the girl behind the front desk lowers her magazine and says, "Jeannie's away until next week."

Harlow stills, completely thrown off. "What?"

"Jeannie," the girl says, and snaps her gum. "You want to book in with her, right?" The girl—sixteen, maybe seventeen, Harlow guesses—looks confused, her nose wrinkling. "She did your cut, right? Jeannie is the only one who does short that good."

Inexplicably Harlow finds herself warming, and she touches a hand to her hair self-consciously. "I did this," she says.

"Really?" The girl laughs. "Shit. Jeannie might be out of a job."

For a second Harlow isn't sure if this girl is laughing at her or not, if she's being made fun of or not. Harlow takes her in: long hair the shade of golden sunlight, green eyes, freckles over pale skin. Lips shiny with gloss and winged glittery eyeliner that shimmers every time the girl blinks.

Pretty girl, Harlow thinks. *Don't have time for pretty girls.*

"Sorry," the girl says now. "You don't want an appointment. So what do you want?"

It's lazy and cheap for Harlow to think what she does, to think *What I want is for you to kiss me,* but it's what comes anyway. Won't happen for a thousand reasons but especially because even a kiss means some level of intimacy and Harlow can't let anyone in like that. Even if all she will dream about for the next week is what it would feel like to hug this girl, or wake up with her breath on Harlow's neck, or press their palms together.

Even if all she wants is to be laid down and to let this girl— or not this girl, any pretty girl, any of the dozens she has tucked away in her mind—do to her whatever she pleases, while Harlow doesn't have to think about anything, while she only has to lie there and say *yes no more less yes there yes.*

"You okay?"

Harlow focuses, the girl in front of her looking amused, the three stylists working in the salon glancing over curiously without taking too much attention off the delicate processes in their hands.

"Sorry," Harlow says, and she shuts that side of her brain away, a black film over indulgent, untimely thoughts. "I was wondering if you could tell me how to find Severn House?"

She makes her voice bright, inquisitive, a little uncertain as if she *thinks* that's what this place is called, she *thinks* that's where she's trying to go. In the back of the salon two of the stylists pay no attention to her, but a third turns away from the client in her chair, one hand resting on a shiny black cane as she gazes at Harlow curiously.

"Severn House?" the girl says. "That old haunted house in the woods? I thought that was empty."

Haunted? Harlow scans the girl's face, wondering whether she means it, or if she's fucking with Harlow. "What do you mean by haunted?"

"You know." The girl leans forward. "Ghosts and shit. I mean, that's what everybody says. That's why nobody's lived there in years. They say a woman in white will get you if you go too close." Her serious expression cracks, and she cocks an eyebrow. "I mean, if you believe in that shit."

Harlow steps closer and lifts one shoulder. "Maybe, maybe not," she says. "But—wait. What's your name?"

"Sloane."

"Sloane," Harlow repeats, nodding. "I'm doing some research that involves Severn House, in a way. But I can't find directions on my phone, so I'm wondering if you or anybody in here can tell me how I might get there." She raises her voice on this last part, making sure they can all hear her.

Sloane swivels in her chair. "Mom," she calls. "You know how to get to that weird house in the woods?"

"Yeah." The same stylist who had turned to look at Harlow—this girl Sloane's mom, it seems—reaches up to toy with a silver earring. "I can tell you. But I can also tell you that Sloane's right. There's nothing there except an old house that's been empty for a long time now, and probably enough potholes on the way in to fuck your car up."

Harlow smiles. Now that's she paying attention, the woman does look like the girl at the desk: her hair a darker blond, her eyes a little harder, like she doesn't take anyone's shit. "That's all right," Harlow says. "I'm working on my thesis, and it's on my list of locations to visit. I'm looking at architecture of the Northwest. It's, like, stupid boring to anybody who isn't an architecture student, I know." She finishes with a laugh, like she's embarrassed by her fictional choice in academic study.

It does exactly what she intended, though, the expression on the woman's face changing, relaxing. She's not some ghoul seeking out the site of a tragedy; she's just a college student hustling for a good grade. "Hold on," the stylist says. "Let me draw you a map."

When the stylist—Adelaide, she tells Harlow her name is—has finished sketching out a loose approximation of how to get to the house, and Harlow has thanked them all for their help and apologized for interrupting their day, she tucks the map in her pocket and turns to head out.

"Good luck," Sloane calls.

Harlow turns back.

"With the ghost," Sloane says. "And your thesis." She smiles slyly, like she knows exactly what bullshit Harlow is running.

"Maybe I'll come back," Harlow says. "If I have any more questions."

Sloane picks up her magazine and pops her gum again, a sharp snap. "You do that," she says.

11

The rain comes down harder as Harlow gets back in her car, keeps on driving through the town, until she's back at the point where it is more forest than civilization. This is it, according to the hand-drawn map she's holding up to the wheel with one hand. *On the outskirts of town, as if you're leaving. And then look for the turn, the road that peels off and carves through the trees.*

Harlow has to squint through the rain, but there it is—a narrow opening in the foliage, and she turns sharply, pulling the car into the space that would be so easy to miss if you didn't know what you were looking for.

The road starts off smooth, even, but quickly becomes rough, the car juddering over knotted roots and mud slicks and dips that should be refilled. But the entire way in, Harlow gets the sense that no one has repaired this road in years, and no one will. When she glances in the rearview, it looks as if the trees are closing in behind her, covering the path she's just taken. Like she's being swallowed up, deep in the belly of the forest.

And then, out of nowhere, the trees open up and the dirt track spits Harlow out into a wide, flat dirt lot. And emerging from the earth—there it is.

Severn House.

Harlow comes to a stop parallel to the low stone wall that surrounds the house, marking out exactly where the woods end and the house begins. At least, that's what it seems to Harlow.

She cuts the engine and gazes through the rain at the building in front of her. It's not as imposing as she imagined, as the name *Severn House* conjured in her mind—not a looming, large mansion, but a weathered, warm-looking cottage. Or Harlow can imagine the warmth that should be there: light spilling out of the windows surrounded by creeping vines, the wild front yard carefully tamed and beaten back into organized chaos, gray smoke pluming from the chimney peeking up from the roof.

"Okay," Harlow says to herself, steeling nerves and shaking off the comments Sloane made. Harlow is the type to believe in what she sees, nothing more, nothing less. "Here we are."

When she gets out of the car, she is first struck by the softness. The rain—cold and sharp as it is—runs through the surrounding woods like a quiet creek, the soft patter of drops onto heavy leaves. Beyond that is the sound of birds calling faintly, and maybe the scratch of some small animal running across the forest floor, but that's all. She can't hear any road noise, or neighbors fighting, no one's TV blaring or the excited yelps of kids playing. It's only the woods, the house, and Harlow.

She lets herself through the low metal gate; it swings open far more easily than she anticipated, like it has been waiting to let somebody in. Up close the house looks battered but still beautiful. It's clear than no one has lived here in a long time, but Harlow can see, if she peels back the years in her mind, how it might have looked when this was the place her mom called home.

Home.

Harlow's breath catches sharp in her throat. Home is not a thing she's ever had. Nowhere has ever been the place where she can retreat, fall back into. She's never been the girl to envision a future where she leaves *home* and comes back later, showing friends, girlfriends, colleagues, around the place she grew up. And she hasn't really thought about the lack of it that much; the absence of a thing can sometimes *become* the thing, in a way. But she has always wondered about the place her mom came from and now she is seeing it for the first time and it hits her, hard, how the girl Cora Kennedy existed inside this space before the woman Cora Ford ever had to exist. *This is where my mom grew up,* she thinks. *This is where she learned how to walk, to talk, to snap back at her mom in petty arguments. This is where she dreamed and figured out eyeliner and danced in her bedroom to her favorite songs.*

And: *This is where she was when her own mother vanished. This is the place she came back to, absent of that woman. This is the place she ran from, terrified of the things that existed here in this town.*

A drop of rain runs into Harlow's eye; she rubs at it roughly, hiding her face from the emptying sky, instead peering down at the empty ceramic pots clustered by the front door. The kind of things that held flowers once, sure, but that also probably hid a spare key, in the way that people in small towns like this liked to do. So trusting and eager to please.

Harlow scuffs the toe of her boot through the layer of dirt covering the path to the door. *There's no way a key is still beneath one of those pots,* she thinks. There is no way fate would let her in that easily.

She follows the path to the door and lifts the pots one by one, until on the third try she sees it: a dull brass key, carefully placed on the ground, as if waiting for her.

Harlow picks it up, and her first thought is how similar it is to the safety-deposit box key. The bronze gleam, the potential to unlock secrets.

Then she slides the key into the lock and twists.

When Harlow steps inside Severn House, she almost feels like the building sighs, relief at a living presence inhabiting it after so long.

It is similar inside to out: softer and smaller than first imagined, in a calming way, in a way that speaks to the history of this house.

Harlow walks through the warren of rooms, marveling at the continuing quiet. Downstairs there is a kitchen with a big white sink and chalk paint on one wall, a living room, another room lined with shelves, and a dining room. A small nook sits next to the dining room with a door leading to the outside: the kind of spot to kick off muddy boots, leave your rain-drenched coats and umbrellas. Through the windows she can see the low wall outside, crumbling in places, falling apart from a lack of love.

Upstairs there are three bedrooms, one at the front of the house with a view out onto the forest and a soft-green tiled bathroom connected. The other bathroom sits between the two smaller bedrooms, a different shade of tile, and floral wallpaper wilting away from the wall in areas, strips peeling away and hanging loose like drooping dandelion petals right before they fall.

That is all normal. Expected.

What Harlow doesn't expect, though, is that the house is not empty like she thought. No: it is filled with the remnants of the family that once lived here.

That is the part that sends a tremor through her. It is as if the occupants—her mom, Harlow corrects, and the sisters—walked out of here in the middle of an ordinary day. The rooms are packed with furniture—dense couches in the living room, a white-painted table in the kitchen, carved wooden chairs in the dining room. In the small downstairs room there are still books on the shelves, as if someone might pull one off when they get the idea. And upstairs, in the bedrooms—hangers in the closets, beds draped in dusty covers, picture frames on the walls.

Harlow pretends not to see it all at first, the same way she pretends she doesn't hear the groan of the stairs or the settling of the beams in the ceiling from somewhere above. At every turn this place subverts her expectations, like it wants her to understand that Harlow doesn't have it or the truth behind it figured out yet. It's almost too much, facing the house with all this history left inside it.

But she can't ignore it. Can't stop herself from sinking down onto the edge of the bed in the right-hand corner of one of the smaller bedrooms—there is another bed in the opposite corner, the shared space of two younger sisters—and twisting her fingers into the aged fabric of the covers. She knows instantly which bed belonged to her mom, which side of the room was Cora Kennedy's. There are still posters tacked to the pale blue walls—the Cure, Sofia Coppola's *Marie Antoinette*, a woman with blond hair and a piercing through her outstretched tongue whose name Harlow doesn't know. There is still a series of water rings on the nightstand, buried beneath a thick layer of dust, her mom always sloppy in those little ways.

Harlow inhales the still air, the dust that has been sitting undisturbed since her mom left—

She stops. *Wait*, she thinks, *is that right? I have no idea. I have no idea who left first, and why. Did Mom go first, and her sisters followed in her footsteps? Or was she the last one here, holding out hope for Eve to come home?*

The rain drums against the window, a reminder that the world out there still exists, and Harlow laughs, a loud echoing sound that ricochets off the pale walls. "I have no fucking clue," she says to the figures pinned up on the walls, holding her hands up and ignoring how they shake. "I have no idea what happened here. I'm so fucking stupid."

Like, what? What did she think was going to happen? That she'd walk into this house and suddenly know all, know whether her mom had had a reason to be so afraid, know what happened to Eve, know where her mom's sisters went? That she'd step into the past and be able to see it all unfold in an instant?

I am so fucking stupid.

• • • •

Harlow leaves Severn House behind and drives back into town.

She finds a small, quiet place to eat dinner, sitting at the bar with her iced tea and burger and listening to the murmur of chatter around her. The people of Crescent Ridge going about their normal lives, unaware of Harlow's journey.

She wonders how much those people know. How Crescent Ridge remembers Eve, her mom. The girl at the salon—Sloane— she said that shit about a haunting, like people think Eve's story is a joke. But the stylist who gave her the directions—Sloane's mom, Adelaide—she was cautious answering Harlow's questions, as if she was wary of outsiders and intruders, the way Harlow must have appeared to her.

Maybe it's somewhere between, Harlow thinks. Somewhere between what those who were around when Eve vanished remember, and what those who have grown up only occasionally hearing about a tired old story that never got an ending think. After all, with no scandal, no salacious details, there isn't much for people to gravitate toward. People like a little drama in their real-life tragedies.

She stays at the bar as the evening draws in and the people around her shift from families and tired-looking workers in business casual to tired-looking high school—maybe college—kids toting textbooks and laptops. Harlow thinks of her own laptop, tucked away in her duffel in the trunk of the car. The wad of cash nestled beside it. Stupid to leave it there but also stupid to carry it on her, because how does she explain an inches-thick stack of bills to the first wrong person to catch a glimpse of it? She can only hope that this town is not the kind of place where people regularly break into people's cars, where your valuables are semi-safe as long as they're hidden out of sight.

It'll be better once she's in a motel, she thinks, and the money is locked away in a safe.

But as she thinks it, she can feel the dread building. Going to another motel, giving another fake name, pretending that she's on her way to somewhere else even though this is it, now. Her end destination, the last place on the list. But what end? She came here with no real plan, no idea beyond *find the house, discover the truth.* As if it was going to present itself.

"Hey, everything okay?"

Harlow opens her eyes to see the waitress who took her order earlier standing in front of her, a tub filled with dishes balanced on her hip. Harlow forces a smile. How many times has this girl asked that question, and how many people have ever answered it honestly?

"Yeah," Harlow says. "Absolutely perfect."

12

It's not so much a decision Harlow makes as one that was already made for her, decades ago.

She traces her way back to the edge of town, back to that hidden turn into the trees, without the use of the map this time. The road feels easier and smoother as she drives, headlights illuminating the woods.

There's something calming about the dark. Harlow has never been afraid of it, even when perhaps she should have been. The night, after all, has always been the time when she could take off the disguise and go back to being herself. The night has always been there for her.

When she gets to the house she parks in the same spot as before, but this time she takes her duffel out of the trunk, her mom's bag too. She carries them through the gate and up the path, and uses the key she pocketed earlier to open the door.

Inside is still and dark, and Harlow drops the bags on the floor, takes a deep breath of the years drifting through the air.

"Hey, Mom," she says. "I'm home."

BEFORE

Cora tiptoes downstairs earlier than she would like, but she still hasn't managed to shake the lifelong habit of shallow sleep, only ever a few murky feet from alert and awake.

It's still dark as she pours a cup of coffee, the same insistent rain from last night pouring out in the woods, intense wind whipping leaves right off the branches and up to press against the windows of the cottage. She remembers last night, the way her lips felt bee-stung after she kissed Ruby, the text that arrived as she was quietly climbing into bed: **i can't stop thinking about u.**

If only today weren't *the* day. Then Cora would go find Ruby and make Ruby say it out loud, tell her she feels the same way. She's so bright, Ruby, like her namesake, trying to hide it beneath her layers of black and her bored tone of voice. Cora sees right through it, though. She always sees her.

Cora doctors her coffee with so much milk and sugar it turns a sweet caramel color, savoring her first sip as she walks into the living room and takes a seat in the oversize armchair, then picks up the guitar leaning against the arm. She contemplates the strings, shiny and bright with newness.

She sets her coffee on the floor and straightens up. Why not? It is a special day, after all.

Cora touches her fingers to the strings and closes her eyes as the notes come, plucking with her barely formed calluses.

"Do you have to do that right now?"

Clementine's irritated whine comes from the hallway, and then Cora opens her eyes to see her younger sister stumbling into the living room, one of Cora's sweatshirts thrown over her shorts-and-tank pajamas. "I absolutely do have to do it right now," Cora says without stopping her playing. "How else would I annoy the shit out of you?"

Clementine makes a face and throws herself down on the couch. "I don't know," she says. "Try breathing."

Now Cora stops, sets the guitar down, goes to the couch where Clementine has burrowed in and curls up next to her sister. "Shut up," Cora says. "Or I'll tell Christina all about that belly button ring of yours."

That's enough to make Clem bolt up, kicking at Cora and catching her shin. "You won't. You *promised* you wouldn't tell her."

Of course Christina appears in the doorway then, all rumpled but goddess beautiful, like the oldest Kennedy sister always is. "Tell me what?"

Cora tries not to laugh as Clem slices a hand across her throat, her eyes wide and wild. As if Christina doesn't already know. There are no secrets in this house anymore, not between the three of them. But still she says, "Tell you that Clem is the one who broke the green vase."

Christina rolls her eyes and crosses her arms over her full chest, brown-skinned Botticelli leaning against the doorframe. "Oh, I hated that vase."

She joins them on the couch and the three of them become almost one, Cora sinking against Christina's softness, Clementine's arms finding their way around Cora's waist. This is how it has been for the last two years, since the day Eve Kennedy vanished.

Since the day their mother disappeared.

Cora finds herself practicing her saddest, most sorrowful look. Today might bring visitors to their hidden house, and they have to keep up the facade they began on that day two years ago. *We have to pretend*, Christina, eighteen then and suddenly in charge, said. *Whatever we do, we can't let them know the truth. Okay?*

Sad faces in the handful of articles online, mournful eyes at the gatherings outside town hall, asking in careful cracked voices that if anyone knows anything about where their mother has gone to please, *please* share that information. *We just want her home. We just want her to be okay.*

Cora brushed her teeth for ten minutes straight afterward, trying to get the taste of the lie out of her mouth.

"I'm hungry," Clem says, breaking the silence.

"You know where the kitchen is," Christina says.

Clem sighs, such petulant teenager shit. "I thought you were making French toast."

"I don't feel like it. You want it, you make it."

"Fine."

Their words bat back and forth over Cora's head, and she smiles as Clementine reluctantly extricates herself and slinks off toward the kitchen, calling out, "I'm not making you any!"

Once she is gone, though, Christina pushes Cora away. "Look at this."

Christina reaches for her laptop on the coffee table, opens it, and brings up the local news site. Cora watches over her shoulder as the page loads, her chest tightening as the familiar photos appear: the three of them, standing on the town hall steps looking into the far distance, and then the picture of her. Eve.

She was always beautiful, their mother, especially so in this photo. Cora always wonders who took it, when. Where she was. They never took pictures of her. But here she is, pale white skin and strawberry-blond hair, a wide smile like she was all sweetness. She was—is—the perfect subject for a good Missing White Woman story; of course she is.

Cora reads the headline: TWO YEARS GONE: WHERE IS EVE KENNEDY? Not creative, but accurate, she'll give them that. It's the first story they've run about Eve in the last year, anyway. As much as she was—is—the perfect subject, the truth is that a story can't sustain itself when there's no news, no rumors, and even the wildest conspiracies have burned out.

She glances at Christina, wearing a worried look on her face and chewing her thumbnail. "It is what it is," Cora says, in a way that's meant to be reassuring but only sounds uncaring. "I mean— we just have to get through today. It's one day."

"A special day," Christina says, exactly like Cora had thought earlier. "We're supposed to go to the memorial at twelve."

"We will," Cora says. "We'll dress up nice, we'll put on our faces, and we'll go play our parts. Then they'll leave us alone for another year."

She says it like it's so easy, and maybe it can be. They'll go into town, make small talk, quietly thank people for coming, and let people admire them—so strong, so brave, the Kennedy girls—and that'll be it. One phone call afterward with whichever fresh cop has been assigned the job of checking in, and it will all be over again.

Cora stands and holds her hand out to her big sister. "Come on," she says. "I want French toast too."

Christina looks up at her, unconvinced, but allows Cora to pull her to her feet. "One day," Christina says. "That's it."

"That's it." Cora nods. "That's all."

13

The first thing Harlow sees when she wakes is sunlight streaming in and illuminating dust swirling through the air.

She blinks once, twice, slowly as she watches the motes eddy through the air. *Where am I?*

She sits up and gazes around the room, her slow morning brain piecing it together. Yes: she is in Severn House, where she has decided to stay. Where she fell asleep last night at some unknown hour, passing out fully dressed on one of the living room couches, with not even a blanket to cover her.

It's as if she only registers the cold in that second, and she shivers as she stands, stretching her aching arms high over her head. *At least the rain has paused,* she thinks; from the light through the window, it seems like today might be a bright day, the kind with clear skies, where even the sight of the sun without any real warmth is enough to give you hope that you'll make it through the rest of winter.

Now Harlow looks around the living room, taking it in. Maybe it is strange for her to want to be here, but technically, legally—this place belongs to her now. At least, that's what she has put together from her mom's will. It names Harlow as her mom's sole beneficiary, bestowing on her all of her mom's worldly possessions.

And according to the deed, Severn House is one of those possessions.

So Harlow has decided to stay right here. No motel, no fake name. She must still be careful, she knows; it's so drilled into her, the rules from her mom impossible to ignore. But there are ways to ask the questions she needs to without breaking all those rules. She will have to walk the line to do it, but in this town she will unearth every secret she can find, all the things that people have thought safe and buried for years.

But she can't get caught up thinking about that now. First there are issues of practicality to attend to.

Harlow's first thought would be power, but she already flipped a switch last night, to see what would happen, and was surprised by the hallway lights coming to life. *If there's power, then that means someone has been paying an electric bill,* she thought. It could have been her mom, but then that would have left a paper trail connecting Cora Kennedy to whoever her mom had decided to be. The risk of the safety-deposit box was one thing; it made less sense for her mom to have taken the same risk to keep the lights on in a house she was trying so hard to leave behind.

She pulled out the photograph, the three sisters together, and examined it as she stood in the glow of the lights. Maybe one of them, then?

That could be her first connection to them, Harlow realizes now as she walks into the kitchen. They might not be here in Crescent Ridge, but one or the other of them might still be connected by this. At the very least, the mystery of which of the three of them is behind the light in this place is one she can begin to solve pretty easily. A solid, stable start, she thinks.

At the big white sink Harlow turns the faucet on and is unsurprised to see water running out. She puts two fingers under the stream and holds them in the cold, waiting to feel if it shifts, and it does: lukewarm, then mild, then hot enough to scald. She snatches her fingers back and turns the water off, smiling. Hot water means she can shower; electricity means she can cook, turn the heat on, formulate her plans under glowing light bulbs.

The trip she makes into town is quick and efficient. There's a decent-size supermarket, and she fills a cart with essentials— cereal, milk, boxes of mac and cheese, cleaning supplies, Diet Coke.

Back at the house she starts the process of shaking out the stillness of the last twenty years. Harlow is not a neat freak, never has been—she and her mom were happy to wear the same clothes three days in a row, to ignore the smears on the TV screen, to leave dishes in the sink until they couldn't put them off any longer—but if she's going to be living in this place, she wants it to feel like she can breathe without inhaling something that might kill her.

She pulls the old comforters off the beds and shoves them into the washer along with the sheets and too much detergent. The dust and grime is wiped off every surface she can see, and she opens as many windows as she can to let air circulate. Gets down on her hands and knees to scrub wet cloths across the kitchen's tile floors, the wooden boards of the stairs. Gets down on her knees again to pry up a floorboard in the bedroom closet, where she hides away her escape essentials—the money, the IDs, the papers from the safety-deposit box.

All of it takes longer than Harlow thought, and by the time she has pulled the sheets out of the dryer and remade all the beds, it's dark outside again. She's sweaty and covered in dust, and so she peels off her clothes and steps into the tub, bracing herself for the hit of cold water from the shower. When it turns hot she relaxes, letting out a long slow breath as the water pounds her skin. She should feel wrong, she knows, being in this house, but in a way it's no different from any other place, another new house full of other people's possessions. And she doesn't feel so afraid, here. She thought she would, but now, as she steps out of the shower, she thinks maybe she has only ever been as scared as her mom told her to be. Has always done what her mom told her—changed her name, left her lives, kept the secrets.

Not anymore.

She makes and eats some macaroni and cheese, washes the single pot she used, and then sits down on the living room floor, her laptop balanced on the sloping coffee table, background music filtering out of her phone.

She can't expect the truth to reveal itself to her so easily. It's going to take work.

So she needs to make a plan.

Harlow pulls out the old newspaper article with Eve staring

out. She looks as pensive as ever, her eyes locked on Harlow's. *Help me,* it seems like she's pleading. *Find me.*

She can't just go around town and start asking people, like she asked about the house. That was one thing. Asking about Eve's disappearance? It would be so utterly stupid of her to act like there isn't the possibility of danger here. There's a difference between taking charge and being plain reckless. Even taking the idea of there being someone in this town willing to hurt Harlow, who has already hurt her family, off the table—in these kinds of towns, people don't like newcomers who show up and start running their mouths. It's going to take more finesse than that.

"What I really need is an ally," she says as she runs her thumb over the newspaper print. "Someone who knows this place, who I need to talk to."

A girl's face appears in front of her: green eyes, freckles, a sly smile. *Sloane.* Sloane?

Harlow turns it over in her head. Sloane is from here and obviously not shy. Sloane seems like a girl who likes to get into things. Sloane seems like the exact kind of girl Harlow would align herself with, in a normal situation. She's already off thinking about it: *I could become a gum-popping girl, who gets acrylics and makes sure to listen for all the dirty secrets being spilled over the sinks. I could be—*

No. She's not going to *be* anyone. Only Harlow Ford.

Harlow Ford will go ask Sloane—carefully, *don't forget to watch yourself*—about the cops around here, about who has been around long enough to have worked on Eve's disappearance. She'll tell Sloane enough to get her interested, snippets of the truth that would make her mom so mad to hear Harlow say out loud.

"But you're not here, are you, Mom?" Harlow speaks it to the ceiling. "So I have to figure out this mess—a mess you *left* me—my own way. You aren't here to make sure I follow every rule. You don't get a say anymore."

She nods, faking confidence to herself, like she believes she can start doing her own thing as easily as that. Like it doesn't make her heart beat faster to imagine going out there and being herself. But that's what she's going to do. Yeah—Harlow Ford will go to the library and pick through the archives to see what else is out there. Harlow Ford will find out exactly who pays the bills for this house, and maybe find out where at least one of her mom's sisters is.

She nods again as it starts to come together in her head. Yes, Harlow Ford is going to do all of this. Harlow Ford is going to get what she wants.

Harlow puts herself to sleep in the same bed her mom used to sleep in, beneath the same sheets, looking up at the same ceiling with a spider crack running from one corner. With the curtains closed, the night is almost entirely shut out, only the slightest gleam of moonlight slipping around one edge. Harlow curls up, rubbing her feet together as she imagines she is her mom. What she would have seen sleeping here: her younger sister dreaming peacefully in the bed opposite, the same moonlight.

Tears drip over the bridge of her nose and down her face, creating a little stain of sadness on the freshly washed sheets. Something about the dark, lonely quiet of the house mutes her earlier resentment, making space for memories of the moments they did have. For the connection that used to tether them, even if it was delicate, always in danger of snapping in two. "I miss you, Mom," she whispers into the dark, allowing that locked box inside her chest to open only a crack, for the sadness to smother the flames of her bitter anger. "I really fucking miss you."

When she finally falls asleep, Harlow dreams of broken glass and the taste of blood.

She startles awake.

For a moment, again, she isn't sure where she is, but then she recognizes the empty bed across from her and the posters looking down and that ceiling crack.

Harlow rolls over, groaning as she wipes a hand over her face and checks the time on her phone: 3:42. Her heart is beating fast and she sits up, the noise she *thought* she heard already fading, if it had ever even been there at all. "Stop," she says to her chest. "It was a dream. A stupid nothing dream—"

The ceiling above her creaks.

Harlow looks up, mouth still open. *What was that?*

She sits still for a minute, waiting to hear it again, whatever it was—the noise of the house settling, or a branch from one of the taller trees outside whipping over and hitting the house. She sits still, trying to slow her heart, quell the insistent sudden fear that tells her she's not safe in this house. *Fuck that girl Sloane,* she thinks, *and fuck her stupid ghost.*

The noise doesn't come again. Harlow stares up at the ceiling in the dark. Her eyes refuse to adjust and she knows how this goes, how she always yells at the girl in the horror movie who leaves the safety of her bedroom to go in search of a strange sound and ends up on the wrong end of a knife or baseball bat or length of rough rope. *Stay your ass where you are,* she'd tell the screaming starlets. *Is it that hard?*

Now here, with her own strange sound, Harlow realizes that yeah, it is that fucking hard. She can't lie back and return to sleep as if nothing is wrong. She doesn't want to lie here panicking all night, not when she has work to get started in the morning. But if she leaves the room and finds somebody outside—

Harlow stops herself, pinching the skin on the inside of her left elbow. *Stop. Who could possibly be here? No one knows I'm in town. I don't think anybody is watching this place, waiting for any of the girls to return. And even if they were and they saw me—what do I mean to them? They wouldn't even know who I really am. So what, their immediate plan would be to creep inside the house and hide out, waiting until they can get me? Come on, Harlow. You're smarter than this.*

She takes a deep breath and throws the covers off, getting out of bed. Unplugging her phone, she turns the flashlight on and points it toward the door as she makes her way over. Once at the door she stops and casts her eyes around for something to hold, as a precaution. *No,* she corrects: not as a precaution. That's the other thing that always frustrates her about horror movie girls— they pick up their weapons but wield them so shakily, no intention behind their movements. You have to know what you're willing to do, Harlow knows. Better be ready to stab with that knife, or bash some brains in with that baseball bat.

Her gaze roams the room, tripping over the dresser with its empty surface, the closet filled with nothing but hangers, her own bag stuffed with clothes.

And then her eyes catch on the ceiling, illuminated by that glimpse of moon around the curtain's edge—on the line running across it.

Without thinking too much Harlow flips on the light switch, wincing at the shift from dark to bright white, and now she can see it clearly, and she starts to laugh as her body relaxes. The crack in the ceiling that earlier petered out in the middle of the room has spread, little fissures through the white paint and no doubt into the plaster and brick above. That was it. That was all the sound was.

Harlow turns the light back off, her heart rate beginning to slow, turns the light on her phone off too. There's no intruder, no one waiting for her. It's just that apparently the entire structure of this house might fall in on her at any time.

She laughs harder, the sound filling the quiet air. Then she gets back into bed and prays to the ether that she won't be crushed by rubble during the night.

14

When Sloane looks up at the sound of the door opening, she doesn't seem in the least bit surprised. "Back so soon," she says, putting down the book she's reading this time. "Jeannie actually is in today, if you came back for her."

Harlow rolls her eyes—that's what this girl wants, isn't it?

Then she remembers that she's not supposed to be doing this, not supposed to be acting. She's not trying to become Sloane's shadow, falling in line to stay safe.

She shakes herself and pushes the sleeves of her black denim jacket up. "Actually," she says, "I came to see you."

Sloane changes when Harlow says that—an almost imperceptible lifting of her chin, her shoulders pulling back. "Oh, really," she says. "What, you want to complain about my mom's directional abilities? I do run the HR department here. Department of one."

Harlow glances back beyond the front desk to see if Sloane's mom is there, and she is, but standing half inside what appears to be a storage closet, unloading something from a stack of boxes. "I do want to say thanks to her," she says. "But that's not why I came."

Now Sloane is the one to roll her eyes. "Well, spill—" She stops, frowning. "Wait. I didn't even get your name the other day."

"It's Harlow." She swallows. "Harlow Ford. And I'm not an architecture student doing thesis research."

Sloane smirks. "That much was obvious," she says. "So what's the deal, Harlow Ford?"

It's a thrill to hear her name from Sloane's glossy lips. Harlow tries to ignore it, meeting Sloane's gaze as if it doesn't affect her at all. "Do you like mysteries, Sloane?"

They get coffees from the place two doors down, and then even though it's cold and gray again, the brief sunny interlude of yesterday well and truly gone, they take their drinks to go and walk down the main thoroughfare to a square outside the town hall Harlow had driven past.

Sitting on a bench facing an empty fountain, Sloane gestures impatiently. "Okay," she says, "we have the coffee, we're out on a clandestine meeting—what is it?"

Harlow looks at the empty fountain and wonders if there are any water-stained coins left sitting on the bottom. "I came here, to Crescent Ridge, because of my family," she starts. *Careful, careful. Draw her in.* "See, that house—wait. Let me tell you the whole story."

Sloane leans in, and Harlow keeps her smile to herself. *She's into this. Good.*

"So one day last year my mom gets a call, right?" Harlow says. She keeps her voice light, like yesterday, and only just stops herself from tossing her no-longer-there hair back. "From somebody who says they're an attorney and we have to come to this reading of a will, and at first my mom's like, sorry, *what*? But then she calls my grandma who says yeah, your uncle—your dad's brother—he just died. But the thing is my mom didn't grow up with her dad: her parents had an ugly divorce when she was a kid and she basically hardly saw her dad after that—I mean, I've never even met him, and he's my grandfather. So this uncle of hers—my great-uncle, I guess—had gotten some kind of property from his wife after she died. And *she* got it from *her* sister." She pauses to laugh at the confused look on Sloane's face. Yes, it's complicated, this fake family tree—exactly how Harlow wanted it to be, landing on the perfect iteration sometime last night when she was planning her next move. Take a little bit of the truth (dead family member), come up with a distant relative (never knowing they existed feels pretty distant), throw in a family rift or two (who doesn't love an ugly divorce?), and like magic, a cover story that sounds real enough for people to believe, but way too boring for them to look into.

"Hold up," Sloane says, frowning in concentration. "So . . . your great-uncle, his wife, her sister . . ." She nods. "Okay, got it. No, hold up again—so the property . . ."

She trails off, one eyebrow raised, and then Harlow nods. "If you're thinking it's this Severn House place, then yeah. You'd be one hundred percent correct. And—" She holds her hands out, palms to the sky, and shrugs. "If you're also thinking, *Oh my god get to the point,* then the point of all this is that me and my mom, we go to this will reading—my mom *drags* me there—and it's a good thing she did, because it turns out that somehow *I* have now inherited this house." Harlow claps her hands together. "Fucking *surprise,* I guess!"

Sloane's mouth drops open. "So you *own* that house now?" she says. "Oh my god. I mean . . . cool? Welcome to town? Hope you like your neighbors the woods and absolute darkness?"

Harlow winces, playing along. "Yeah, the house is not exactly a dream, but let's be real, this was probably the only way I was ever going to become a homeowner." She gives a small smile. "But I didn't just come here to spend my break cleaning up a dusty old house that somehow now belongs to me. See, because of the whole divorce and my mom's dad being pretty much a deadbeat piece of shit, we really had no connection with that whole side of the family. So I had no idea who my great-uncle's wife was, or her sister, the one who the house came from in the first place. But last year, after all of that, I started doing some research and—"

Sloane cuts her off. "And that's when you found out that the woman who lived there—"

"Disappeared," Harlow says, and she laughs, a strange sound like she's almost amused but also knows this is so awful, like of course she has to laugh, because it's so completely weird and not something that would ever happen to her, a normal girl with a normal life. "I think her name was Eve or something?"

Sloane nods. "Eve Kennedy," she says. "Yeah. I've heard about it. But—" Sloane looks at her, curious. "So what was with the story yesterday?"

"You mean, why did I lie?" Harlow waves a hand in front of her face like she's embarrassed, like of course lying is a weird thing for her to do, just like being connected to a mysterious disappearance is weird. She wants this girl Sloane to believe she is normal, like her. Nothing to hide, no intense trauma, certainly not careening from a car accident that killed her mom to the place she was running from, not at all.

Harlow fights the temptation to touch the bruise on her forehead, that she had spent a long time covering up with makeup before she left the house. She's not entirely convinced she succeeded, isn't sure whether Sloane can see the mark shining through all the concealer and her hair swept over it. It hurts less today, at least—the pain in her head has reduced to a dull ache, and while her entire chest and rib cage is still sore, she can grit her teeth through it so nobody else knows.

She's aware Sloane is still looking at her, waiting for an answer, and Harlow sighs. "I don't know," she says. "I guess in a way I feel like . . . weirdly protective? I mean, sure I never met this woman, and I never even heard of her before all of this but—she did go *missing.* It's kind of grim. I didn't want to show up here and have people thinking I was some asshole getting my kicks from digging into some poor missing woman. And I also didn't—don't—want to let people know that I'm related to her right away, in case they start asking me questions or getting way too involved. Does that make any sense at all?"

Sloane takes a long pull of her coffee—iced, even in this weather—and then says, "Yeah. I get it." She rakes a hand through her long hair, leaving her beautifully disheveled. "So. You're here.

You're looking at this house that's yours, now. And . . . is that it?"

She's asking even though she knows that's not it, Harlow can already tell. She's asking, because she wants to know what Harlow's really doing here, because she's intrigued, now.

Harlow flicks her tongue out to wet her lips. "Tell me," she says. "If it were you, and you just found out that somebody you were related to vanished into thin air almost twenty years ago— wouldn't you want to *know*? Wouldn't you want to find out what happened? Whenever I see that some girl has gone missing some-where, or you hear those stories, you know the ones, I always feel—it pisses me off, and it makes me so sad, because how can a person be around one day and gone the next and no one ever bothered to find out what happened?" Her heart hammers fast as she says this, the closest thing to the truth that she has told Sloane so far. *Careful.* She can feel more bubbling up, coming to a scalding, boiling need: *This missing woman, that's where my mom came from, and I want to know what happened to her to make my mom so afraid. I want to know if Eve is dead, or if she might be alive out there, somewhere. What if she's alive out there, has been for all these years?* Without a body and a definitive end, it's so hard to say it's over. Harlow doesn't know how to face the idea that in one swoop she both found her grandmother and lost her. The woman who made her family, who she never got to know.

Sloane places her half-finished coffee on the ground, straight-ening to look intently at Harlow. "If it were me," she says, "I would be doing exactly what you're doing. Hello, a mystery? A missing woman? A haunted house? No fucking question, I would want to find out."

Annoyance flares in the pit of Harlow's stomach when Sloane says the shit about the haunted house. She wants to tell her that this isn't a joke, to take it fucking seriously, but that would be too dangerous. The version of Harlow she's giving this girl, she can't be too emotionally invested. For that version, this is a curiosity, a somber mystery that she's found herself connected to. She can't let on exactly how close to this she really is.

But beneath the annoyance, there's a swell of excitement, too. This is the closest Harlow has been to playing herself in her whole life. People always say lying is addictive, but Harlow already feels that the opposite can be true. It's a little thrilling, skirting so close to the truth, almost revealing herself. *Almost.*

"I don't really know much about the whole thing beyond that she went missing," Sloane's saying now. "I think I've heard it brought up maybe, like, half a dozen times in my whole life. And then there's the house, but people just tell stories about it. No one even goes there, it's not even fun like that. So I don't think I can really help, but you know who might? Ruby, at the salon. She's my mom's cousin—my mom moved here and lived with Ruby, until she met my dad. Ruby's lived in town her whole life. She would have been here for all of it. I bet she remembers." Sloane tips her head to the side. "You know, it is weird, now that I'm thinking about it. It's weird that I've never heard much about this, about Eve. You would think it's the kind of story people would talk about more."

"Yeah," Harlow says, trying not to let the bitterness seep through, keeping that light, curious-girl voice going. "You would think." She shakes it off. "So you think Ruby wouldn't mind talking to me?"

"Not if I ask her nicely." Sloane stands, takes out her buzzing phone and makes a face at the screen before putting it back in her pocket and looking at Harlow again. "In fact, if we get back there now, she can probably spare some time. She had a cancellation this morning." And she smiles, her tongue peeking out between crooked teeth. "See? It pays to know the front desk girl."

15

"Eve Kennedy?" Ruby steps away from the mirror, sounding perplexed. "You want to talk to me about . . . Eve Kennedy? Why?"

Sloane nods in Harlow's direction. "I'll let her explain that."

Then Ruby is staring at her, expectant, and Harlow finds her mouth is dry suddenly. She feels stupid, expecting her flimsy story to work on another person, relying on it to give her enough cover to keep her out of danger. But what choice does she have, if she wants answers?

Ruby's still staring, light eyes ringed with dramatic liner. She's dressed all in black, like the other stylists are, but where they are mostly in jeans and bleach-stained T-shirts, Ruby wears a combination of gauzy layers over tights with runs, cinched at the waist with a corsetlike belt. She's tall, imposing, tattoos visible on what little of her skin is exposed. Regal, almost.

Harlow swallows and forces her shoulders down, her weight on one hip. "I'm kind of doing some family research," Harlow tells Ruby. "And it turns out this Eve—" She inserts a note of uncertainty here, like she's not used to saying Eve's name yet, like she might not even be sure if she got the name right. "It turns out I'm related to her, and actually I inherited that house out there in the woods, but I only just found out about any of it. All of it."

"She means she just found out that Eve Kennedy disappeared," Sloane says, smiling like she's *so* helpful.

Harlow glances at Sloane, and then back to Ruby. "Right," she says. "So I'm . . . interested in finding out what happened. And Sloane said you lived here when it happened, and you might talk to me about it."

Ruby looks to Sloane and shakes her head. "You have such a big mouth," she says, but then she puts a hand on Harlow's shoulder, turning her. "Come on. I'm due a break. Let's go out the back."

Harlow lets herself be steered through the salon, glancing over her shoulder at Sloane as they disappear into the darkness.

They're in a small back room piled high with boxes, a counter with a couple of cabinets and a sink running along one wall, just enough space for a tiny table and a love seat in the middle of it all.

Ruby gestures at the green velvet chair, indicating for Harlow to sit, while she opens a mini refrigerator and takes out a soda. "You want one?" she asks. "Or water? Coffee?"

Harlow can feel the coffee she drank with Sloane sitting cold in the pit of her stomach. "No," she says. "Thanks."

Ruby closes the refrigerator, leans against the counter, and cracks her soda, the hiss of it filling the quiet. "So," she says after a moment. "How exactly are you related to the Kennedys?"

Harlow perches on the edge of the love seat—it's more form than function, the legs spindly enough to feel like they won't even take her weight—and says, "It's complicated. My great-uncle was married to Eve's sister. We didn't really have much of a connection with that side of the family, though, so I didn't know anything about what happened to Eve before last year."

Ruby raises the soda to her lips. "What happened last year?"

Harlow wonders how Ruby keeps her deep-dark-red lipstick from smearing. It's perfect, her Cupid's bow sharply defined, the color dramatic against her pale white skin and platinum hair. "He died. My great-uncle," she clarifies. "That's when I found out about the will. He never had any kids. I guess I was the only one really left for him to pass the house on to."

"That's gotta be a fun surprise," Ruby says. "Nothing better than finding out about long-lost relatives only when somebody dies."

Harlow laughs a little. "Super fun," she says, and she feels like she delivered the story well, that Ruby is buying her version of events.

Ruby sets the soda down and folds her arms across her chest. She looks tired, circles under her eyes. If she were guessing, Harlow would say she was maybe a few years older than her mom, but she's not always the best judge of age. "And Sloane told you to come talk to me about this," she says, and it's not a question. "Well. I don't know what answers you're looking for, or if you think there's some crazy interesting story behind Eve's disappearance, but whatever it is, I don't know how much help I can be to you. I didn't even meet Cora until after Eve was gone."

"Cora?" Harlow's whole body jolts to attention at hearing her mom's name come out of Ruby's mouth. *She knew her. Ruby knew my mom, way back when. She knew her before any of this started—* or no, not before, because Ruby just said Eve had already been gone when they'd met, and that's interesting. It means that her mom didn't leave Crescent Ridge when Eve vanished; she stuck around after, and if she stayed then maybe it wasn't something to do with Eve's disappearance that made her run. Or maybe it was and her mom just didn't discover the thing that scared her until sometime later.

Harlow steadies herself, hopes that she has contained her reaction fast enough so that Ruby didn't notice, can't tell how much Harlow wants to explode open with questions. What was her mom like back then, when she was a teenager herself? What did they do together, where did they hang out? What made her mom laugh? *Did you ever go to that lake with her? Did you see her all bright and shiny in the sun coming off the water?*

Ruby doesn't appear to have noticed Harlow's response. She only shifts her weight and says, "Yeah, Cora. Eve's daughter? One of them, at least. Isn't that why Sloane told you to see me, because I was friends with Cora?"

Harlow shrugs. "I guess," she says. "I didn't know Eve had kids, is all."

Ruby buys the lie. "Really? Shit. I guess we're starting from the top," she says. "Yeah, okay. So this is what I know at least. They lived out there in the woods, just the four of them—Eve, Cora, and the other girls, Christina and Clementine. Their dad died when they were all pretty young, I think. They were, like . . . not shut-ins, but they didn't come into town a lot. Cora was home-schooled, up until Eve disappeared. She got her GED after that.

That's when we met, in class—I dropped out of high school after I went on a two-year bender or whatever. And we never really talked about her mom because—what do you even say? I always figured if she wanted to talk about her, she would. I wasn't going to be one of those bitches who tried to get all the gory details and all that. But as far as I know—what the news said and the story that went around town—Eve went out for groceries one evening and she never came home. That's when I started seeing the girls around town, and you know what I always remember thinking? How it felt like they were these mythical creatures, finally emerged from the forest to grace us mortals with their presence."

Harlow can imagine that too, how it would feel to see those three laughing girls in the photographs in the flesh, beaming their brightness onto everyone.

But she frowns a little, confused, too. "When you say you started seeing them then," she says, "when you say you met Cora in class, you don't mean you never met them before that. Right?"

"No, that's what I meant."

"But they lived here," Harlow says. "Their whole lives. Right?" It doesn't make sense, this vision Ruby is painting of the lesser-spotted Kennedy girls, not with the world Harlow has been creating in her own imagination.

"Sure," Ruby says. "But I told you, they were homeschooled. They didn't come into town. They kept themselves to themselves out there in the woods. At least until Eve was gone, and I guess they had no choice, then. Had to start looking after themselves."

Suddenly the images Harlow has conjured up—Eve getting her wine and chatting to the sales assistant, her mom in high school weaving through packed corridors and smiling at everyone who said hi to her, her mom with Christina and Clementine out at the county fair eating too many funnel cakes and flirting on the Ferris wheel—they all fracture. Spider cracks like the one in the bedroom ceiling, spreading across the glossy visions. If they were homeschooled, then that means no Friday night football games, no sitting in the cafeteria holding court. If they kept to themselves in the woods, that means no sepia-toned days out, no Eve marching her trio of little girls through town to pick up flowers from the market stall and cupcakes from the bakery.

It sounds, to Harlow, as if Eve was keeping the girls close. Hiding even.

It feels familiar. Like what Harlow has spent her whole life doing with her own mother—except where they were moving, Eve kept them still.

Maybe that was their downfall, Harlow thinks, because if all this is true, then perhaps what she's been thinking is wrong. Perhaps the danger didn't start when Eve vanished—it began far before that.

It seems, to Harlow, like Eve was trying to keep the girls safe.

"Harlow?"

She snaps back to attention. "Sorry," she says. "It's just a lot to try and piece together. So—" She pauses, unsure whether saying what she wants to is too strange, too callous. *Ask the questions if you want the answers,* she thinks. "Are you still in touch with Cora? Do you think there's any way you could connect us?"

I am sick in the head, she thinks. *Asking this woman to connect me with my own dead mother.*

Ruby gets a faraway look on her face, something altogether

softer than her expression has been previously. "No," she says, "no, we don't keep in touch. I haven't seen her in years. She left town a couple years after Eve went missing, and I never heard from her again."

Yeah, that sounds like my mom, Harlow thinks. But she makes a mental note of another piece of information Ruby has given her: two years. That's how long her mom stayed in Crescent Ridge before taking off.

Ruby rubs at her nose. "There is someone who might know where she's at," she says. "My older cousin Tommy married this chick who was a cop right around the time Eve disappeared. I don't know, she might have some idea of where Cora is, be able to connect you two. Or maybe she could answer your questions about Eve better than I can, at least."

A sourness rises in Harlow's throat. She should tell Ruby that Cora Kennedy is gone, Cora Kennedy is dead and there's no talking to her ever again. But she can't, of course, so instead she swallows the sour down and says, "Yeah, that would be cool," even though she doesn't trust cops in the slightest. But if she wants to know what went down officially, how hard the authorities tried to find Eve, and maybe what theories they had about her disappearance, then this is the best way of getting that information. "If you don't mind."

"I'll have to ask my cousin," Ruby says. "They split up a few years ago, but I don't see why she wouldn't do it. Marcy's pretty decent."

"Marcy?"

"Marcy Sheffield," Ruby says. "Here, give me your number, and I'll pass it along."

Ruby hands Harlow her phone, and Harlow taps her name and number in the contacts. When she gives the phone back, she catches sight of the tattoo on the back of Ruby's hand: a traditional heart with a blue banner wrapped around it, rippling in a forever suspended wind. The banner itself says *however far away* in crisp, clear script. "Wow," Harlow says. "I love that. Does it mean anything?"

Ruby holds her hand up to look at the piece, as if she forgot she even had it despite it being right there in front of her all the time. "Oh, yeah," she says. "It's a line from this song by a band I love that you've probably never heard of, you're such a baby. They were big before even *I* was born, anyway. I got it for—" There's a split second of hesitation. "For a girl I loved a long, long time ago."

The line echoes in Harlow's mind. *However far away, however far away.* God, why does that sound so familiar?

Then a memory hits her: she and her mom in the car, on a perfect autumn day, her mom sliding that same Cure album into the CD player as Harlow began to sink into sleep, on their way to the next life.

She looks up at Ruby, and Ruby is watching her curiously, something so sad in her eyes. And Harlow knows the truth of it all in that moment, what Ruby and her mom had been to each other, what this tattoo means, and it takes the air right out of her.

She wishes she could tell Ruby that her mom held on to those songs, at least. That she might have abandoned her, but she didn't stop thinking about her.

Again, of course, she can't.

So she looks away first, fixes her gaze somewhere to the left of Ruby and says, "I hope she loved you, too."

16

Harlow waves to Sloane, busy shampooing a customer, as she heads out of the salon.

She spends the rest of the day walking around town, trying to imagine this place as her mom saw it growing up here. It's small, like one-high-school small, but serpentine, roads wrapping around each other and lanes revealing new corners, tucked away stores in the center of town and hidden houses farther out.

She walks until her feet are sore, boots rubbing a blister on her heel, and drenched through from the slow but insistent rain. By the time she makes it back to her car the shops on the main street are closing, the restaurants and coffee shop the only ones still lit up. Harlow looks toward the salon and sees it's in darkness too.

She drives home, to the house, and this time the drive down the narrow track feels a little more claustrophobic.

When she's in the house, it feels a little smaller. She imagines what it would be if this was the only place she went, if that was how her mom and her sisters lived. Homeschool lessons at the table in the kitchen, reading sessions with the books piled on the living room shelves, spending the rest of their time occupying themselves playing in the woods. Fine for a little kid, maybe, but imagine the boredom escalating as they got older. You can't make friends in the woods. Were they good girls? Did they abide by their mom's paranoia, like Harlow has always done? Or did they brush it off and convince themselves it was no big deal to sneak out to that party they'd heard about, to walk a couple miles so they could hang out at a diner with all the other kids their age?

Harlow flicks on the lights as she walks through to the living room, dusk already beginning to creep through the woods. *You're getting ahead of yourself,* she thinks. She doesn't even know if she's right, in her hunch that Eve was trying to hide them out here. Maybe it wasn't like that, or maybe it was, but Eve had been better at covering it than Cora was. Imagine if Harlow believed they moved so much for fun, because her mom liked to travel, liked the change, rather than because there was somebody after them. Maybe she could have felt more normal then.

It's not until she focuses in on the living room that she senses it. It's small, at first, a humming feeling that something is off. But then the more Harlow looks around the room, the louder the humming becomes, the more everything feels ever so slightly *wrong.*

First there is her laptop, which she is sure she left at the edge of the coffee table, but now sits crooked in the center. And the blanket on the couch—it's still undone, lazily tossed over the cushions, but it looks—*too* rumpled, somehow. As if it hasn't been thrown but rather carefully arranged, strewn in a way that says *I was like this before.* And there, by the bookshelves—was that book on the top shelf always leaning sideways, or is Harlow imagining that before now it stood perfectly straight?

Harlow swallows, a sudden charge in the air. She can't push out the thought in her head: *Someone has been inside this house.*

Without thinking too much, she makes her way to the kitchen and pulls a knife from the butcher block, the metal dull from the years but the blade still sharp. For the second time in less than twenty-four hours Harlow finds herself on edge and about to search the house for an intruder.

This time, there is no convenient evidence to the contrary that stops her.

Harlow moves on light feet, blood rushing in her ears. *How could somebody have gotten in?* She has the key from under the ceramic pot outside, hooked onto the ring with her car keys. *Yeah, because that's the only way someone could get into this house,* she thinks. *As if they couldn't just smash a window if they really wanted.*

She keeps a tight grip on the small knife as she moves quickly from room to room, each time flicking on the lights and expecting to see some figure throwing themselves at her, the bright flash of light maybe enough to throw them off for a second, long enough for Harlow to get the knife into their flesh.

Except in every room all she finds is emptiness. The same still air, the corners of dust that she couldn't quite reach, and nothing else out of place. In her mom's bedroom—her bedroom now—Harlow uses the last of her panic to search under the floorboards for the cash she's hidden there and finds every note present.

Search over, she sits on the edge of the bed and wipes one hand over her face, dropping the knife onto the covers with the other. *Maybe—*

She squeezes her eyes shut, trying to remember. Maybe she *did* leave her laptop in the center of the table. And the blanket— how would one fake toss a blanket over a couch like that, anyway? How would Harlow ever remember what it looked like before, when she'd thrown it off her shoulder? Then the book—Harlow hasn't even paid attention to the books before today. So yeah, it could have been standing perfectly straight before. But it also could have been leaning.

A haunted house, she thinks. *They say a woman in white will get you if you go too close.*

Blame Sloane for putting the ideas in her head, for sparking her own wave of paranoia.

Back downstairs she makes sure the front door is locked and leans against it, sinking into the quiet of the house. Somehow, now, knowing that she is fully alone is both a gift and a curse.

BEFORE

After the remnants of breakfast are half cleaned up, crumbs swept onto the floor to be dealt with later, and dishes soaking in the sink, the girls get ready for the memorial.

Because Christina is the oldest, she gets the shower first, like she always has, but then Cora breaks the order and lets Clem go next. While Clem is in there, Cora goes through their shared closet and pulls out a dark blue dress with thin straps and buttons up the front, and a black turtleneck to go underneath. She lays the clothes on Clem's bed along with a pair of thick tights—the wind is cold; Cora can tell by the way it sings through the trees outside. When Clem walks in wrapped in a towel, she makes a face at the clothes on her bed. "Are you for real?" she asks. "I'm not a baby, Cora. I think I can pick out my own *appropriate* outfit."

"Don't get bitchy," Cora says. "I just didn't want you to take anything I might want to wear."

"So you pick out *your* outfit, then." Clem rolls her eyes as she opens her underwear drawer. "Are you going to shower or what?"

Cora does, staying under the hot water for too long until it becomes cold again and her skin starts to chill. When she steps out of the water she averts her gaze from the mirror. On days like this it's harder to look at herself. To see the parts of her mom that live in her face looking back at her. It's as if her mom is watching her, accusatory, questioning. *Why haven't you found me? Why are you going along with this charade from the town? Where am I, Cora?*

By the time she steps into their shared bedroom, Clem is gone, although the dress Cora picked out remains, tossed on the floor now. Cora bites the inside of her cheek as she picks it up and slides it back onto its hanger. Clem talks a big game about how she's no baby, not a little kid, how she's fifteen and that means Cora and Christina should treat her like they treat each other, but then she does petulant shit like this. Like, would it have been so hard for her to put on the fucking dress? They're going to be standing up in front of a large audience today, with cameras on them. An audience that probably has a thousand theories about what happened to Eve, although none of them have ever panned out. That doesn't matter, though, Cora knows: people make up their minds about things like this. People decide not to believe them when they say *We have no idea where she is; no, she didn't give any indication that anything was wrong; no, she didn't talk about leaving; no, she didn't have a boyfriend, not that we knew about.* Especially when the woman missing is beautiful and still young and white, and the daughters she left behind are the wrong kind of young, feckless, Black, too close for comfort in a lot of people's eyes.

Cora pulls out a black denim skirt, not too short, and a prissy white blouse she bought especially for her first GED class, back when she didn't know how people dressed for something like that and wanted to make a good impression. Not to be the home-school weirdo coming out of the woods.

As she dresses, she forgets about the mirror on the inside of the closet door and can't help but catch a glimpse of her back, the part where her smooth brown skin is marked by a jagged lighter line, the scar snaking across and up toward her shoulder blades.

"Hey." Christina's voice comes from the doorway. "You almost ready?"

Cora drops her shirt, but not fast enough for Christina to miss what she was looking at.

Her older sister crosses the room. "Let me see," she says, and Cora drops her hands, lets Christina gently tug the back of her blouse high enough to reveal the scar again. "Hmm," she murmurs, and her fingers touch it lightly. "It's fading, I think."

"Not fast enough."

"I'll put in a call to the universe."

Cora allows herself a small smile at that. She turns to face Christina, tucking her blouse into her skirt. "What's Clem wearing?" she asks. "Please tell me she at least put the tights on."

"She's wearing a perfectly respectable black dress," Christina says. "And the tights, yes. I mean she'd be insane not to—it's fucking freezing today."

Christina is quiet for a moment while Cora searches out her own tights and shimmies into them, frowning at a hole in the left toe. *Too late to change,* she's thinking, when Christina breaks the quiet. "Do you think they know?" she asks quietly. "The cops? Do you think they have any idea at all?"

Cora's head snaps up, staring at her sister. "No," she says. "I don't think they know anything. They're fucking useless like all the rest." She lifts one eyebrow. "Does that make you feel better?"

"A little," Christina says.

From downstairs Clem's yell echoes. "Are you two ready? We're going to be late!"

Cora reaches out and squeezes Christina's hand. "Well, we don't want to be late," she deadpans. "Whatever would people think of us then?"

17

When Harlow wakes in the morning, she's disoriented again, lost in space for a second. But it takes only that second to remember where she is, acclimatizing quicker each time she wakes.

In the bathroom she brushes her teeth as she waits for the water streaming out of the shower to warm up, and considers her next steps. This is, she knows, something she learned from her mom, this desire to constantly be making a plan and writing a checklist of things to do, some kind of order to carry through the noise. That was how her mom used to do it, a habit Harlow didn't recognize until she was older, because when she was a tiny kid, it felt like chaos every time they moved—the packing, the driving, the nights in a motel until they could secure their own place. But as she got older, she learned to pay more attention, and then when she was older still, twelve or thirteen, her mom started to make Harlow do it with her. *Okay,* she would say as they sat in the car eating whatever fast food they'd picked up, *what's next?* New phones first always, because a phone could be tracked; a job for her mom, because even less than legit landlords wanted to know there was money coming; then the apartment; then school for Harlow, enrolled under her newest name, and all this while they were trying to remember those new names and realizing what they had left behind this time and her mom always, still, looking over her shoulder for their pursuer.

Harlow spits and rinses, staring at herself in the mirrored cabinet door. The steam from the shower fogs the glass, giving Harlow a ghostly mist around her reflection. Next item on the list today: call the power company and find out what's going on there. Somebody has been paying the bills, keeping the house running, and she's not sure who, or why. For her mom to have been paying bills on this place the whole time—it doesn't make sense, when she was trying so hard to get away from this town, to not leave a trail that anyone could follow. But if it wasn't her mom, logically it can only have been either Christina or Clementine, and it doesn't make sense to Harlow why either of *them* would be keeping the lights on in a house neither of them has lived in for seemingly years.

Harlow strips off her boxers and shapeless gray T-shirt before stepping into the hot water and closing her eyes. It's soothing, the pressure on her stress-tight muscles and the warmth radiating through her cold bones. It helps the ache in her ribs, still slowly subsiding.

She lets the water run through her hair and thinks about those sisters. Christina. Clementine. They don't know that their sister is dead. She thinks of the photographs, the three of them laughing together, looking as close as sisters can be, and wonders how they could have gotten to this place, a place where one of them could cease existing and the other two don't even know it. *Did they ever know where Mom went? Where did they go, when they left this place?* Did they run like her mom had gone at the same time but in different directions, or did they trickle out one by one, until there was nothing but the empty house left behind?

Harlow steps out of the shower, watching herself in the mirror again. She touches her fingers to the edges of the bruise on her forehead, wincing slightly. "Should I try to find them?" she asks her reflection. *Don't they deserve to know their sister is gone?*

She dresses in dark jeans and a thick black sweater of her mom's, pulled on over damp skin because it's too cold to wait. She finds herself gravitating toward the dark, here, in a place where she doesn't have to pretend as much. A uniform of black jeans and sweaters, and a black denim jacket she found in a thrift store three towns ago, boots that also once upon a time belonged to her mom but that Harlow had long ago claimed for herself.

Staring into the cracked mirror on the dresser she covers the bruise and draws on eyeliner, like she imagines her mom and Clementine would have done years ago, fighting over the space in front of the mirror and which makeup belonged to who and who was taking longer. That's what Harlow imagines life is when you have a sister: endless bickering fights, moments of teasing and skewering and annoyance that only cover up how deep the love goes. Especially for these girls, who had nobody else, it seems. Just the three of them and Eve, protected from the world out here among the trees.

Downstairs she starts on her work for the day. First she searches through drawers in hopes of finding a decades-old bill somewhere to start her off, but most of the drawers in both the kitchen and the living room are empty. There's a dresser in the dining room, but it doesn't open, the lock stuck tight with glue, and Harlow wonders if there was something in there that somebody never wanted found, or whether it was just Eve getting tired of the girls playing with things they shouldn't and finding a way to keep them out, permanently. *That's the problem with everything,* she thinks: *too many possible meanings, things that could be significant or mean nothing, occurrences that could be warnings or not.* Did Eve keep them out here because she was scared, or because she enjoyed the simplicity of it all? Did her mom run because of what happened to Eve, or was she just desperate to escape the claustrophobia of the woods? Things changed, depending on how you looked at them, depending on how much weight you were putting on them.

Harlow remembers coming into the house yesterday, that sensation that someone else had been inside. See, right there—a tipped-over book on the living room shelves: gravity, or the touch of a hand?

She takes out her phone and writes a text to Sloane, an attempt to swipe the chill sensation away and tell herself she wasn't afraid at all, that it's just a joke, really: **totally thought there was a ghost in the house last night. i'm blaming u for putting ideas in my head**

Before she can put her phone back in her pocket Sloane replies: **omg stop it**

listen if u need an exorcism u know where i am

or maybe just somebody to hold ur scaredycat hand

Harlow's cheeks warm, and she shoves her phone away. Come on. Focus. *Do not get distracted reading into harmless texts.*

She finds no bills, but there is a sticker on the inside of the cabinet that hides the fuse box, with a date stamped on it and what Harlow hopes is the name of a still active company. In the living room she opens her laptop and hot-spots off her phone to search for the company, finding that yes, they're still in operation and still providing power to the county that Crescent Ridge resides in.

From there, it's surprisingly easy to make it through to an actual person. It's harder to keep her voice steady when she tells the customer service rep on the other end of the line that she's sorry but no, "I don't have all the account details because I believe my mom was the account holder and she—she died very recently. I'm trying to chase up all these different things and she wasn't the best record keeper, but I have her social security number and her financial details and—"

She doesn't have to finish, because the rep rushes to assure her it's okay and that they can issue her temporary access to manage the account until Harlow can provide them with a death certificate and the proper account closure procedures can begin.

Death certificate.

Harlow pushes that aside and says, "Thank you, that would be perfect."

There's the click-clack noise of typing on the other end. "And I'm assuming you want to keep the additional account holder's access open too?"

"The other account holder?"

"Yes," the rep says. "You can have up to three people named on the account, one as the primary—so you'll be given temporary primary access, the . . . deceased account holder still has primary level, and the additional user is able to access the account and make payments but not make any changes. Did you want to leave it as that?"

Harlow's breath quickens. "Can I just check who that person is?"

"One sec . . ." More typing, and then: "Christina Kennedy. Is that okay?"

Harlow nods before she remembers the rep can't see her. "Yes," she says quickly, "yes, that's fine. Thank you for your help."

An email pings into her inbox as she hangs up, a set of temporary login details. Her mom *and* Christina are on the account. *So does that mean*—Harlow can't track her own thoughts. Were her mom and Christina in contact, then? Were they both paying the bill? Is her notion that her mom and the sisters had no contact wrong—was it only Harlow who her mom kept away from them?

Harlow uses the new details to log in, navigates to the account personal settings page, and there in front of her are her mom's details, her email, a phone number that Harlow knows for sure is a million years out of date, and an address they never lived at. But under that, there is Christina. An email address, a phone number, and her address. Just like that, a way to get in touch with this woman Harlow only a week or so ago didn't know existed.

She stares at the view from the living room window. She's getting used to the different kind of cold here, the wind constantly shh-shh-shushing through the trees. She's always been good at adjusting—new towns, new apartments, all that. But things here feel different. The moves she's making now feel different. This is not a place where no one knows her or her family at all; she's making ripples by being here, and she'll leave a wake when she goes. These are not strangers who she can convince to let her in, become her friends, and then abandon when she feels like it: this is her family. Her blood.

Before she can think too much, she taps the number into her phone, presses call, and puts the phone to her ear.

It rings twice, three times, and then a soft voice answers. "Hello?" When Harlow says nothing, the woman speaks again. "Hello? Is anyone there?"

Harlow swallows, her throat desert dry suddenly. "Hi," she says. "I'm—I'm looking for Christina Kennedy?"

There's a moment's silence, and then: "It's Diaz, now. Christina Diaz. But—who is this?"

"My name is Harlow," she says, fast, so she can't back out of it. "Cora Kennedy—I'm her daughter. I'm Cora's daughter."

18

The silence on the other end hangs for so long that Harlow begins to think Christina is gone, that she's waiting for air to respond.

But then there's a small noise, like a half-swallowed sob, and Christina says, "Cora? Cora Kennedy? She's your mother?"

Was, Harlow wants to say. *Was my mother.*

But one thing at a time.

"Yes," Harlow says. "And you're—you're her sister, right?"

"Yes. Yes, she's my—but how did you even find me?" Christina says, and Harlow thinks this is confirmation: Christina has been running too. Changing her name, hiding as somebody else. But then Christina says, "I haven't spoken to her in—god, I didn't even know she had a kid. I've been trying to find her for so long. And now—you found me."

There's an awed hush to Christina's words, and Harlow's interpretation of things shifts a bit: so it isn't that Christina has been running too, but that her mom ran so far her own sister couldn't even find her. *Of course she did.* Paranoia ruling everything—after all, if there was something really bad going on, wouldn't her sisters have run too? But instead of the three of them taking off, her mom had left them behind. Maybe had even convinced herself they were to be feared, as well.

"How old are you?" Christina's saying. "Does she know you're talking to me? Is she there? Can I talk to her? Oh my god."

Oh my god, Harlow thinks too. *Maybe this was a mistake.* How do you pick up the phone and find it's your sister's kid on the other end, a kid you didn't know existed, from a sister you lost touch with years ago, and then the kid tells you *Surprise, actually! She's dead.*

Harlow presses her fist into her thigh. "This is really—really hard to say," she starts, faltering. *Tell her quick, get it out there and over with so that this woman doesn't spend another second more thinking her long-lost sister has come back to her.* "I'm just going to say it. My mom is dead. She died a week ago. There was a bad car accident. And so—yeah," she finishes. "That's that."

"Oh my god," Christina says, and there's that same half sob as before. "No. *No.* I don't believe this. She can't be—" The line goes muffled, and Harlow can faintly make Christina out in the background, something like *No, honey, I can't play now. Mommy's sorry.*

Harlow feels sick. Maybe there was a better way to deliver the news. Maybe she shouldn't have told her at all. But that would be worse, Christina out there not knowing Cora was gone. *Like Clementine still doesn't know,* she thinks. "Christina?" she says. "Are you there?"

The line clears. "I'm here," Christina says, and she sounds

steadier now. "I'm sorry. It's such a—I always thought I'd see her again. Someday. But you—are you doing okay? Is your dad okay? Where are you—do you mind me asking? Where you're living now?"

Harlow holds back a laugh at the absurdity of what she's about to say. "Okay. This is going to sound so weird. But I'm in Crescent Ridge."

"You're—"

"And I don't have a dad," Harlow continues, cutting Christina off. "It was just me and Mom. I didn't even know about you, actually, or Clementine. Or your mom. My grandmother. I literally just found out that all of you exist and about what happened to your mom and this place and I don't really know what I'm doing or where to go so I came here to, I don't know, figure some shit out? Find out about my family?" In a rush Harlow is crying, her voice thick with it. "So I guess I wanted to call and speak to you to tell you about what happened to Mom but also to maybe ask you some questions, or find out if—"

Now Christina cuts her off. "You're in Crescent Ridge?" she says. "Right now?"

"Yeah." Harlow hiccups, turning it into a laugh. "I'm staying in your old house, actually."

This elicits a sharp intake of breath from Christina, and Harlow begins to form the question in her mind: *I know this is really weird but I'm kind of starting to get freaked out about being all on my own here, and I would really like to meet you and talk to you about everything, so maybe—I don't know, would you be able to come out here sometime soon? No pressure or anything—*

But she doesn't get the chance to ask before Christina speaks again, all business now. "Okay. Hold on. I'm booking a ticket now. I'll be on the first flight I can, okay?"

"What?"

"I'll be there as soon as I can," Christina says. "You shouldn't be out there all by yourself, dealing with this. So you know what, I have your number now—I'll have to make a couple calls to figure some things out but I promise you, I'll be on my way to you as soon as I can."

"But . . ." Harlow doesn't know what to say. "You're coming here?"

"Of course," Christina says. "We're family. This is what we do."

19

Harlow can't settle in the house, not knowing that Christina is at every moment moving closer toward her, on her way back to Crescent Ridge. She can't stop thinking of all the things she wants to ask Christina: Did she run too, or was her mom alone in that? Does she know where Clementine is, how Harlow can get in touch with her? What was it like growing up in this house? Why did she and Cora lose touch? What does she believe happened to Eve? What does it feel like, coming back here?

She goes into town, feeling a little like a stalker as she heads toward the salon, hoping Sloane will be sitting behind the front desk. But there's another girl at the desk, and Harlow veers off before she reaches the door. She pulls her phone out, thinking about texting Sloane again instead, but stops before she gets that far. *Don't come on too strong.* They just met and Harlow can feel herself becoming too intense too fast, the feeling of being closer than usual to her true self enticing her to put way too much trust—no, not trust: honesty—into this burgeoning new friend-ship.

Friendship. Yes, that's what she's going to call it, even though she thinks Sloane is beautiful in a way that makes her want to kiss her eyelids and press her palms either side of Sloane's ribs. Of course she would have a crush on the first girl she meets who seems cool. There are a lot of things in her life that have not been normal, experiences she has missed or skipped over entirely, but it's nice to know that she can still do the whole homoerotic is-she-or-isn't-she intense friendship thing.

So she won't look like she came here just to see Sloane—as if anyone is actually paying enough attention to her to think that, or notice her at all—Harlow veers into the bookstore a few doors down. It's quiet in there, and when the dark-skinned guy behind the counter wearing a shiny collection of pins on his jacket collar asks if she needs help, she shakes her head. She points at the arm-chairs at the back of the store, clustered around a display of mys-tery paperbacks. "Is it okay if I sit?" she asks. "I'll buy something, I swear."

He shrugs and smiles in a way that tells Harlow he's too stoned to care. "Have at it," he says, and goes back to processing a delivery.

Harlow browses the shelves, running her fingers across a rain-bow of spines, until she finds something that catches her attention. She sits in one of the chairs and makes it through three chapters of the apocalypse fairy tale before she can't keep still any longer.

She takes the book up to the counter, a crumpled twenty in her hand, and pays. Then she goes next door to the coffee shop and orders an iced tea, and as she hands over a ten this time, she starts thinking about all the money she's spent over the last week or so. The hotel in North Langston, the car, gas and motels and supplies as she made her cross-country drive. The food and cleaning supplies for the house, the book, the tea. Some things far smaller than others but still, it's all beginning to add up. And sure, her mom left her that money, but it's not going to last forever. Especially not if she keeps on spending at the rate she has been.

Her mind wanders as she waits for her drink. Because what is she going to do? She has that money, but when it runs out, that's it. *Well, there's the life insurance,* she thinks, although she has no idea how much might come to her from that, and besides, it doesn't feel like something she should count on. Not while she doesn't have a number in mind, at least. Plan for the worst, expect—usually, the absolute fucking most terrible worst. Maybe she could sell the house, but who would buy it? She doesn't even know that she could bring herself to do it, to sell the place where her mom grew up, even if that's part of the reason her mom left it to her, to help take care of her.

"Peach tea?" the barista calls out, and Harlow snatches it up, noticing the makeup of the coffee shop's current crowd—office workers swinging through, parents with kids in strollers, older guys coming in for black coffee and bagels, kids her own age on winter break like Sloane.

Harlow takes her iced tea to a small table by the front window. Okay, even if she *does* sell the house, and there's life insurance money, she'll still need to make money on her own. She won't be able to live off that for the rest of her life, unless her mom secretly had, like, a million-dollar policy on herself.

So she'll need a job, and for that she'll need a diploma, mini-mum. Harlow sips her iced tea and winces at the brutal sweetness of it. This is all the shit she has never really considered before—what she would do after high school, what kind of life she might lead. There was never any room for her to think about it because she knew what her life was and how it was going to continue: her and her mom and the running. College wasn't an option, not if it meant staying in the same place for years, vulnerable.

A raindrop rolls down the window, racing along a path traced earlier by someone else's finger. Harlow does the same thing, pull-ing her finger along the damp glass on a path of her own choosing. *But now I'm here,* she thinks. *And I'm making progress, and if I can find out what really happened to Eve, what my mom was really run-ning from, then maybe I can stop. Then a diploma and college and whatever comes after—*

With all her questions answered, that future might be the kind she can actually reach for, but god—right now it feels like a pain-ful stretch.

Then, on cue, her phone buzzes on the tabletop. It's a text, from an unknown number: **Hi. This is Marcy Sheffield—Ruby gave me your number. She said you'd like to ask some questions about a relative of yours. Are you able to meet me this evening at Monroe's? Looking forward to hearing from you.**

It takes Harlow less than thirty seconds to answer: **Is six okay? I'll meet you there.**

Monroe's, it turns out, is a diner on the outskirts of town, the way Harlow drove in. It gleams bright in the evening dark with a neon sign and the lights of the bowling alley beside it, two pins knocking into each other over and over.

Harlow parks and checks her reflection in the rearview mirror before she gets out of the car. She wants to seem serious, not like she's some idiot kid on a morbid voyeur chase. She licks her pinky finger and rubs off the smeared mascara under both eyes. Better.

As soon as she walks into the mostly empty place, a white woman in a blazer and white button-down waves at her.

"Harlow?" the woman says when Harlow reaches her table.

"Yeah," she says. "How did you know—"

"An educated guess." The woman sticks her hand out. "Marcy Sheffield. Pleasure to meet you."

Harlow shakes her hand, suppressing a smile. Marcy looks somehow exactly like Harlow had pictured from that one single text message: older, formal, a little uptight. Her button-down is perfectly white and crease free, her dark blond hair pulled back into a neat twist, and on the table the sugar packets have been organized by color. "Thanks for talking to me," Harlow says as she slides into the booth. "I know it's weird. I show up out of the blue like this. . . ."

Marcy purses her lips, but there's a gleam in her eyes that says maybe she's not quite as rigid as she looks. "To tell you the truth, I wasn't all that surprised," she tells Harlow. "I always had a feeling this would come back. Of course, I didn't quite expect the person who came looking for Eve to be a long-lost relative."

"No?" Harlow says drily. "I can't imagine why." Then she leans forward, elbows on the sticky table. "Who did you expect?"

It's an indulgent leading question, she knows, but she wants to hear Marcy say it. "I always thought one of the girls might come back," Marcy says. "Eve's daughters. But it's been a long time since anyone heard from them, so maybe that's wishful thinking on my part."

"Did you know them well?" Harlow asks it carefully, trying to sound more curious than desperate, desperate to hear more people talk about her mom. "The girls?"

"Not well," Marcy says, "but I did spend some time with them, when I was working. I suppose I got the impression they weren't the kind of girls to let something terrible happening to them fade out with no consequences." Marcy glances over at the counter and the girl with long pink braids behind it. "Taylor, could I get a tuna melt?" she calls out, and looks to Harlow. "Anything for you?"

Harlow scans the menu, suddenly ravenous but also aware of the talk she had with herself earlier, not wanting to burn through too much of her cash on cheeseburgers and onion rings. "I'll just get a grilled cheese," she says.

"Are you sure?" Marcy pats the table. "It's on me. Get whatever you want."

Politeness makes her resist for a second, but then Harlow says, "Actually, I'll have a cheeseburger and fries, and onion rings, and a Diet Coke. Please."

Marcy smiles. "Did you get that?" she says to the girl behind the counter, who nods and disappears into the back.

Marcy turns her attention back to Harlow. "Okay," she says. "So. What would you like to know, exactly?"

"About Eve?" The waitress appears with her soda then, and Harlow takes it and gulps down half of it in one go, her teeth turning icy.

"About whatever it is you think I can help you with," Marcy says. "I'm an accountant now, but back then I was part of the county police, as I'm sure Ruby told you."

Harlow looks at her in surprise. "You left? You're not a cop anymore?"

"God, no." Marcy looks down at herself. "Why? Do I still look like one?"

If anything Harlow had thought that when Ruby said Marcy *used to* be a cop, it meant she was retired now. Truthfully, yeah, she does still look like a cop—one of the grim, cold ones who rose up the ranks by doing everything her superiors wanted, so that now she could sit in an office all day and use that same power to get what she wanted done. "I don't know," Harlow says carefully. "I guess I didn't really think too much about it. Why did you leave?"

Marcy smooths an invisible speck of lint off her blazer. "Oh, I was just a kid when I joined," she says. "So naive. I thought I was going to be a good guy and protect people, you know. All the things they feed you. Then I started actually doing the job, and I realized it's not like that at all. Mostly it's people who are power hungry looking for ways to put smaller people down. Especially in a town like Crescent Ridge, where we mainly have petty crimes—it didn't feel good to me trying to put some kid away for possession when I knew half the guys on the force had done the exact same thing when they were in high school." She pauses and her eyes widen, as if she realizes only now what she said. "I mean—I don't mean to say what happened to Eve was a small thing. That was different, obviously."

The waitress brings their food, sliding plates onto the table. "If you need anything else, just yell," she says.

Harlow watches the waitress walk back to the counter, a bounce in her step that sets her braids swinging, pick up the pot of coffee, and go over to refill a customer's cup. Maybe Harlow could be a waitress, in a place like this. Remember her regulars' orders and develop a shorthand language with the weed-smoking cook in the back. Maybe she could be the weed-smoking cook, even. Stashed away in the kitchen throwing together eggs and bacon and hash browns, club sandwiches and fries. Come home to an apartment of her own smelling like grease and sore from a hard day's work.

She looks back at Marcy, taking a dainty bite of her tuna melt. Maybe she could be like Marcy—go to school, get a degree, and become someone who tells other people what to do with their money. Spend her days in smart little suits, in a sleek office, with a secretary who answers the phone and goes to get coffee for her.

Harlow's stomach growls, and she puts a pause on her fantasizing to take a big bite of her burger, ketchup leaking out the corner of her mouth. She catches it with a finger and wipes it off on a napkin, a bright smear across the white surface. "Can you tell me?" she asks. "How it went down, from your side? All I know is what I've read online. That Eve didn't come home one day and the girls—her daughters—reported her missing the next day, and then she was never seen after that. Hasn't been seen since."

Marcy's neatly filled-in eyebrows knit together, and she shakes her head, putting her sandwich down. "Well. That's about the sum of it," she says. "She was last seen at the grocery store. After the girls reported it, we did a few drive-bys of places she was known to frequent, but it was a long shot—as if she would have spent all night at the hardware store. After that, a large-scale search of the woods was organized, but after a few days of looking, we hadn't found anything to indicate she was in the woods or that anything out of the ordinary had taken place out there. We also ran her license plate, her credit cards, put her photo in every database we had . . ." She sighs. "Nothing."

"What about a boyfriend? An ex?" Harlow asks. "What about the girls' dad?"

"She didn't have a boyfriend that anybody could point to," Marcy says. "She kept pretty much to herself. Some people might call her reclusive, with the way she decided to homeschool the girls and how she retreated from the community, but I think it was understandable, after—well, you see, the girls' father is deceased. He died years before she went missing. So all in all, there wasn't much to go on. Everyone who did know her found her to be a sweet woman, quiet but nice enough to talk to. We couldn't figure out any motive for anyone wanting to hurt her— no debts, no drugs, no jilted lovers, no hidden family issues . . . it truly just seemed as if she'd up and vanished into thin air."

Harlow tilts her head to the side. "Or as if someone completely unknown to her picked her off the street and took her."

"Well." Marcy presses a hand to her throat. "That was something else we considered. But there were no unusual sightings reported. When we found her car—that was a little strange, but the only prints found on it belonged to her, and to the girls. But I suppose—it could very well be a possibility that that's what happened. Back then I was an entry-level officer. I tried to hear and see everything, but I wasn't in charge of anything. I wish I could be more helpful." She moves her hand away, and it leaves behind red marks on her pale skin, the shadow of her own grip. "Tell me," she says suddenly. "Why did you really want to talk to me? Why are you so interested in knowing what happened back then?" Her gaze skips around Harlow's face. "After all, it's not going to bring her back." A pause. "Eve. Your grandmother."

Harlow has just taken another bite of her burger when Marcy says it, and she half chokes it down, caught by such surprise. When she's swallowed, she takes a gulp of her drink, feeling everything moving painfully through her throat and catching somewhere behind her ribs. "I don't know what you're talking about," she says eventually, weakly. "I don't—"

Marcy raises her eyebrows. "I'm still a good enough cop to remember that there was no sister of Eve's, no other family on that side. Which would make it difficult for you to be, what was it—the distant niece of her sister's husband?" She sighs loudly. "And you look like them. The girls. You look so much like them. I may not be a cop anymore, but I'm not completely out of it, Harlow."

Harlow doesn't know what to say. She hadn't counted on being caught out like this, hasn't prepared any backup story or anything. Didn't think anyone would pay close enough attention to figure out who she actually was.

But now Marcy Sheffield has, and Harlow can tell from the look in her eye that she's not going to just let Harlow go without getting her own answers.

The diner is quiet, but Harlow still looks around. There's a guy a few booths down half-asleep over his plate, a tired goth in the back typing on a laptop, and a woman in scrubs forcing eggs into a toddler's mouth. Safe enough, Harlow thinks. *If safe is something I can ever really be.*

She meets Marcy's gaze. "Cora," she says softly. "Cora was my mom."

She sees Marcy catch that past tense. "Was?" Marcy says. "Oh, no."

"It's okay," Harlow says, even though of course it isn't. She cannot face saying it all right now and then going home and having to deal with the consequences of unlocking that box in her chest. "But you want to know why I'm here, and that's why. My mom died, and she never really talked about her family. I didn't even know about Eve or that I *had* aunts until recently. So I came here to . . . learn more about my family. When I said that, I wasn't lying. I haven't lied about that part at all."

Marcy nods slowly, and she looks sad. "It was just you and your mom?"

"Yeah."

"So now it's—"

"Just me." Harlow holds her hands out, fingers spread wide. "Yeah."

Marcy twists the small gold stud in her right earlobe. "Why lie at all?" she asks. "I don't understand."

Of course you don't, Harlow thinks. *I bet your mother told you to tell the truth, that lying was a bad thing that bad girls did. I grew up with Cora, and Cora taught me how to lie, so that's what I'm doing, it's what I always do.*

Harlow breathes in slowly, feels her lungs inflate to the point where her busted ribs hurt with the movement, and lets it all out in a heavy exhale. Marcy may have figured out who she is, but she doesn't need to know the rest. Harlow can't tell her the rest, because after all, she barely knows this woman, and as much as Harlow would like to fully trust her, being on her guard is another one of her mom's lessons that she cannot shake.

Marcy's waiting for an answer, though, so Harlow tells her the only thing she can think of. "I don't want people to know who I really am and start treating me like their own personal true crime entertainment," she says. "I just wanted to come here and be able to find out about this traumatic thing in my family without having people staring at me everywhere I go or running to talk about me online. That's why I made up some extra details." Harlow sits up straighter and puts her shoulders back. Actually, maybe she *can* take a little truth. "And I think it's fucked up that someone could disappear into thin air and no one seems that bothered about it. I think it's fucked up that three girls were left without their mother and no one did anything for them. I think it's fucked up that my family has been treated this way."

To that Marcy says nothing. She only nods, looking grim, as if she knows she has no legitimate rebuttal. Then she picks up her sandwich, and Harlow picks up her burger, and they eat in silence.

When Marcy is finished, she brushes the crumbs from her fingertips and says, "I could reach out to some old colleagues and see how they can help you. If that's okay with you."

Harlow allows herself to smile then, a mixture of relief that Marcy is on her side, that her half-truths are fully believable, and nervous energy at the thought of finally getting to speak to some-one who *really* knows something. "Sure," she says. "That would be great."

Marcy reaches across the table as if to touch Harlow's hand but then seems to think better of it. "Okay" is all she says. "I'll get right on it."

20

Harlow can't sleep.

She spends a few hours tossing and turning, legs tangled in the sheets, and then gives up and steals out of bed.

She slips downstairs in the dark, trailing her hand along the wall, the stair railing, because she doesn't know this place in the dark yet. Sometimes it seems like she feels a pulsing beneath her fingers. Like the house has a heartbeat of its own.

Harlow puts on her boots and her jacket and leaves the house behind. She's aware she's not at all adequately dressed for the cold as she steps into the dawn chill in her pajamas and jacket, legs bare, but she almost doesn't feel it. Or it feels good, a wave of wind over her skin, washing away the troubled night.

The sky is beginning to turn from night to dawn, the subtle shift of black sky to deep morning blue, as she sets off into the woods, making sure to keep in a fairly straight line—the last thing she wants is to get lost, find herself unable to untangle the route back to Severn House.

It's quiet out among the trees, only the small sounds of nature: wind through the leaves, the creak of high-up branches, birds and their morning chorus, the subdued trickle of a creek. Harlow likes the way her footsteps sound as she strides out: the snaps of small branches, the rustle of fallen leaves underfoot. She ignores the small thorns that scrape her skin and the leaves that sting.

When she has walked far enough, maybe too far, she finds herself in a clearing. A small piece of flattened land, the raw stumps of forgotten trees speckling the surface. Harlow tips her head back to stare up into the foliage, rising dark greens and reds and browns beneath the watery first glances of the sun. Harlow forgets the feeling of claustrophobia she had the other day, winding her way back through the woods. There's nothing claustrophobic about this open space, no one around for miles, all the sounds and senses of the natural world hovering under the cloudless sky.

Eyes closed, Harlow pulls in deep breath after deep breath, until her bones feel like liquid and all she can smell is the sharp scent of evergreens. Within the moments when the wind dies down, Harlow can even convince herself she feels warmth from the winter sun, real *warmth* on her face. Those moments end as quickly as they began, but Harlow stands still anyway, grateful for even that short reprieve.

She feels tiredness coming over her and decides to head back, hoping that this time when she crawls into bed, she'll be able to sleep.

When she opens her eyes, Harlow sees something between the trees.

It's so fast, she isn't sure if she actually saw it. But then—there, again: a flash of white, and then a loud snap that echoes through the morning.

On edge suddenly, Harlow curls her hands into fists. "Hello?" she calls out, embarrassed by the tremor in her voice. She clears her throat and calls again. "Hello?"

Now she is extremely conscious of what she's wearing, or rather not—she has no protection from the elements, and little to protect her against somebody or something else in these woods. The entire way she had assumed herself alone, because who else would be here? There are no other houses for miles; she's checked the maps online, and the track from the main road ends at Severn House, with no other turns before that point. Even Christina, the person most connected to this place now, is a flight away. She thought she was safe out here all alone.

They say a woman in white will get you if you go too close.

Harlow wishes she could claw Sloane's words out of her mind. They're infectious, she thinks, making her susceptible to fear. Turning her into the kind of person who thinks she hears noises from nowhere, sees things that aren't there. Of course Severn House is not haunted, because ghosts are not real, and the only people who bother making up stories like that are people who are too bored with their own lives, who look to tragedy for entertainment, gory tales to feed their appetite.

Harlow stands frozen for a while longer, waiting for another glimpse of the white thing between dark trunks. But when several minutes have passed and she has seen nothing, she comes back to life, turning and rushing back the way she came. All the way to the house, she tells herself that the bird or rabbit or whatever other creature it may have been didn't mean her any harm, and that her fearful reaction is just that—a programmed reaction, a physiological response designed to protect her from perceived threats.

By the time she arrives back at the house, Harlow has relaxed, her heart rate only a little elevated, and purely from the walking now. She lets herself into the house and definitely does not allow herself to give in to the idea that what she saw was no animal. That it looked, to her, like a human figure dancing around those trees. That it really was a ghost.

She's awoken by a knocking at the door.

Harlow stumbles out of bed and pulls on clothes in a rush, jeans and a muted khaki sweatshirt that is the first thing she pulls out of her duffel. Then she rushes down the stairs, unsure what time it is or how long she's been asleep—she remembers returning from her walk in the woods and eating cereal before she climbed back into bed and finally sank into an uninterrupted sleep. Or uninterrupted until now.

The knocking comes again, and Harlow skips the last stair, taking three long strides to the door. "Hold on," she calls, fumbling at the lock. There's no peephole or anything, no way she can peer out to see who has come down to the woods.

But then the door unlocks and Harlow swings it open and there she is.

Christina.

It's unmistakably her. The woman standing on the doorstep looks almost exactly like the girl in the photographs: a couple inches shorter than Harlow, like she is shorter than her mom in the lake photos, with the same full figure and long, romantic curls. She is older, obviously, but it only shows in the slight hardness of her features, the softness of youth gone now. She's so beautiful that for a moment Harlow is taken aback: even in the gloom of the woods she is radiant.

And then when she smiles, nervously, tentatively, Harlow sees her mom. She sees herself.

"Harlow?" Christina says, then, awed: "I didn't know whether to believe it. I didn't know whether to believe it was true but it is—it's you. Of *course* it's you."

Harlow lifts one hand, face-to-face with another blood relative for the first time in her life, and she doesn't really know how to respond to that. "Hi" is all she says in the end. "Do you want to come inside?"

But Christina lunges forward, pulling Harlow into a hug that startles her with its ferocity. When the surprise fades, though, she allows herself to sink into Christina's hold, reaching her arms around her aunt and holding on tight. Then she begins to cry.

21

They are in the kitchen, and Harlow thinks she should be the one making the tea, finding cups to drink from, but instead she's sitting at the small table as Christina does all of that. She moves around the space with ease, as if it hasn't been almost twenty years since she last stepped foot in this house. Although maybe it hasn't been that long—Harlow is assuming, basing her guesses on her own history, how long her mom had been gone from here. Maybe Christina, the one who keeps the lights on but doesn't even have her name on the deed, stayed longer after Eve went missing. Maybe she comes back from time to time to check in, to make sure the pipes haven't burst and the walls stay standing.

"Is it strange?" Harlow asks the question before she can think it through, and once the words are out it's too late.

But Christina lifts the kettle off the stove and pours, steam pluming off the boiling water. "Being back here?" she says, understanding immediately. "Yes." Then she shakes her head. "And also no. I've imagined coming back here a lot. What it would be like to see this house again. And it was strange, coming back down that track and seeing the house appear in front of me. Like a dream. But everything is so the same that it feels a little like I never left."

"People say it's haunted, you know." Harlow accepts the cup of deep purplish-black tea that Christina places in front of her. "They say a woman in white will get you if you come too close."

"They really say that?" Christina sounds surprised, wounded, even, and Harlow realizes too late that of course the ghost in the story is Eve, and of course Christina doesn't want to hear how people think her missing mother is no more than a ghost.

"Well," Harlow says, trying to walk it back, "at least I heard that's what some people say. But it's stupid. And anyone who says it is an asshole."

"They're bored. Boring little people with nothing much to say."

Harlow watches her aunt—her *aunt,* here, in the flesh—take the seat opposite and brush her long hair off her shoulders in a practiced, effortless sweep. Harlow's hand instinctively moves to her own absent curls, and she bites the inside of her cheek. "Why did you leave?"

Christina smiles that mirror-image smile again. "God, going in with the easy questions first, I see."

"I've been trying that approach." Harlow shrugs. "It hasn't really gotten me anywhere so far."

Now Christina laughs. "Jesus, you are just like her, you know? Oh my god, I had forgotten. So stubborn, so determined. Jesus. It's so nice." And then Christina is the one crying, her head dropping into her hands as her shoulders shake.

Harlow starts to reach out, then changes her mind, drawing her hand back to herself. She lets Christina cry and feels tears fill her own eyes, hot and heavy, although her breathing stays steady. Sometimes it's like this, a flow of uncontrollable weeping without anything else, like her body is overloaded on emotion and needs a way to get it out but doesn't want to interrupt everything else.

After a few minutes Christina lifts her head and sniffs loudly, wiping her nose with the back of her hand. "I'm so sorry, I really am," she says. "About so much. Your mom. Cora," she says softly, to herself almost. "That she's gone. And that she was gone all those years before, too, I—if I had known you existed, I would have tried harder to find her. I did try, you know. But she didn't make it easy, and after a couple years I couldn't keep trying. But if I had known about you, I think I would have kept going because I would have wanted to be there for you. For the both of you."

"So she did leave first," Harlow says.

"What?"

"I've been trying to figure it out," Harlow says. "The order of things, you know. Which one of you left soonest, and who stayed here the longest. You didn't answer me before, about why you left."

Christina looks away, as if she had been hoping she'd dodged that question neatly enough. "There wasn't much to stay for," she says. "You're right. Cora left first. Took off one night and left us a note that said she was okay, but she couldn't be here anymore, and not to worry about her. A *note*. Like we wouldn't worry just because she told us not to. And after everything we had been through with our mom . . . first she vanished, and then Cora, except Cora went by choice. It took a long time for me to accept that."

Harlow imagines Christina coming down the stairs one sleepy morning, the unwilling matriarch of a broken family, to find Cora's scrawl on a Post-it stuck to the fridge. *Took off one night,* Harlow repeats in her mind, and she sees her mom again, as she was before she died, so ready to flee.

"What about Clementine?" Harlow pushes her rapidly cooling tea away, leaving a smeared wet ring behind on the tabletop. "What happened to her?"

"She stuck around for a while longer," Christina says. "She was the youngest, you know. I tried to make things okay here for us both. But after a while she wanted to leave too, and I wasn't going to stop her. And then it was just me here and it seemed stupid to stick around in the hope that Mom might reappear as suddenly as she'd vanished and so eventually I left too."

Harlow squeezes her shoulders to her ears. "So that was it? You all broke apart and never spoke again?"

"Oh, no," Christina says. "Clem and I stayed in touch. She wanted to, like . . . be out there, you know? She ended up becoming a flight attendant. I mean, how much further can you get from a quiet life in these woods? She comes to stay with us during the holidays, sometimes, if she's not working."

"She does?" Harlow swallows. "Do you have any pictures of her? Like, from now?"

Christina takes her phone out. "Sometimes she sends me pictures when she's working," she says. "Where's the . . . okay, here. There she is." She turns her phone to show Harlow a picture of a grown-up Clementine in a navy-blue uniform, a pencil skirt and short-sleeved blouse. She's posing, a bottle of champagne in her hands, one eyebrow cocked, hair pulled back from her face.

Harlow breathes out slowly. Clementine looks the least like the younger version Harlow has seen, her hair lightened to a honey blond and her teenage self vanished, but there she is, just like Christina said. Real and out there in the world, somewhere. "Do you think I could have Clementine's number?" she asks quickly. "Or her email?"

"Sure," Christina says. "But—" She gets a pained look on her face. "Let me tell her about Cora, please. It's going to—it's going to wreck her. I don't think she ever got over how Cora left us. That she took herself away like that."

Harlow tries to piece this—her mom abandoning her sisters—together with the things she already knows, all the reasons her mom gave her for why their life was the way it was: there was somebody looking for them, someone on their tail, and they couldn't be caught, it wouldn't be safe. When Harlow saw that clipping about Eve and found out about her disappearance, it seemed to make some kind of sense: her mom was running from what happened to Eve. But now Christina is here saying that she stayed, and so did Clementine. *If they knew something more about Eve's disappearance, if they knew who was involved or even suspected,* Harlow thinks, *then wouldn't they both have been as afraid as Mom was?* But evidently they hadn't been. Not scared enough to leave without letting anyone know where they were going. Not scared enough to abandon their true identities and spend the next however many years hiding.

So what is it? Harlow wonders. *Did my mom know something they didn't? Is that why she was the only one to vanish herself?*

"How come my mom's name is on the deed to the house?" she asks. "You were the oldest. You were left in charge, right? How come it wasn't you?"

"It was, for a while. We only changed it over a few months before Cora left. I had gotten into some trouble with credit cards," Christina says, and she looks tired. "It wasn't easy trying to keep us all going on minimum wage and all that. I didn't want to risk anyone coming after the house or anything, so we switched it over, just in case. But nothing happened anyway. I guess I worried about everything a little too much, but what else could I do?"

Harlow pulls at the cuff of her sweatshirt. "And you're on the utilities," she says. "That's how I found you."

"Yes." Christina nods. "I've been listed on those, too."

Keeping the lights on, for all those years. Like a signal in the dark. A flare to guide the lost home.

Christina is looking at her intently. "What are you thinking?" she asks.

"I don't know," Harlow says, and it's true. It's hard to make everything fit together: her mom left, but Christina and Clementine stayed, so what had her mom run from? Without knowing, it seems, Christina was safe. Felt safe enough, at least, to carry on with her life and move on—

"Oh!" Harlow says, because she has remembered on the phone the other day hearing Christina call herself *Mommy* to somebody. "Do you have a kid?"

"I do," Christina says, and if she's taken aback by the sudden switch in topics, she doesn't show it. "I have a son, Otto. You want to see?"

Harlow nods, and Christina scrolls away from the image of Clementine, swiping a few times before she turns the phone over and holds it screen-out in Harlow's direction again. "There. That's Otto, and that's my wife, Mila."

Harlow reaches for the phone. "Can I?" she asks, and Christina nods. Harlow takes the phone and holds it close to her face. The little boy—maybe four or five, Harlow isn't good with kid ages—has a dimpled grin and messy caramel curls, his face pressed close to a woman with bright blue eyes and pale skin, dark hair cropped in a similar length to Harlow's own. Christina is in the picture, too, her face pressed close to the boy's other cheek, radiating joy. "Wow," Harlow says, and feels a tightening in the pit of her stomach. "He's gorgeous. And so is she. You're so lucky." She tries to tamp down the flicker of jealousy because how fucking pathetic is it to be jealous of a little kid who has done nothing to her? Except she is. Looking at that photo, all she can see is the secure life Christina has made for herself and her child, and it's so far from Harlow's experience that she wants to cry again. It's like there were two paths out of Crescent Ridge: one led to stability and happiness, and the other to perpetual panic, and her mom chose the latter. It was easier for Harlow when she could tell herself there had been no other choice, that her mom was doing the best she could under the circumstances, but she'd always doubted it, and here was the irrefutable proof. There had been another life possible for them.

Christina takes her phone back, apparently unaware of the emotions swirling inside Harlow. "I am lucky," she says, and talking about her family brings that same glow to her face. "It took us a while to get pregnant, and then we had a couple of losses before we got Otto. But I wouldn't have it any other way."

Harlow pushes her chair back abruptly, screeching across the tile floor, startling Christina. "Sorry," she says. "I just—I have a photo to show you, too."

She runs up the stairs and into the bedroom she's claimed as hers, and digs through her duffel bag for the photographs from the safety-deposit box. When she has them, she pulls the lake picture out and takes it downstairs, handing it to Christina as she comes back into the kitchen. "This is what my mom left for me," she tells her. "This is the first time I had any idea that you existed."

Christina takes the photograph by the very edges, and her hands shake the slightest amount. "Oh wow," she says softly. "Look at us." She lets the photo drop to the table but bends over it, her long hair falling forward. "This was after. When we were trying to make it on our own and pretend like everything was okay. Or I was, at least." She looks up at Harlow. "I was the oldest. I had just turned eighteen when our mom went missing. They let us stay here together—or I should say, they let Cora and Clem stay with me instead of going to foster care or a group home or whatever. But it was hard, because suddenly I was in charge of everything and I didn't know how to be their sister and their fake mom at the same time. Still," she says, "we had some good times. While we were still all together."

Harlow can't avoid it any longer, asking the questions she really wants the answers to. "What happened to Eve?" she says. "What do you think happened? How did it happen?"

Christina sits back and picks up her tea but doesn't drink it, only taps her nails on the china. There's a strange expression on her face—both sad and soft, angry and quiet. "I was thinking," she says, "on the flight. About what I could tell you. What answers I could give you. It was all I could think about, the whole way here, even after I was off the plane and in the cab and walking up to that front door. And I knew whatever I could think of was going to disappoint you." She shakes her head. "I don't want to disappoint you, Harlow. I want to help you, I want to be able to give you everything you want and need and make everything make sense for you, but the truth is that I can't. I can't make things make sense for you because they don't make sense for me."

She holds a hand up as Harlow opens her mouth to interrupt. "Here's what I can tell you," she says. "We lived a quiet life in this house. Our dad died when we were so young I barely even remember him. Mom kept us close after, and sometimes it sucked but mostly it was okay. We were homeschooled and again, sometimes it sucked but mostly it was okay. We would have been lonely but we had each other, and at least we weren't bored trapped inside a school building all day. We liked our life. We grew up. One day Mom went into town to run errands, but she never came back. We waited up and then decided we were being stupid, she obviously forgot to tell us she would be out late, and we went to bed. When we woke up in the morning, she still wasn't back, and that was when we started to panic. That was when we made the call." She rakes a hand through her curls and sighs. "And then we lived through the investigation, what there was of one, and our pictures in the papers and online and waited for someone somewhere to call in a tip or a sighting or something they'd overheard someone say in a bar, but nothing real came. It really was like she'd vanished. I don't know how else to explain it. And I've spent *years* thinking about it. How is somebody there one minute and gone the next? But it turns out—I started looking into it, looking up missing people cases and the statistics around them—it turns out a lot of people vanish."

"But they don't," Harlow says, and she can hear the hot frustration in her own voice. "People don't just disappear into nothing. It's not physically possible."

"You know that," Christina says, "and I know that. But it doesn't stop there from being these situations we can't explain. She was supposed to come home, and then she didn't. When it comes down to it, that's all we have."

Christina looks at Harlow, and Harlow has to make herself not look away from the eyes so like her mom's, and then she realizes Christina is probably feeling the same thing. Both of them looking at a face haunted by another. Christina reaches across and glides her fingers over Harlow's bruise, like she has seen right through the makeup, like she can see right through Harlow. "I wish I had more to give you, but that's all I have."

Harlow is the first one to look away.

22

Harlow has to park farther away from the main strip this time because the street is taken over by a small market, tents pitched up and down the center of the road. She walks up from the small lot she found off a side street and takes in the trinkets and things for offer on the stands: hand-carved animal figurines and crocheted baby blankets and fresh preserves to spread on fresh sourdough. There are a decent number of people milling around the market, and Harlow is comforted by this, relieved to be another person passing by the stalls, a sense of anonymity. She has had enough of being herself today already.

She left Christina at the house, slipping out with promises to be back shortly: *I need to run some errands, get some fresh air, pick up some groceries, no no it's fine, you stay here, of course of course.* Left Christina gazing around as if taking in the house for the very first time, her hand resting on the stair railing as she started up them. When the door closed and Harlow was on the outside, Christina locked within, then she could breathe.

Christina is a real person, she found herself thinking. *Clementine, too. They are real and they exist and Christina is here now and—*

She had to bend over, catching her breath hanging like that. It was overwhelming, was all. Years and years of wondering and now so much happening all at once. Her mom dead but Christina alive, and here for Harlow to talk to. And yet—still, Harlow had so few answers to her many, many questions.

Walking toward the salon now, she sees Sloane at the front desk through the glass, sees how Sloane sits up when she sees Harlow approaching and she gets this weird expression on her face. It turns Harlow's stomach—in a good way, an electric way, a scared-at-the-newness way, because none of her fake friends have ever looked at her like that. Like they actually *wanted* to see her, like her presence made their day *exciting.*

Maybe it's because she's being more of herself than ever before. Not telling Sloane the whole truth, obviously, but—she hasn't put on a personality to mold herself into a shape she thinks Sloane would like. She isn't hiding every single part of her, only the ones that would be too dangerous to share. And in a way she's glad that she stuck to that rule, at least, because it means that Sloane doesn't know how fucked up everything is. It means that when Harlow goes in there, she isn't going to have to talk about her life in hiding or her shattered family or her dead mom.

So she smiles and enters the salon. "Hey," she says.

"Hey," Sloane says, and pushes back from the desk, revealing bruised bare knees under a short green dress. "Mom! I'm taking lunch now!"

Before Harlow can even hear Adelaide's answer Sloane has her coat in one hand and Harlow's wrist in the other and they are back out the door, escaping.

Sloane takes them to a drive-through where they get burgers and fries and a chocolate shake each, and park in the farthest corner of the lot to eat. "I only have a half hour," Sloane says as she tears the top off a honey mustard sauce. "So how goes the distant-family-trauma excavation?"

"Oh, you know. A curious mystery with no answers," Harlow says easily, like she barely even cares anymore. "Doesn't every family have one of those if you go back far enough?" She watches as Sloane takes a bite of her burger, somehow managing to not disturb her bright red lipstick. Today Sloane's hair is in a high ponytail, and her eyes are outlined with geometric green liner that matches her dress. She looks ready for spring, instead of the cold wind rattling the car. "Do you have friends?"

"What?" Sloane looks at her, speaking through a full mouth. "Do I have *friends*?"

"Yeah," Harlow says, turning a little so her back rests against the window. "In town. From school or whatever."

"I mean, yeah," Sloane says, and she swallows. "But also no? I guess? I mean, most of my friends went away to college this year. They were a grade ahead. Only me and this girl April are seniors now. But at the start of the school year she got this girlfriend who didn't like me, even though April swore that wasn't what happened and she like, *totally needs to get to know you and you need to get to know her*, except I wasn't invited to hang out anymore so how was I supposed to do that? I don't even know what I did to that girl to make her hate me. We only met a few times. But it's . . . whatever. I have other people I can hang out with. I have the girls at the salon. Why are you even asking me that?"

Harlow can imagine exactly why this girl April's girlfriend doesn't like Sloane, and it has a lot to do with the way Sloane is looking at her right now, curious and sparking with excitement. Girls like Sloane, sometimes they don't even know how much they give off, how magnetic they are. It's a way of being to them, not anything particularly special or interesting. April's girlfriend, Harlow imagines, was probably worried that April was in love with Sloane, or that she herself would be, soon enough.

Girls like Sloane, Harlow thinks. *They have no idea what they do to girls like us.*

"I was just wondering," Harlow says. "Why you'd want to hang out with me."

Sloane rolls her eyes. "Feels like you're fishing for compliments," she says. "But okay, fine. I like interesting people. You seemed interesting. And I was right, wasn't I? Hurry up and eat your food before it goes cold and I have to get back."

Harlow laughs and plucks a few fries out of the bag. "Didn't your mom ever tell you not to talk to strangers?"

"No," Sloane says. "She runs a salon—all she *does* is talk to strangers."

"Fair."

"Besides, don't you ever get bored with all the people you know?

Like, everybody here is *boring* to me," Sloane says. "I'm over it. I'm over this town, I want to—god, I want to travel, go to cool places, get high in Amsterdam and surf in Portugal and climb a mountain or something. Don't you want to *climb* a fucking *mountain*, Harlow?"

She leans over and grabs Harlow's arm as she says that last part, her whole upper body pressing into Harlow as she shakes her and makes Harlow laugh again. "I can say for certain that I *don't* want to climb a mountain," Harlow says. "I've watched too many documentaries. I don't want to be frozen up on some rock for a thousand years."

"Okay," Sloane says, "then what *do* you want to do? Money no object, no reality, no mom nagging at you to just *go to cosmetology school and get your license that you used to want!* I mean, just for example. Where would you go?"

Harlow closes her eyes and imagines a map, all the distant places she's heard of but never seen, the cities and countries and wide-open stretches of ocean that she knew she could never see because her life was with her mom, running and hiding and running again. Her only fantasies lately have been of what boring job she might get one day, as if she couldn't possibly think any further than that. But here is Sloane asking her to think, asking her to go further.

She opens her eyes. "Japan," she says, surprising herself.

"Oh yeah?"

"They have those trees, right?" Harlow says. "Cherry blossoms, and tons of people go to see them bloom. I want to go and see them bloom."

"Cute," Sloane says, and when Harlow glances over at her, she's wearing a wicked smile on her face.

"Don't make fun of me," Harlow says, flipping her the bird. "You asked!"

"Who said I was making fun of you?" Sloane grabs for her hand before Harlow can go back to her fries, her fingers cool against Harlow's, her thumb rubbing over Harlow's knuckles as she examines her hands.

"What?" Harlow pretends to not care at all about Sloane's touch, as if her heart rate didn't just skitter upward. God, she's so fucking predictable. All it takes is one pretty girl paying her even the slightest bit of attention and she melts, completely malleable. She would do whatever Sloane asked right now, all for just a touch of their hands. "What are you looking at?"

"You should come get your nails done at the salon," Sloane says finally. "Look at these raggedy cuticles."

Harlow snatches her hand back. "My cuticles are not raggedy," she says, and only now does she notice that her nails still bear the final few peeling pieces of the pink polish she painted on when she was Meredith Bloom.

A lifetime ago.

"Whatever you say." Sloane picks up her shake and swirls the cup around. "Or come to my house and at least let me paint them. If we're going to be friends, I can't have you running around town in chipped polish. My family has a reputation to uphold, Harlow, really."

Sloane painting her nails in her bedroom, just friends, just innocent fun. "Maybe," Harlow says. "But only if you'll paint them black."

23

Sloane drives them back, only five minutes late to the salon. "See you later," Harlow says when she hops out of the car, except her voice lilts up at the end, like it's a question, like she's hoping: *See you later, maybe?*

"Text me," Sloane says. "So you can come over and we can play salon."

"Yeah," Harlow says. "Sure."

She leaves before Sloane can see the flush on her cheeks, hurrying back to her own car in the parking lot. She gets in and is about to start driving back to Severn House when she remembers the excuse she gave Christina for leaving and decides to get the groceries she promised.

She drives to the store she visited the other day and is drawing up a list in her head—more bread, fresh milk, maybe some kind of real food and ingredients so Christina doesn't think she can't take care of herself—when her phone rings.

She stills when she sees it's an unknown number. There are only a handful of people she would even expect to call—Sloane, now Christina, maybe Marcy Sheffield—since she tossed her old SIM card with all her contacts from before. And unknown numbers were definitely a no on her mom's list—*only answer when it's someone you recognize, in case whoever's on the other end can somehow trace you right to your exact location.* Except now it doesn't really matter, does it? Harlow has brought herself back to the place her mom was determined to leave, so if someone wants to find her, she's sitting prey.

Harlow takes a deep breath and puts the phone to her ear. "Hello?"

"Hi," a deep voice on the other end says. "I'm looking for Harlow Ford?"

Harlow's pulse kicks up a notch. "Who's asking?"

"This is Vincent Harris," the voice says. "Marcy Sheffield spoke to me and asked me to reach out to you. I believe you're looking for information on your grandmother's disappearance."

Her pulse settles some. Marcy said she was going to talk to old colleagues—clearly she didn't waste any time. "Yeah, I'm Harlow," she says, and it makes her uncomfortable down to her bones to be handing out her name over the phone so easily, but she supposes it doesn't really matter anymore. Enough people know her now—Sloane, Ruby, Adelaide, Marcy—that she can't hide, not in the way she's used to. "So. You're like, a cop, then?"

Vincent laughs, an infectious sound, and Harlow tries to build a picture of this man in her head: a beat cop in his late fifties, maybe early sixties now, close to retirement, who has spent his entire career fielding petty crimes in Crescent Ridge. Or maybe he actually is what Harlow thought Marcy was, a yes-man who rose through the ranks to get to power, spending his money on sharp suits and shiny watches. "Actually, no," he says. "I am not now nor have I ever been a cop. I'm a private investigator. I worked alongside the investigation."

Harlow's defenses go right back up. "Private investigator?" she says sharply. "So someone paid you to look into the case?"

"No," Vincent says, his tone attempting reassurance. "I was brought in as a useful set of eyes. Sometimes the police do that, when they're having a hard time breaking a case."

"But you didn't," Harlow says. "Break it."

Vincent is quiet on the other end of the phone for a moment. "No," he says eventually. "But I would still like to talk to you about the case, and your grandmother. Your mother, too. Marcy told me she . . . passed away." When Vincent says it, he sounds remorseful, and Harlow wonders how many people are out there who might mourn her mother, if they knew she was gone. How many people is Christina going to have to tell? How many people is Harlow going to meet who she *can't* tell? People like Ruby, who so clearly loved her mom. "I'm very sorry for your loss."

Harlow flips down the visor and watches herself in the tiny mirror there. "Thank you." The image of Vincent Harris changes in her head: now he's the kind of man who wears vintage suits with patches on the elbows, keeps a scruffy beard, and has a file cabinet with records of every case he worked on that has gone unsolved. *I watch too many shitty cable dramas,* Harlow thinks.

She flips the visor back up. "Can you meet tomorrow?"

She arranges a time and place—the same diner where she met Marcy; it seems right, and besides, it's one of the four places she actually knows in town—and then says, "Thanks for calling. I have a lot of questions about what happened."

"I'll be glad to help you with what I can," Vincent says. "See you tomorrow."

Call over, Harlow tosses her phone on the passenger seat and breathes out. A private investigator.

It's becoming clear to her that there's almost zero chance of finding out any new information about Eve's disappearance. But she didn't come to Crescent Ridge just to find out about Eve—she wants answers about her mom, too, and although she had at first assumed the two were connected, now she's not so sure. The fact that Christina and Clem stayed after her mom left, that Christina didn't seem at all afraid to come back—maybe Harlow is looking at this all wrong. If she wants to know why her mom was running, then perhaps it's time to start asking questions about Cora Kennedy, instead.

BEFORE

Cora tugs at her blouse. She forgot how itchy it was, and now she's stuck wearing it for this whole memorial thing, too late to go back to change.

"Stop." Christina digs her elbow into Cora's ribs.

"Sorry," Cora says, but she fusses with the material again, pulling it away from her skin. "I fucking hate this shirt."

Clem clicks her tongue against her teeth, a petulant habit left over from her ten-year-old self, a surefire sign she's about to say something equally petulant. "You're not allowed to say *fuck*. Christina said no cursing while we're here. So like, put a dollar in the jar when we get home."

"*You* put a dollar in the jar—"

"Can you both shut the fuck up?"

They're standing in the wings of the main chamber in the town hall, the mayor out onstage making his introductory speech to the reporters and TV cameras that make up the entire audience.

The press conference before the actual memorial part of things. "Worse turnout than I expected," Cora overheard the mayor murmuring to his aide earlier. "This is all the press we could round up?"

"There's a story about a break-in at the aquarium in Hanneford," the aide whispered. "I think a lot of them diverted there."

"Hanneford?" The mayor shook his head. "Christ. All that money we spent on the renovations and no one's going to see them."

Cora leans out as far as she can manage without being spotted by the meager collection of journalists occupying the first row of seating. *Coming in second to some stingrays whose house got robbed? Good going for a case two years old and cold, really,* she thinks.

Christina yanks her back. "Will you stop everything you're doing?"

Cora shrugs her grip off. "I was only looking."

"Yeah well, don't. Think about what you're going to say instead."

"I know what I'm going to say," Cora says. "You know, and Clem knows, and I know. It's the same thing we said last year, and the same thing we said when it happened."

Christina's face remains grim. "I hate public speaking," she says, and her skin is a little pale, Cora notices, a lack of blood.

She reaches for her sister's hand and squeezes tight. "You'll be fine," she says. "We'll be fine."

Christina doesn't say anything, but she squeezes back, and their hands stay clasped until the moment the mayor beckons them onto the stage.

Cora isn't good at public speaking either, and the lights from the couple of cameras still seem extremely bright to her, and her mouth is dry when it's her turn to speak. But she manages to get through it, only stumbling a couple of times as she makes her plea to the public for any assistance in finding their mom, and then, like last time, a direct plea to their mother: "Mom, if you're seeing this—we love you. We miss you so much. Please come home, if you can. We'll be waiting."

The cameras click and whir and Cora wills herself to keep her hands still as Clem speaks, her voice wavering and full of tears. *Do not touch your shirt. Do not touch your shirt. Do not—*

Then their part is over and they're hustled offstage while the police captain makes his speech, which is somehow more about statistics and solve rates than about Eve.

In the wings an officer waits for them, a smile plastered on her face. Cora softens a little; she doesn't hate this one. Officer Marcy Sheffield, barely older than Christina with the acne to show it. She wears too much perfume, and her hair is always pulled back so tight Cora can only imagine the headache, but she's also honest and not prone to saccharine platitudes like some of the other officers they've come into contact with. It's been a while since they saw any of the Crescent Ridge police, Cora thinks. Only Officer Sheffield and the captain, when he asked them to come to his office to discuss this memorial/press conference.

"You did good," Officer Sheffield whispers. "Do you have coats? It's starting to snow a little."

"Yes," Christina says. "The mayor's secretary hung them up in the office, I think."

Officer Sheffield collects their coats for them, and Cora shrugs hers on while Christina whispers something into Clem's ear. Clem looks pale, her bottom lip trembling. *Perfect,* Cora thinks, because it isn't over yet—now they have to go outside to meet everyone who has come out to hold up a candle and stand in silence for a minute, as if that will magically bring Eve back.

Officer Sheffield goes ahead to make sure everything is ready, and Cora hurries to walk on the other side of Clem, touching her hand to the back of Clem's dark green coat, passed down by Cora. "You were great," she says, attempting a reassuring tone. "Honestly."

"I hate this," Clem says. "I want to go home."

"One day," Christina says, and she glances over the top of Clem's head to Cora, and she can tell they're both thinking the same thing: only one day, but that might be all it takes to break them. "And the hardest part is done, right? Now we go out there and say thank you to everyone for coming, and then we can go home and really soon it'll be tomorrow."

"And we won't have to do this again for a whole entire year," Cora says.

Clem nods as they push through the main entrance and out onto the steps. "Yeah," she says. "I know. I know."

Officer Sheffield was right: it's begun to snow, heavy flakes drifting down and landing on already wet ground. It won't stay, Cora knows, but she always likes falling snow. How clean it looks, how soft, as if—cliché but true—someone were up in the clouds pouring confectioners' sugar into the air.

They make it down the slick steps and stand in the square, the fountain at the center gurgling icy water over the stones. Maybe the snow is the reason for the small crowd outside, Cora thinks as she looks around at the people gathered. It's more likely the same reason there weren't more journalists inside—the truth is, people have lost interest in Eve. There is only so long that being a beautiful missing white mother can sustain a story without any other information, and yes, it's longer than most, but it's wearing off now. Cora can feel it in the air when she's walking around the grocery store, or picking up coffee at the independent place that just opened, or dawdling through the weekly farmer's market: the thrill is gone. People no longer look at her and immediately turn away to whisper to the person beside them. She doesn't get stopped in the cereal aisle by older women who want to hug her. The middle school girls hanging around the square with their overpriced pink drinks don't giggle uncertainly when she sits on the benches looking over the fountain. And outside town their story has been overtaken by newer, more captivating cases—the elderly man two towns over who was found half-decomposed in his trailer, and the teenage couple who vanished from Rutherford Hills, and rumor is there's a serial killer making his way through Vancouver. *And of course,* Cora thinks with a wry smile, *can't forget the aquarium break-in.*

Christina elbows her again. "What are you smiling at?" she says through gritted teeth, the rest of her face carefully neutral. God forbid anyone should think they're arguing. God forbid anyone should notice anything about them at all.

"I was thinking how Mom would have hated this," Cora says. "All these people, looking at her."

"They're not looking at her," Clem says. "They're looking at us."

"Maybe," Cora says as Officer Sheffield makes her way over to them again. "But all they see is her, really."

"Okay, girls?" Officer Sheffield hands them a candle each, long and white with a piece of card wrapped around the middle to catch the drips of wax. Cora isn't even sure why they're doing this shit with the candles—it's the middle of the day; there won't be any pretty imagery of hundreds of flickering flames in the gathering dark.

But she takes her candle and holds it out when Officer Sheffield produces a lighter. "Let's go," the officer says.

They join the small crowd, and the mayor is the one who leads this part, raising his voice as he tells the gathered about how *vital* Eve was and how much the town misses her, the *energy* and *lightness* she brought. Then he introduces someone from the local community choir, and a woman with tear tracks down her deep brown skin steps forward and begins a rendition of a song Cora has never heard before. Cora wonders if the tears are from some deep sadness this woman has for another woman who she's never known, or if it's only the sharp wind.

The song goes on too long, and Cora can't stop scanning the faces of those who have come out today. She recognizes maybe a quarter of them, not by name, but as the family she sees at the store and the guy who runs the old pizza place, things like that. Over the last couple of years she and her sisters have gotten to know Crescent Ridge more than ever before—without Eve, they've had to venture out of the woods by themselves, at first anxious because of it but quickly settling into new routines, making new familiar places.

The woman is still singing, voice straining to reach too-high notes, and Cora is still scanning, and then her gaze lands on a face she really does know. Tucked next to the fountain, her white-blond hair blowing from under a knit cap, is Ruby. She's watching the singer, and Cora is glad, because as long as Ruby isn't looking at her then Cora can keep the two of them in a place where none of this matters, where she and Ruby exist separate from the tragedy of her life.

But right then, as the singer finally ends, Ruby's eyes slide over and lock onto Cora's. She holds the stare for a long moment before lifting her hand, and her mouth moves silently, but Cora sees what it is that she's saying.

Are you okay?

Cora looks down, blinking away the snowflakes landing against her eyelashes and the hot tears suddenly dripping down her cheeks.

She was okay, until this moment, until she realized she can no longer pretend that Ruby and everything they are to each other exists somewhere far away from her real life. It's not like she didn't realistically know that Ruby was aware of this, of what happened to her family and who she is, but *god* she liked to believe none of it mattered. When she and Ruby are together, she wants it to be about them, driving fast and listening to the same old songs and the kisses that say the things they can't. But of course there is no version of Cora that exists without all this trauma, and she was stupid to act like there ever could be.

She looks back at Ruby and mimics her motion, lifting her hand, holding it there. *I'm okay,* she mouths back, even though it's far from the truth.

Then there is the silence, and the flickering of the candles in the snow falling thick and fast, and Cora leans over and whispers into Christina's ear, "We were wrong. It does look beautiful."

24

When Harlow gets back to the house, Christina is sitting at the kitchen table, staring at the photograph Harlow gave her, and when Harlow touches her on the shoulder, she jumps and then pretends she hadn't been scared at all, a smile to cover everything. Then she tells Harlow she's booked a room in town, and Harlow thinks for a moment about asking Christina to stay at the house, the two of them there together, but the idea of it feels too strange, and besides, that fearful flinch Christina gave before more than shows exactly how she'd feel about staying here.

It reminds Harlow of her mom. Another thing the sisters share: that on-edge feeling, the urge to shy away from Harlow's touch.

She'd be lying if she said it didn't hurt.

Harlow drives Christina into town and drops her off at one of those bed-and-breakfasts she saw when she first drove into Crescent Ridge, and then she goes back to Severn House by herself to spend another night alone, listening to sounds that may be real or may be only her imagination.

• • • •

In the morning she heads to her meeting with Vincent Harris.

The rain comes down heavy today, the sky blocked out by nothing but low gray clouds bringing gloom. Harlow flicks the wipers on full speed, an incessant swish-swish-swish back and forth as she drives to the diner, finds a spot in the corner of the lot, and parks. She runs the short distance from her car to the entrance, but even those few seconds are enough for her to become soaked, water dripping off the end of her nose as she enters the diner. She ignores the droplets tickling down the back of her neck as she looks around the diner, scanning for someone who fits her imagined vision of Vincent Harris. The only other people inside look as tired as Harlow feels: truckers fueling up with big breakfasts, a few women in scrubs, an elderly man at the counter.

Harlow peels off her jacket as she slides into a booth. The same waitress who was here when she met Marcy Sheffield comes over; her braids have gold beads added now, and they click when she nods her head at Harlow's request for coffee. As she leaves, the bell over the door chimes and in walks a man similarly dripping from the rain, and Harlow only glances at him for a second before she decides no, he is not the man she's come to meet, and goes back to drawing patterns in sugar on top of the table.

But then there's a shadow over her sugar art, and a voice says, "Harlow? Harlow Ford? Vincent Harris."

Harlow looks up, taking her second look at this man. He's nothing like the images she put together as they talked on the phone—well, not nothing: every version of the private investigator she imagined was white, and so is this man, with dirty-blond hair falling loosely to his chin and a beard to match. Bright blue eyes behind black-framed glasses. Everything on him black, actually: rain-darkened coat, boots, jeans, sweater that looks expensive, the kind Harlow likes to run her fingers over in department stores she can't afford to be in. He looks more like he'd be at home in one of those stores, actually, offering custom suit tailoring to unfashionable men naive enough to believe if they bought whatever he was selling, they too could look as good as him.

She realizes then that he's holding his hand out for her to shake, and so she does, at the same time saying, "Hi, yes, Harlow."

Vincent Harris smiles and gestures to the booth. "May I?"

"Yes. Sure."

He slides in and takes off his glasses, holding them up to the diner's buzzing lights. "Some weather, huh?" He sets his glasses on the table. "So. On the phone you said you had a lot of questions about your grandmother's disappearance. Why don't you tell me what you know first, and I can see if there's anything I can add to that."

Harlow swipes the sugar off the table, letting it fall to the sticky floor like snow. "Wow," she says. "You're all business, right? Straight to the point."

Vincent looks apologetic. "Busy day," he says. "I have another meeting in a half hour."

"It's fine," Harlow says, and she kind of means it: it's nice to not have to replay the whole sorry-for-your-loss thing again. "But actually—"

She's been thinking about it all night. She wants to know why her mom was running. But it's not like with Eve—there's no easy story she can conjure up to put distance between her and the details. If she wants to use Vincent for help with this, then she's going to have to tell him the real truth, things that she didn't tell Marcy Sheffield. Things she's never told anyone.

She eyes Vincent. Is he trustworthy? He's an absolute stranger. But he's an investigator. That means he has knowledge and skills she doesn't, skills that might actually get her somewhere.

The warning bells ring loud in her head: in doing this, she'll have to break every remaining rule her mom made, every behavior that has become second nature to Harlow.

Look at you, Harlow thinks. *You've made it this far. Broken enough of the rules already.*

If I want to get anywhere close to the truth, I have to do this.

She takes a deep breath. "I think I've learned everything there is to know about Eve's disappearance," she tells the investigator. "Or, everything that's possible to know right now. Maybe forever, I don't know—it doesn't seem like there's going to be a shiny new lead any time soon, not when nothing's come up in the last twenty years—"

"So you don't want my help with Eve," Vincent says, and he glances at his watch—silver and heavy—like she's wasting his time. The very ends of a tattoo creep out from under the watch, intricate lines twisting together.

"It's my mom," Harlow says. "Cora Kennedy. I think you can help me with her."

When Vincent looks at her now, it's with pity. "I thought her death was an accident," he says. "The police will be handling the investigation, but it seems pretty straightforward. Traffic collision, yes?"

He's done his research, Harlow thinks, and then realizes how stupid the thought is: he's an investigator. Looking into things is literally how he makes his living. "Yes," Harlow says. "But it's not about the accident. I want to know—" She pauses as the waitress returns and pours steaming coffee into her mug, then looks at Vincent.

"Can I get you anything?" she asks.

"I'll have some of that," Vincent says, nodding at the coffeepot in her hand.

Harlow waits until she's finished pouring and is on her way back up front before she continues. "I want to know about why she left Crescent Ridge in the first place," she tells Vincent. "I think there might have been something else going on in her life that made her leave, not just Eve going missing."

Vincent takes a sip of his coffee and grimaces. "That'll wake you up," he says, and then: "What exactly makes you think there was another reason for her leaving?"

"A lot of things," Harlow says, and steels herself. *You have to do this. You can't keep all the secrets forever. Look where that got Mom—got you.* Under the table she squeezes her hands into fists and begins. "Like the fact she didn't leave until two years after her mom had disappeared. And the way she was . . ." Harlow trails off, her face warming. It's guilt, she knows: telling him about her mom's insistence that someone was after them—it's like a betrayal, almost. As if she's saying, *Hey, I know, my mom was crazy. Can you figure out why she was so fucking weird?*

"The way she was what?" Vincent looks curious now.

Harlow forces herself to continue despite the guilt. "She

thought somebody was after her. So now I'm wondering if there was some kind of trouble she got into before she left, something completely separate from Eve."

Vincent's nodding before she's even finished speaking. "Could be," he says. "Did she have any boyfriends that caused issues? Did she owe anyone money?"

It strikes Harlow as darkly funny, how these are the same questions that swirled around Eve. As if both she and her daughter brought their troubles on themselves, by maybe getting involved with the wrong men, or trusting the wrong people with money. As if maybe they should have been smarter, taken their own safety more seriously, and then people wouldn't have to be asking these questions at all.

Harlow runs her finger around the rim of her coffee cup. "She never had any boyfriends that I knew about," she says. "No girlfriends, either." Harlow's not naive; she's never thought her mom was completely single and celibate, that there weren't numerous lovers over the years, but anyone there was never made it to the point of meeting Harlow. "I always felt like she got spooked after my sperm donor, you know?"

"So your father was the last person she was really involved with?" Vincent asks. He pulls a pen and a small black leather-bound notebook from his pocket and flips to a clean page. "What's his name?"

Harlow's face warms more, her cheeks burning. "I don't know," she says sharply. "He wasn't important. He *isn't* important."

"He's important if you want to get these answers," Vincent says, his voice the same even and calm tone, no reaction either way to Harlow's defensiveness. "Do you have any idea of his identity? Any way of locating him?"

"He didn't want anything to do with us," Harlow says. "That's all I know about him."

Vincent shrugs. "Okay," he says mildly, scribbling something down. "And any financial issues?"

"We got by," Harlow says, but on this she is less certain. Fifteen thousand dollars, in *cash*, is a lot for one person to have amassed, especially over a lifetime of bar work and temp jobs, especially while on the run with a child. Money was another thing Harlow didn't attempt to press her mom on, though: there were questions she knew not to ask, and answers she was never going to get. Now, of course, she regrets being so reticent. Regrets letting her mom control everything, hide every detail she deemed Harlow too young or stupid or naive to know.

Vincent writes something else in the notebook and then closes it. "Okay," he says, glancing at his watch again. "Here's what I think we should do. You should, if you can, look at your mom's financials. Do you have access to them? Bank accounts, any credit cards, things like that?"

Harlow frowns, one hand diving back under the table to worry at a loose thread in the ripped knees of her jeans. "I don't know," she says, cautious, thinking of the wad of cash from the safety-deposit box. "She didn't really let me in to all that. But I can try—maybe I can call around?"

"You should try," Vincent says. "You want to look and see if there's any debt she might have had that she kept hidden from you, or any unusual activity on her accounts."

"Unusual how?"

"Large withdrawals," Vincent says. "Or large deposits. Any indication she might have been receiving or sending money to anyone. You'd be surprised how often these things come down to money."

Harlow nods slowly. She doesn't even know if her mom had credit cards, or if she did, what name they were under. "Okay."

"A list of acquaintances would be helpful," he says. "Any friends, former romantic partners, colleagues—anyone who strikes you as important. Then I can start looking into people and assessing their connections to your mother. See if anything particularly . . . *interesting* comes up."

"I can do that," Harlow says, even though she can count the people her mom might have called friends over the years on one hand.

"And then—" Vincent takes his wallet out and fishes out a couple of bills. "Any details on your father could be useful. You might want to think about doing one of those ancestry DNA tests. Again—you'd be surprised how often custody disputes can turn *extremely* ugly."

"Custody?" Harlow repeats incredulously. *Is he suggesting my father could have been the one after us? Like, he* wanted *me?* No: not possible. Her mom would not have kept Harlow's dad away from her if he'd really wanted to be involved. She might have hated him, but she wasn't cruel like that.

Are you sure about that? a small voice in her head whispers. *After finding out all the shit she's hidden from you—after finding out she did keep your other family from you—you still really think she couldn't have been capable of that?*

"We should follow all potential avenues," Vincent says. He takes a card from his wallet and hands it to her. It's not as fancy as Harlow would have expected, his name in plain black font on a somewhat flimsy card, not the glossy weighted paper to match the quality of his rich-boy sweater and watch. "Listen, I have to get going now, but here's my details. Send over that list of names as soon as possible, and I'll get things going on my end."

"Okay," Harlow says, and she has to look up at him as he stands, towering over her. "Thank you. For meeting me, and helping." She thinks of that fifteen thousand, several thousand less now, that she's tucked beneath the floorboards at the house. "How much is this going to cost?"

"Don't worry about it," Vincent says, and his bright blue eyes soften, become misty almost. "Everyone in my line of work has a case they couldn't stop thinking about, long after the fact. So don't worry about my fee. I'm as curious as you are."

Harlow tries to hide her surprise, her relief. It makes her feel like she was right to trust him—he's not after her money; he just wants to help, out of a sense of duty, or something like it. And she's glad she doesn't have to pay—that money has to last her. Her mom meant for Harlow to spend it on rent, not on private investigators. "Thank you," she says.

"No problem," Vincent says, and he raps on the table, two quick knocks like punctuation at the end of a sentence. "Speak soon."

Then he's gone, back out into the driving rain, fading into the gloom.

Harlow takes a mouthful of now-lukewarm coffee and tries

not to think about the thing that has never, would never have before this, occurred to her:

Was it my father she was running from?

Harlow jumps out of the car and runs through the rain again, this time to the salon. But when she nears, she notices the darkness behind the windows: nobody inside, no music making the windows vibrate, and no Sloane behind the desk. She steps back and examines the opening hours. Today: *closed.*

Harlow swears. There goes her distraction. She hides in the doorway as she texts Sloane. **hey where are u?** she taps out. **salon's closed?**

Sloane's response flies back: **always closed thursdays. shopping with Ruby rn, hit u up later?**

Harlow slides her phone into her back pocket without replying and sprints back to her car. Once she's inside, the rain becomes percussion on the roof, and she cranks the heat high as she thinks about what Vincent Harris said, that thing about her father—

"Don't," she tells herself, hands forming a loose hold on the steering wheel. *Don't think about it, don't think about him—*

It's useless, of course. Now all she can think about is this phantom man somewhere out there who she has, before now, never truly given more than a moment's thought to. And maybe *that* is the real strange thing, maybe she's the weird one for not caring more, but it isn't some exaggeration or some act that she hides her longing behind—Harlow has really never thought about the man who contributed half her DNA in any way more than *Huh, that's interesting.* Why would she think about him? For all

Harlow's frustration with her mom's secrets, her penchant for hiding things, the one thing that never bothered her was how little her mom was willing to share about her father. What did Harlow need to know about him that she couldn't parse from the fact that he didn't have any interest in *being* her father, or in being with her mom? Every feature on her face belongs to her mom— to her entire matrilineal side, actually. Her skin the same shade of warm brown as her mom's, her eyes that look like Christina's, the smile that all four of them share. And she learned everything about life from her mom: how to ride a bike, how to wing her eyeliner, how to change a flat tire. *He*, whoever he was, wasn't any part of that. He didn't want it, and Harlow didn't want him.

Except.

You'd be surprised how often custody disputes can turn extremely *ugly.*

Harlow leans her head against the window, the rain running rivulets on the other side. Vincent Harris has put it in her mind, and she would like to ignore it but when she tries it out as a puzzle piece, it's alarming how well it seems to fit. *My mom finds out she's pregnant,* Harlow thinks. *She doesn't want him involved. He won't agree to that. So she takes off, so that he can't ever have me.*

Or maybe: *He says he's not interested, and I'm born, and we live our lives for a couple years, and then out of nowhere he shows up. Says he's ready, except now Mom doesn't want him at all. So she takes off.*

Or: *He doesn't care, but his family does. They have money, lawyers, and my mom has nothing, and she knows what will happen and she doesn't want to lose me so—she takes off.*

Harlow knocks her head against the glass repeatedly, softly, but enough to start a dull ache throughout her skull. *I'm almost eighteen,* she thinks. Not that long to go until she becomes a legal adult, not subject to custody or the whims of one parent over the other. But her mom showed no sign of slowing down, of giving up their transitory life once Harlow's birthday came and she would be free from any potential court-ordered anything to do with him.

She watches one lone raindrop sliding down the glass, a solo race to nowhere. If this is it, if she's on the right track now—why would her mom have continued to keep her hidden after so long? What kind of man must he have been, to elicit such fear, to put the panic in her mom's eyes that Harlow saw during every late-night escape?

She closes her eyes and envisions a different version of events— not a father wanting to see his child, but demanding it. Forcing it, forcing contact, forcing her mom to say yes, tight grip on fragile bones, harsh threats in a soft tongue. The kind of man who wouldn't let a thing like legality or technicality stop him from taking what he wanted. Harlow. Her mother. Taking what he saw as his.

No. Harlow bites down on her cheek and opens her eyes, flicking the radio on and turning it up loud, as if she can blast the thoughts away. Suddenly she is exhausted and overwhelmed. Can't think about it anymore, not today.

The voice is there and doesn't even scare Harlow this time. *Can't,* the voice says, *or won't?*

25

Harlow drives home, her mind turning everything—her father, Christina, the memory of fear in her mom's eyes, the image of a faraway Eve—over and over as she winds through the woods. Right when she pulls up to the house, she gets a text. It's Sloane: **wanna come over and order pizza and get stoned???**

Harlow doesn't even have to think about it. **send ur address**, she types back, and when Sloane does, she puts it into her phone and then swings a circle in front of the house, retracing her path up and out of the trees this time.

Sloane's house isn't hard to find, a ticky-tacky box in a development of identical ticky-tacky boxes. Harlow follows the numbers upward until she gets to 147, and then she pulls into the driveway, parking behind Sloane's car.

Sloane answers the door in sweatpants and a white tee scattered with tiny holes and thin enough that Harlow can see her pink lace bra beneath it. "Welcome to Casa Prescott," Sloane says in what Harlow thinks is supposed to be a British drawl. "Do come inside. But take your shoes off, because Addy Prescott *hates* outdoor shoes inside."

Harlow unlaces her boots and leaves them at the bottom of the stairs, neatly lined up together. "Your mom and I feel the same," she says.

Sloane rolls her eyes. "Whatever. Come on, let me give you the tour." She swings one arm to the left. "Here you will find the usual rooms of a house." Then she points upstairs. "And up there, even more rooms! Let's go."

Sloane bounces up the stairs, and Harlow follows at a slower pace, taking in the framed pictures that line the staircase—a selection of Sloane's school pictures, shots of the salon's grand opening, Sloane and her mom cheek to cheek across the years. "Is it just you and your mom?"

"Huh? Oh, yeah," Sloane says over her shoulder. "My parents got divorced when I was, like, four or something. I don't really see my dad much."

Me neither, Harlow wants to say. *It was just me and my mom too,* she wants to say, but then she'd have to tell Sloane about her mom's death and open everything up, and that's not why she came over. She wants to take a break from thinking about everything. She does not want to tell Sloane about theories and ideas and wild speculation about her mom's state of mind when she ran from this cold town. She does not want to bring up her father or the private investigator or Marcy Sheffield. And she does not want to think about how the longer she's in Crescent Ridge, the less sure she becomes of what little she thought she knew. No: Harlow is sick to death of all of it.

She can't help imagining what she'd be doing right now if things were normal—well. *As normal as my life ever got,* she thinks. Like, if that eighteen-wheeler hadn't hit them, and her mom hadn't died, and they'd carried on speeding through the night until they reached their new town, then by now she'd be settled in to a new school with a new identity and a group of people she called her friends. Maybe goth girls this time, the kind who wear impossible platforms and pure-black lipstick and always have a tampon to spare in the school bathrooms. Maybe right now she and her new goth girl friends would be getting bubble tea and smoking in the back seat of someone's mom's car.

"Harlow." Sloane's at the top of the stairs now, waiting. "Earth to Harlow."

Harlow looks up at her standing there, the soft roll of her belly curving over the waistband of her sweats, the way Sloane's eyes slant down at her. Then again, in all of her hypothetical *right now*s, she wouldn't have Sloane.

"I'm coming," Harlow says. "What was that about getting stoned? Because right now I'd like to be high enough that it feels like my brain is no longer connected to my body."

Sloane takes Harlow by the wrist as she reaches the top of the stairs. "I have exactly the strain for you," she says. "Jesus, you're like ice. You wanna borrow a sweater?"

They spend all afternoon in Sloane's bedroom, which is like the inside of a disco ball, or at least that's how Harlow's stoned brain sees it: pink walls, trinkets everywhere, clothes spilled on the floor, tiny twinkling lights wrapped around fake-flower garlands and draped from the ceiling. She eats breadsticks one after another after another as Sloane flips through her high school yearbook, telling stories Harlow laughs at without following about people whose names she can't keep up with. They watch an old cheerleader movie and blow raspberries against their palms any time one of the characters says something egregiously homophobic, and then decide that they can probably dance just as well as them and attempt the routine from the end credits, tripping over the piles of shoes that Sloane keeps littered across her floor and laughing so hard they can't breathe. They lie down, heads touching, on Sloane's bed and watch the galaxy projected on the ceiling swirl and shimmer, and Harlow takes another hit off the joint Sloane rolled and realizes this is the first time she has had fun being Harlow.

"What?" The word comes out of Sloane slowly, like she's on half speed. "Say again?"

Harlow frowns. "Did I say something?"

"Something about being Harlow," Sloane says, and she moves, hooking her leg over Harlow's. "Something about fun."

"Oh," Harlow says, barely able to think about her words with Sloane's leg on hers like that, with Sloane's hair tickling her shoulder. "I think . . . oh, yeah. I never got to be Harlow before. You know? So it's like, did I even ever do shit I liked? Or was I pretending to have fun because that was what the fake me would have done? And how do I even know where the other versions of me stop and actual Harlow me starts? It's weird."

"You're not fake," Sloane says, not understanding Harlow's real point. "You're just weird. I'm weird. Everyone's weird."

"We could have been friends," Harlow said. "If I met you. In one of those other places. But I wouldn't have been me. Harlow me. I would've been, like . . ." She catches herself before she starts in on the fake names. *Nonono we're not going there remember, this is distraction time, nice time, this is Sloane who thinks we're normal, remember?*

"Boring," Harlow finishes instead. "I would've been too boring for you."

Sloane makes a noise like she's choking, but it's laughter. "Hello? You have a mysterious vanished relative. You, like, *inherited* a haunted house—"

"It's not haunted."

"If you say so."

"I told you I don't like it when you say that."

"Um, no, you didn't."

Harlow squints at the ceiling, her eyes following a planet-shaped swirl traveling past the light fixture. "No, I didn't, did I," she says, remembering and laughing. "Well. I don't. And I don't want to talk about that place anyway."

"What do you want to talk about?"

Harlow lets her head fall sideways and is surprised—but not as much as she should be, she knows—to find Sloane turned half on her side and watching Harlow from under heavy eyelids. "I don't know," she says, trying to keep her gaze focused on Sloane's eyes, not roaming over her face, down to her mouth. "What do *you* want to talk about?"

"Hmm." Sloane rakes a hand through her sunlight-golden hair. Then she takes that same hand and brings it to Harlow's face, running a finger over her cheek, across her jaw, and under her chin. Her touch is warm, soft. "I don't really want to talk. I don't think you do either."

Harlow is conscious, suddenly, of the rise and fall of her chest in her borrowed sweatshirt, her breathing fast and uneven. She knows better than to fall for this. The not-stoned version of her does, anyway, except she's very stoned, and she's very electrified by way Sloane is moving her foot along Harlow's leg now, her toes pressing into Harlow's calf. *Don't be stupid. She does not like you. She's a pretty girl. Pretty girls don't like you.* She repeats it over and over in her head, but it doesn't stop her from saying the next thing, so very quietly. "What do I want?"

"I think you want me to kiss you," Sloane whispers. "Do you, Harlow?"

Harlow nods. What else can she do? She nods, and Sloane grins and tightens her grip on Harlow's chin. Pulls her closer and puts her mouth on Harlow's and at the same time presses the entire length of her body against Harlow's, and Harlow gasps her surprise into Sloane's mouth. If she weren't so high she would be overthinking this moment but she is and it's her body in control of her brain, not the other way around, so she puts her arm between them and slides her hand up beneath Sloane's shirt, her palm pressed against the delicious soft flesh.

Sloane hooks her leg higher around Harlow's and then without really knowing how she got there, Harlow is on her back, Sloane on top of her, and there's a moment when Sloane slips her tongue out of Harlow's mouth, and Harlow takes a sweet breath and thinks of how she wanted this from the moment she first saw Sloane in the salon. Tried not to think about it—her—too much. And now it's happening, Sloane looking down at her with those sea-green eyes full of hunger, and Harlow makes a noise she's never made before and lets her head fall back, her throat open and vulnerable.

Then Sloane is kissing her there, delicate touches of her mouth to Harlow's skin, and then—

From somewhere below there is the sound of the front door slamming. It is followed by a woman's voice calling out: "Sloane? Why are all the lights on down here?"

Sloane bolts upright. "Shit." She scrambles over Harlow and goes to the windows, which she throws wide open, icy wind slicing through the moment they were wrapped up in. "My mom's home early," she says. "She can't know we were smoking in here."

Harlow sits up, dazed, touching her fingers to her swollen lips. She feels a second or two behind Sloane, a lag on her understanding of the situation. Oh, right: the interruption, her mom, the weed.

"Harlow!" Sloane points. "There's air freshener in the top drawer." She looks around and takes in the crusts in the open pizza boxes, the half-demolished bag of salt-and-vinegar chips, and the ashtray on the nightstand. "I think she's going to know," Harlow says. "Besides, isn't it legal here? It's not a big deal."

"It is to my mom," Sloane says. "She has this whole not-in-the-house thing."

Harlow leans over and opens the top drawer of Sloane's nightstand. "Okay," she says, and sprays synthetic rose scent into the air.

But she is only thinking about what would have happened if they hadn't been interrupted.

"Help me put some of this shit away," Sloane says.

By the time Sloane's mom comes upstairs and knocks on the door they are sitting on the floor like two little schoolkids: *nothing going on here, no ma'am, just two wholesome girls watching a wholesome family sitcom.*

"Mom," Sloane says when the door opens and Addy Prescott steps in, in one hand her cane, today shimmering blue, and in the other an already open beer. "I thought your training thing went till late."

"Hi, Ms. Prescott," Harlow says.

"Oh, hi Harlow, honey," Sloane's mom says, and then, to her daughter: "Only half the people who registered actually showed, so we got through things much faster than I thought. Then I went by the salon to check the messages."

Sloane shrugs. "Okay?"

"There was a lovely selection of messages left by Liam," Sloane's mom says, and her face grows stern. "I thought I told you, I don't want your boyfriend calling the shop because he can't get a hold of you. I don't want your drama at my workplace, okay? I'm not going to tell you again."

Boyfriend?

When Harlow looks over at Sloane, she is at least flushed. "Okay" is all she says, in a meek kind of way that Harlow has never heard from her before. "Sorry, Mom."

Adelaide sighs heavily. "Sure you are," she says. She pauses for a second, her gaze drifting around the room, and Harlow knows she isn't at all fooled, but she doesn't say anything about the smell or the debris hastily piled by the trash can. "I hope you've done those assignments that are due after break. I don't want to be called into another meeting—"

"They're done, Mom," Sloane says. "It's all good. Nothing to stress about."

Addy clicks her tongue against her teeth as if she doesn't believe her daughter. After a moment, she raises the beer to her lips, swallows, and then uses it to point at them. "Well, I'll leave you two in peace. Be good girls, okay?"

"Always," Sloane says.

It's the kind of thing her mom would have said, Harlow thinks, if she'd ever had friends over. They're a lot alike, Sloane's mom and her own, with the weariness and the after-work cold one and trying their best as a single mother. It's like Sloane and Addy Prescott are the alternate versions of Harlow and Cora, in the world where they never had to run.

Sloane waves at her mom until the door closes and they're alone again, and lets her hand drop. "She didn't buy it."

Harlow stares at her. As if that's what she cares about most right now. "You have a boyfriend?"

"Oh god." Sloane rolls her eyes. "I could kill her for—no, I don't have a boyfriend. I mean, technically I don't. We're broken up. On a break. Whatever."

"Does he know that?"

Sloane throws her hands up. "Why is everybody making *his* inability to move on *my* problem?" she says, but she can't meet Harlow's eyes.

"Right," Harlow says. "And when did you two break up?"

Sloane pauses. "Last week. I guess."

Harlow gets to her feet, suddenly extremely sober. "Okay, well, I'm not some toy you can play with. Some stupid girl to mess around with while you're boyfriend's off doing whatever—"

"It's not like that, Harlow, come on," Sloane says. "I mean, it's not a big deal, right? We barely know each other. It's not like this means anything."

It's a heavy hit to her ego. *Oh.* It doesn't mean anything to her. *Harlow* doesn't mean anything to her. "Whatever, Sloane," she says, grabbing her keys and phone and what little is left of her dignity. "I gotta go."

"Harlow, don't be like that." Sloane follows her as Harlow rushes out of the room, down the stairs. "Harlow, come *on*—"

Harlow shoves her feet into her boots and makes it outside, pulling the door shut hard behind her.

She waits for a second. Sloane doesn't open it.

She gets in her car and pushes the heels of her hands into her eyes until her vision fractures like the cracked insides of a kaleidoscope.

26

Stupid stupid stupid girl, I knew she didn't really want me, she has somebody she actually cares about and I'm just someone else to pass the time while the one she really wants isn't around, I knew it I knew it I knew it but I let myself fall for it anyway and now what do I have? My only friendship here, ruined. Back to being alone.

By the time Harlow has finished berating herself and driven home, it's midnight dark, the house blending into the trees surrounding it, blurred by the persistent rain.

She swallows as she looks up at the house. In the dark tonight it looks more imposing than she's thought before, and bigger, as if it has grown over the last few days. As if it has swelled larger, taller, reaching up to join the tops of the tallest trees, becoming a looming mansion rather than the quiet cottage she'd first seen it as.

Harlow makes a break for it through the rain and lets herself in; when she closes the door behind her, the sound of the rain quiets, and she stands there for a moment, listening. The silence is broken by the noise of her phone ringing, and she takes it out to see it's Christina.

She pushes off the door and heads into the kitchen, grabbing a glass from the side of the sink as she answers. "Hey, Christina. Hi."

"Hi," Christina says. "How are you doing?"

"Me?" Harlow fills the glass right to the top with cold water, eyeing it, almost daring the water to spill over the edge. *Kissed a girl for the first time, almost had my fantasy come true, and then she told me whatever happened between us doesn't even matter. And did I mention my dead mom?* "Oh, fine. You know. You?"

"Fine, fine," Christina says, and then they both laugh, because they both know the other is lying, because of course neither of them are *fine*. "Oh god, I hate this," Christina says now, and she sounds flat, quiet and tired. "I talked to Clem. I told her about Cora. I told her our sister is dead."

I talked to Clem. Harlow sets her glass down, the water spilling onto her hand, icy. Clementine, still a mystery to Harlow. She tries to picture her, in an airport bathroom exhausted from a long flight, toes numb inside her heels, listening as Christina delivers the news. And what did she feel? Surprise, that it had happened? Or acceptance, like the only real surprise was that it had taken this long for some terrible fate to befall one of them the same way it had their mother? "I'm sorry," Harlow says quietly.

"For what?"

"I don't know," Harlow says, and there's a tremor in her voice. "That you had to tell her that. For bringing you out here. Being the bearer of bad news. All of it."

Christina's sigh crackles down the line. "You don't have to be sorry for any of that," she says. "None of this is your fault. *None* of it. You're just a kid, Harlow. I don't think you get that. You shouldn't have to be doing any of this. You shouldn't have to be facing life without any parents. You shouldn't have the only two family members you know be one person you just met and the other halfway around the world, barely contactable and completely disconnected from any of her responsibilities—" She takes a deep breath. "Sorry."

"Is she coming?" Harlow asks, and then, quickly: "Did you tell her about me?"

"Yes," Christina says. "I mean, yes, I told her about you. But I don't know if she's coming—it's not as easy for her to drop work and go, or—I don't know, Harlow. Maybe she'll show up; maybe she won't. That's kind of how Clem operates."

"I'm sorry," Harlow says again.

Christina ignores it this time, instead saying, "How about we go for dinner tomorrow? Somewhere nice. We can eat good food, and talk, and get to know each other better, and . . . I think it would be nice."

Harlow nods, before remembering Christina can't see her. "Yeah," she says. "I'd like that."

"Okay," Christina says, and now Harlow can hear the smile in her voice, and it makes her feel warm, a welcome relief from all the darkness and bad things. "I'll find a place, and let you know. But now I have to call home, because if I don't read Otto the same story he's heard thirty thousand times, he won't go to sleep."

Harlow smiles by herself in the dark. "All right," she says. "See you tomorrow."

27

That night Harlow wakes in the early hours of the morning again. Or she thinks she's awake; it's hard to tell. Everything is dark, blacker than usual, and she can feel the mattress beneath her, but she can feel the floor, too, the smooth wood under her bare feet. If she turns—thinks *turn*, thinks *look around*—she can see herself in bed, lying there on her back, the covers half thrown off and eyes tightly shut. She is watching herself sleep.

Then she lands in the bed with a soft thud, eyes snapping open and panic catching in her throat as she remembers the sensation of falling, plummeting to her death. It takes a minute to fully come back to herself, her hands grasping the sheets as she realizes no, she's not falling; she's not dreaming; she's not watching herself from the corner of the room. She is in bed and it was all a dream, or nightmare. Night terror.

She pulls the covers around herself, curling into them and rubbing her feet together to generate some kind of warmth. Her eyes begin to adjust to the dark and she's looking at the half-open closet and it itches something in her brain.

Half-open.

She closed it before bed, she thinks. Pulled a dry shirt out of her duffel and then pushed it back into the closet where she's been keeping it, and then pulled the door closed too.

But now it's open.

Half-open.

Harlow's breathing is shallow, and she pulls the covers closer around her body as the room comes into clear contrast. Her clothes on the floor. The empty hanging picture frames on Clem's walls. The gaping black mouth of the closet.

And then, out of the darkness—

Something gleams. The reflection of moonlight hitting something shiny, metallic.

Harlow stops breathing as it falls into place. No: something alive.

Eyes, staring out from the blackness.

No. No no no you are imagining things you are dreaming still you are seeing something where there is nothing.

Harlow blinks rapidly as if trying to clear the vision from her eyes, but nothing changes. She stares into the darkness; somebody—some*thing*—stares back.

And then slowly, slowly, long fingers begin to creep around the edge of the door.

Harlow pulls the sheets over her face and squeezes her eyes as tight shut as she can. "You are dreaming," she whispers, her breath hot in the small space beneath the covers. "You are dreaming, this is a dream, this is a nightmare, it's your imagination, you are going to wake up soon, you are going to wake up, wake up, wake up—"

· · · ·

When she next opens her eyes, it is light. Soft gray morning seeping through the windows, and Harlow opens her eyes to stare at the half-open closet door, but it is not half-open at all. It is closed, exactly like she left it before she got into bed last night.

She's clammy all over, head pounding, and it takes her a few tense minutes to peel back the covers and get out of bed. Cross the room, bare feet on the wood *like I felt when I saw myself, is this a dream too—* no: keeps moving forward until she reaches the closet and takes a deep breath before pulling the door open with one decisive action, and there is nothing inside. Or not nothing, but only what should be there: empty hangers, her duffel, a few boxes with nothing of consequence inside them. No monster lying in wait. No intruder waiting to wrap long fingers around her throat and squeeze.

She checks under the floorboard; the money and everything else is right where she left it.

Harlow nods, over and over and over, as she closes the closet door and goes back to the bed, sitting right on the edge. "It was a bad dream," she tells herself. Like before, she can feel it getting to her—this house. The paranoia her mom instilled in her. The quiet of the woods, swinging from comforting to claustrophobic. She can't be like this. She can't get caught up in imagined monsters and visions. There are far too many real hidden things for her to unearth.

She gets up, deciding to get the day started and put the sleepless, sweaty night behind her. *Maybe it was the weed,* she thinks absentmindedly as she takes the towel off the back of the door.

But on her way out, she can't help but look back, make sure the closet door is really closed this time.

28

When she gets out of the shower there are two texts waiting, one from Sloane and one from Christina.

Her finger hovers over Sloane's message, but she can't bring herself to look. Instead she reads Christina's: **I got us a reservation at Fontinelli's in Hanneford tonight, at 7, if that's okay?**

Harlow texts back that it's fine, perfect even, and arranges to pick Christina up around six thirty.

There are a lot of hours between then and now. Harlow passes them at first by doing what Vincent Harris asked, looking up DNA tests and wondering what she might find if she takes one, if she spits in the tube and sends it away so some lab somewhere can analyze her and tell her exactly where she comes from. Who she comes from.

But then she quickly gets sidetracked reading stories from people who took the test and wished they hadn't, stories of families torn apart and secrets unearthed and plain old parents who didn't want to be. She closes out of the search without making any purchase and thinks about the other information that Vincent told her to look into, her mom's financial records and the list of people she knew, but Harlow can't bring herself to go there yet. All of a sudden this all feels too fast, too much, and she's so tired and there is this constant knowledge in the back of her mind that her mom's body is waiting back where she died, waiting for someone to claim her, and instead Harlow is thousands of miles away focused on something else.

She abandons her laptop and grabs her keys and jacket, rushing out the door. She drives into town to get away from the house and parks on the street like usual but doesn't bother going over to the salon. How can she? She's mad at Sloane and she's hurt, but most of all, she's embarrassed. It's not even really that Sloane is already with someone else. It's that she didn't tell Harlow about him. It's that she decided it would be okay to fool around with Harlow, knowing—*knowing*, it's not like Sloane is oblivious—how Harlow feels, and then when she got caught out, she said it didn't matter. Like Harlow was nothing at all.

And really, the reason that stings, so painful, is because—it's what Harlow deep down feels about herself. She's nothing. There's no real her, just a collection of faded girls she used to be.

She looks at her phone, the number on her inbox, Sloane's message waiting. Before she can talk herself out of it, she opens the text and reads quickly, fast, like ripping off a Band-Aid. **Yesterday was stupid. I was stupid. It didn't mean nothing to me, I shouldn't have said that. Come over today and I can explain about everything. I don't have any friends as cool as you. Talk to me, please?**

Harlow knocks her head against the window. That's a lot of words without actually saying sorry.

And yet she can feel herself wanting to forgive. To go over there and let Sloane paper over everything and push her own feelings down so things can go back to the way they were. Another thing she learned from her mom, evidently: keep everything inside and don't you dare tell another soul what you're really thinking, ever, at all.

Eventually she gets out of the car, and instead of the salon or the coffee shop, Harlow walks over to the square and sits. It's still cold but there's no rain today, and she is sick of being inside, craving the bite of crisp air in her lungs. Weak sunlight breaks through the clouds, more white today than gray, and Harlow tips her head back and closes her eyes as she wills herself to imagine she can feel some kind of warmth on her skin. She puts her head-phones in and puts on an old song her mom used to play when she was cleaning, some country singer rhyming about the trailer park and her mama's broken heart.

But the song is only halfway through when it cuts off and is replaced by the ringing of Harlow's phone.

She opens her eyes, sits forward, and presses her tongue to the ridge on the inside of her cheek when she sees it is Marcy Sheffield calling. "Hello?" she answers.

"Hi, Harlow?"

"Yeah, it's Harlow."

"Oh good, I was worried I'd get your voicemail," Marcy says, and she sounds a little distant, harried, and Harlow pictures her at her desk answering emails and scanning over spreadsheets while talking to her. "I'm calling to follow up on our conversation the other day. I have reached out to a few contacts of mine from my police days, but I haven't heard back from anybody yet. I have to say the lack of response isn't making me hugely hopeful any of them are particularly eager to talk, but I'll chase them anyway. I'm sorry I don't have a more encouraging update."

Harlow reaches to rub the nape of her neck, squinting against what sun there is. "Actually," she says, "I spoke to one of them. Vincent Harris? He called me and we met, so—"

"Who?"

"Vincent Harris," Harlow says. "The private investigator? He told me you'd reached out to him, and he seemed like he wants to help. He had some ideas about things to look into, anyway."

"Vincent Harris," Marcy repeats. "Harlow—" There's a long beat of silence, longer than is comfortable, long enough that Harlow knows whatever comes next isn't going to be good. "Harlow, I've never heard that name before."

At first Harlow thinks she must have completely misheard, because there's no way Marcy just said she's never heard the name Vincent Harris before, because if she's never heard that name then it stands to reason that she doesn't know that man, and if she doesn't know that man then who is he and how the fuck did he know who Harlow was and what she wanted?

"Harlow?"

"But he told me you spoke to him," she says finally. "He said you asked him to call me."

The clicking of keys in the background ceases, and now Marcy sounds concerned. "No," she says. "I promise you, Harlow, I've never heard the name Vincent Harris before. And I certainly didn't speak to any private investigator. I called a few of my old colleagues. County police, that's all."

"But he knew I was looking for information on Eve," Harlow says, and she can hear the way she's trying to convince Marcy, almost—*Come on, really think about it; you must remember him, because he knew everything, and how could he have known if it wasn't for you?* "He knew—" She lowers her voice. "He knew who my mom was. He knew she was dead. And he told me you sent him, and it made sense because you said you were going to ask for help and I thought he *was* that help. He knew—everything."

"Harlow." Marcy says her name sternly, like she needs to make sure Harlow listens to her. "Do not contact this man again. Okay? That's the first thing I need you to do, stay away from him. I don't know who he is or what exactly is going on, but will you promise me that? You won't talk to him again?"

He knew everything.

Sitting there on the bench in the square in the town her mother once called home, Harlow feels the ground drop from beneath her, a wave of dizzying nausea crashing over her. Stupid, stupid, she is so *fucking* stupid. All those years of being extra careful, abiding by her mom's rules, knowing not to trust anyone too much because all it takes is one person, the wrong person—all of that and still she was foolish enough to do it. Let her guard down because he said he knew Marcy, and Harlow had decided already to trust Marcy, because—why? Because Ruby sent her there, and

Harlow had decided to trust Ruby, too, the moment she realized that her mom had loved this woman a hundred years ago, when they were just kids? Or because the moment she'd stepped into the salon and set eyes on Sloane, opened her mouth to mention Severn House, she'd lost all sense of the caution she was supposed to take?

"Harlow? Are you still there?"

Harlow pulls in a deep breath, the cold air stinging. Earlier she had wanted that feeling, and now it's painful, too much. "I'm here," she manages to say. "I'm—" She stops, unsure of what to say next. "If you didn't tell him who I was, then—"

Marcy has already reached the same conclusion as Harlow, it seems. "Then there's really only one way he could know," she says. "He knows your family situation, your name, and details about your mother's recent passing. I would say the person who is paying that much attention is probably not doing it for no reason. I would say that the person with that much interest in you and your family—it most likely didn't start recently."

Out with it, Marcy. "A person like that has probably been watching my family for years," Harlow says flatly. "A person like that might be the kind of person responsible for making a woman disappear. Right?"

"Don't be alarmed," Marcy says, and she sounds different—like she's slipped back into cop mode, Harlow realizes, keeping her voice calm and clear in order to console a worried victim. "Now, it is well known that perpetrators often like to revisit their crimes. I'm not saying that's *definitely* what's happening here, but—"

"But you're not *not* saying it, either," Harlow says. She squeezes her eyes shut as she realizes that Marcy doesn't even know the rest. The person on their tail. Her mom's paranoia, jumping at every little noise, watching for danger around every corner.

"Listen, it's going to be okay," Marcy's saying now, her tone patient, as if she's talking to a child. Harlow thinks about Christina yesterday on the phone: *You're just a kid, Harlow.* "I'll tell my old colleagues, and they can handle this. You have his number, you've seen his face—both of those things should be able to help them look for him. And until you hear from me again, don't talk to him, don't meet him, just—don't do anything."

"I won't," Harlow's saying, but she's checked out of the conversation, up on her feet and running to her car. "I have to go."

"Harlow, are you going to be—"

"Bye. Thanks. Bye." Harlow hangs up and throws herself into the car. She thinks back to the day before: the man sitting across from her in the booth, with his fancy watch and pretty face. The way he'd seemed so genuinely sad about her mom's death.

She swallows. Not sad. Remorseful.

Remorse means guilt, she thinks.

It's all falling apart so fast, but the only thing Harlow can think is that she's pretty sure Vincent Harris is the one who's been on their tail this whole time. And more than that—

She's pretty sure that Vincent Harris—or whatever the fuck his real name is—is responsible for Eve's disappearance.

29

She's breathing fast, shallow panic-tight breaths that pinch at her ribs and send adrenaline flooding her body.

Her fingers fumble at her phone. There are a million thoughts running through her head, but one that is bigger, louder, more urgent than the others, one that she's heard in her mom's voice so many times before: *run.*

Harlow curls over the steering wheel, hitting her fists on the dash. To leave, now, when she's just discovered her family? Abandon Christina and make her escape before she's even gotten to meet Clementine? Once she goes—if, *if* she goes—that will be it, she knows. She won't be Harlow Ford anymore: she'll become one of those girls on the IDs her mom left for her. She'll disappear into the old pattern of things and she'll never really know the answers to all her questions and she'll never see her family ever again. That's what it takes, to stay safe; that's what her mom taught her, and Harlow knows why now.

Vincent Harris, knowing too much, snapping at their heels.

Harlow sits up, an awareness of her surroundings coming back to her. It's quiet around the square, eerily so, and she suddenly has the feeling that sitting still like this makes her an easy target.

She cranks the engine and peels out. It begins to rain as she drives, heavy full drops that explode violently on the windshield. She heads out of town and along the winding roads, but it's only when she's passing by those rows of ticky-tacky houses that she realizes where she's going.

She swallows the shame that followed yesterday's kiss and hears the words of Sloane's not-quite-apology in her head. *It didn't mean nothing to me.*

Whatever it is that she does mean to Sloane, Harlow knows what Sloane means to her: the first and realest friend she's had, even if she hasn't told her the entire truth, even if she is also infatuated with Sloane in an embarrassingly earnest way. When— *if*—she leaves, she'll never see Sloane again, never get to kiss her again or feel the bright intensity of Sloane's gaze on her. And Sloane will be left like everybody else Harlow has left behind, except there will probably always be the question in Sloane's mind, if Harlow's sudden disappearance is Eve playing out all over again.

Harlow pulls up in front of Sloane's house, parking behind a gray hatchback that must belong to Sloane's mom. She sits there for a minute, attempting to even out her breathing and urging the shaking that started somewhere on her way over to cease.

This is reckless, she knows. But she can make it make sense as the last reckless thing she'll do.

Sloane is not the same as the other people she has left behind. She doesn't want to leave her wondering. She doesn't want to leave her with anything less than the truth, and really, it doesn't fucking matter anymore does it, because Vincent has already caught up to her. Her attempts at subterfuge have really been for shit, because who knows how long he's been onto her, onto them? And there is a part of her that wants to do this—to tell Sloane everything—in an attempt to mark her own existence. So that somebody here, somebody she cares about, knows who she is and why she did what she's done and that she, Harlow Ford, was real.

She looks up at the house and then sends Sloane a text: **are u home? i want to talk.**

Sloane's response is instant: **yes, come over**

i'm outside

okay one sec

The rain turns heavier as Harlow walks up to the front door, trying hard not to look over her shoulder for someone following behind. She shelters under the porch roof as she waits for Sloane, and then the door swings open wide and Sloane is grabbing Harlow by the wrist to bring her into the house, the touch so casual, as though what happened yesterday isn't still hanging strange and new between them. "It's freezing, come on," Sloane's saying as Harlow trips inside, and then the door is closed behind them and Harlow's skin tingles as the heat of the house hits her. "Are you okay? You look like you've seen a ghost."

Harlow smiles, and she can feel how the expression pulls strangely at her face. "Maybe I did," she says.

Sloane shifts on the spot, that bright gaze determined and focused. "About yesterday," she says. "I'm an asshole—"

"I don't want to talk about that," Harlow says. "I have to—" She cuts herself off, listening, remembering Adelaide's car in the driveway. "Can we go to your room?"

"Sure," Sloane says, a little taken aback. "One second, though. My dad's here."

"Your dad?" Harlow is the one surprised now. "The one you barely see?"

Sloane lowers her voice. "He showed up out of the blue last night, which—of course he did." She sounds tired. "Let me get rid of him."

"Don't worry," a man's voice says from the kitchen. "I'm on my way out."

Sloane turns in the direction of the voice. "It's not my fault I have other things going on in my life," she says, her voice raised but disarmingly sweet, like she's talking to a child. "That's why me *and* Mom told you to call before you just show up, remember?" She turns back to Harlow, rolling her eyes. "You want something to drink?" Sloane asks, but Harlow barely hears her, caught in place.

That voice. *I'm imagining it,* she tells herself, and again: *You're imagining things, Harlow—*

But then Sloane's dad strolls out of the kitchen, a lazy smile on his face, a hand running through his dirty-blond hair, and Harlow bites down on her cheek so hard she tastes blood, but it's the only way to stop herself reacting outwardly, to protect herself.

Because in front of her, standing in Sloane's house like he owns it, is Vincent Harris.

Harlow's mind flickers and whirs, short-circuiting. Vincent Harris looks at Harlow, his smile unchanging, like they are strangers, and says, "You're not going to introduce me to your friend, kiddo?"

"Don't call me that," Sloane says immediately. "Harlow, this is my dad. Dad, this is Harlow. Okay, you can go now!"

"Slow down," Vincent says, and he holds his hand out to Harlow just like he did at the diner, the first time they met. His smile widens, teeth gleaming and dangerous. "Oliver Prescott. Nice to meet you, Harlow."

BEFORE

It doesn't take long for the crowd to dissipate, but the girls leave before that—or Cora makes sure they are gone before Ruby can come over, glancing over her shoulder to check Ruby is still far back as she drags Christina and Clem to the car. She doesn't want her sisters to meet her here, now. She doesn't want to make this day stranger than it has to be.

Cora sees the flash of Ruby's white-blond hair in the rearview mirror as they drive off and pretends she doesn't feel like a piece of shit.

The snow keeps on falling as Christina navigates the car along the winding roads, down the track through the woods. Cora watches it coming down to distract herself. She wonders what would happen if it got really bad, if they were snowed in to the house and trapped in the woods. She imagines the quiet of it, and the certain knowledge that nobody would be intruding, that it would be just the three of them alone. She imagines hot cocoa and grilled cheeses, and bundling up in their warmest clothes to make snowmen, a thing they've never done before, stick branches for arms and whatever they can find in the fridge for a nose.

"—paying attention?"

Cora rouses, looking at Christina. "What?"

Christina huffs, but there's a smile that tells Cora she's not really pissed. "What are you thinking about?"

"Snowmen."

"Snowmen?" Clem says from the back with a laugh. "What?"

"Never mind," Cora says. "What was I not paying attention to?"

The forest opens up ahead of them and there's the house waiting, a dusting of white on the roof. Picture-book perfection. Christina pulls up and puts the car in park. "I was just saying it went well," she says. "We did a good job. Yeah, I think we all did a good job."

As soon as they get inside, Cora rips off her stupid itchy blouse, sighing with relief as the cold air hits her irritated skin, and she scratches at her waist. "Remind me to throw this out," she says, and Christina grabs the blouse out of her hand as she passes, heading upstairs.

"I'll put it in the donation bag," she says. "Some other little goody-goody schoolgirl might get a kick out of it."

Cora flicks her middle finger at Christina's retreating back. "I didn't know that's not how people dress!" she yells after her. "I hate you."

"You love me," Christina calls back over her shoulder, singsong, and like that the tension breaks. Cora feels the weight lift off her tired spine, the sudden knowledge that Christina is right: they did good. It's over, for another year at least. Like Cora said to Clem this morning, all they had to do was get through the memorial, and now they have, and now normal life can continue, and they can be the girls they've fought so hard to become.

The day returns to what it is, another slow Sunday, and afternoon passes to evening, the sky darkening outside while they resume normal behavior: Christina in the kitchen prepping dinners for the week ahead, Clem at the table doing homework, Cora buzzing around annoying both of them. "Do you need help with your English paper?" she asks Clem. "Remember what we agreed: you bring those grades up to Bs or above and you can go to Tia's family's cabin for spring break. But any less—"

"I know, I know," Clem says, narrowing her eyes at her notebook filled with row after row of her cramped writing. "You know, a C is a perfectly respectable grade for someone who only started going to real school a year and a half ago."

"We never got to go to school," Christina says, stirring a pot of simmering vegetable stock. "Be grateful."

"Yeah, yeah," Clem says, sitting up and pointing at Christina, then Cora. "How about *you* talk to *her* about actually registering for college classes?"

Christina spins away from the stove, waving a wooden spoon accusatorially in Cora's direction. "You told me you did already!"

"I did!" Cora makes a face, knowing she's caught. *Ugh, Clem is such a little rat sometimes.* "I mean, I started to. I just don't know what I want to take exactly and there's a million different—"

"Tonight," Christina says firmly. "You and me, after dinner. We're sitting down and we're getting it done."

"Christina—"

"Don't bother! It's happening, Cora. This is the plan, remember? Clem in school, you in college, me working—you can't back out now. We're all getting a life. Remember?" she says again.

Cora presses her lips together like she's annoyed, but she's not really. Christina is right: this is the plan they made, when they realized they were really alone and could do whatever they wanted, all the things they weren't allowed to before. When they realized that without Eve, they were free.

"Fine," she says to Christina, and then, with a sly glance at Clem: "But just so you know, Clem totally got her belly button pierced two weeks ago."

Clem's mouth drops open. "Cora! I *hate* you!"

"Clementine Kennedy—" Christina, a scandalized expression on her face, heads for Clem. "You little shit! Show me!"

"No!" Clem jumps up and runs past Cora, Christina giving chase, and their infectious laughter fills the house. Cora runs after them in time to see Christina fall onto the couch with Clem on top of her, arms around Clem's waist as she kicks at the air and squeals. "Okay, mercy! Mercy!" She rolls on the floor and pulls her sweatshirt up to reveal the tiny pink gem sparkling in her navel. "Here. Happy?"

Christina bites her lip as she examines the piercing and shakes her head before looking up at Cora. "Well," she says with a dramatic heavy sigh. "I guess it's actually kinda cute."

Clem looks between her sisters, her nose wrinkled in confusion. "Wait. You're not mad?"

Cora can't hold it in any longer, then, and bursts out laughing,

Christina joining her a fraction of a second later. "No, she's not mad," Cora says between breathless laughs.

"I don't care!" Christina says. "I never cared! I just wanted to see how long you thought you'd get away with hiding it."

Clem's eyes flash as she realizes she's been tricked. "Oh, that's it," she says, scrambling to her feet. "You two are *dead*—"

And then there is a hollow, hard knock on the front door.

30

Harlow stares, frozen at Vincent—Oliver—whatever the fuck his name is, whoever this fucking man is.

Sloane's dad. The con-man private investigator who Harlow has just realized poses a threat, who maybe is the reason that Eve vanished, the reason her own mom is *dead*, is actually Sloane's deadbeat father.

What the *fuck* is going on?

Run. Harlow hears the word in her mom's voice again. *You know what to do. Run and don't look back.*

Harlow's muscles tense, ready to bolt. Who he is and what he wants are not important right now. The voice in her head is right, and she's certain now. She needs to get out of here, as fast as she can.

"You know what?" Harlow forces a bright tone, making herself look Vincent-Oliver right in the face before turning to Sloane. "I completely forgot I need to go meet my—somebody. We have dinner reservations. I can't believe I forgot. I'm so stupid! Nice to meet you, Mr. Prescott, and, Sloane, I'll text you later, okay? Okay, all right, bye!'

It all comes out in one rushed sentence, Harlow tripping over her words and then over her feet in her haste to get out, cursing herself for giving away her nerves. She knows Vincent—Oliver, *Oliver*—notices, his fake smile turning cold as she backs up and fumbles for the door, pulling it open and stepping back out into the cold. Sloane only looks confused, rattled by the abrupt shift in Harlow's demeanor. "Wait, what?" Sloane says as Harlow turns now, covering the short distance to her car. "I thought you wanted to talk—Harlow? Harlow!"

Harlow's in the car now, key in the ignition, but when she turns it, the engine stutters and dies. "Don't," she says, smacking her palm on the steering wheel. "Come on, wake up."

But now Sloane is at her window, rapping her knuckles on the glass. "Harlow," she says, her voice muted. "Where are you going, weirdo?"

"I have to go," Harlow says without looking at Sloane, and tries the engine again, getting the same faint whimper of life before nothing.

"Harlow—put the window down," Sloane says, and because Harlow can't think of a reason not to, she does as she's told, rolling the window down so there's a two-inch gap for Sloane to speak into. "What the fuck? I thought we were going to . . . talk about things. Did something happen? Did I say something? I know you're mad because of yesterday but I told you, I can explain. I *want* to explain." She makes a face. "Is it because my dad is here? I swear he's leaving now. He's not even supposed to come to the house, my mom has this rule—anyway, he's going so it's fine, just come back inside and be normal, okay?"

Normal, Harlow thinks. Sloane has no fucking clue. Normal would be getting to explain to your friend why you're leaving town, not taking off with zero notice. Normal would be a family with run-of-the-mill secrets—who got arrested once, who owes money to the IRS, who had an affair with the next-door neighbor. Normal would be meeting your friend's dad and *not* finding out that he's been pretending to help look for the woman he most likely hurt so long ago.

"I can't fucking do this," Harlow says aloud, and she doesn't mean for it to be a response to Sloane, but it does make Sloane step back, her hands up like she has no idea what Harlow's deal is but she knows enough to be freaked out. "Sloane—shit, I'm sorry. But I have to go. Okay? I'm sorry, I really am."

She turns the key in the ignition for the third time, and this time the engine roars to life. Only now does Harlow let herself look at Sloane, on the other side of the glass, golden hair blowing across her confused, beautiful face. For a moment she feels herself weakening, wanting to stay a minute longer, to give Sloane the goodbye she wants.

But then she glances up, and there's Sloane's dad framed in the doorway, aglow from the light inside the house, and he raises his hand in some kind of salute.

"Harlow—"

"Goodbye, Sloane." Harlow reverses out of the driveway, a wide arc onto the rain-slick road, and then she puts it in drive and floors it, leaving Sloane and her liar of a father behind.

• • • •

Harlow drives but doesn't let herself relax. She can't, won't, until she's out of this place for real, the whole town and all the things buried here in the rearview for good. *Go home,* Harlow thinks as she navigates through a descending fog. *Pack up, leave, get out. You can call Christina from the road, say goodbye that way.* There is no time for her to linger, she knows, not when the danger is so close. He made it clear, the way he smiled at her, appearing in the last place she would have guessed: *You can't escape me.* But she has to, now, and she can't see Christina, can't say goodbye, will have to let a shitty phone call be enough. The last call she'll make before she tosses that SIM card and picks up another. This is how it goes, starting over. You leave everything behind. You lose everyone.

Harlow drives but doesn't let herself relax, already thinking about the future unspooling in front of her. It's probably best to go all the way back to where she started this journey, putting that much distance between herself and Vincent Harris. *Where did he even get that name?* And how did he know that posing as a private investigator would be his way in? How did he know about Marcy, and what they'd talked about?

Harlow drives but doesn't let herself relax, and when she sees the gray car gaining on her, she knows she was right not to.

She presses harder on the gas, watching the speed creep up, feeling the body of her hastily purchased and barely inspected car shake as the needle ticks to sixty, sixty-five, seventy. Too fast to be going on these winding roads coated in rain, the view ahead partially obscured, and Harlow has no idea what her next move is, but all she knows is running, so here she is, going as fast as she can.

It's not fast enough: the gray car catches up to her easily, lights flashing bright behind her, and Harlow grips the wheel hard as Vincent presses up close to her. *Too fast too fast too fast,* she thinks as she takes the next bend and feels the car skidding beneath her, her steady grip on the steering wheel the only thing that keeps her on the road. A thousand sharp slices of memory explode in her mind: the snap of her head against the window when the truck hit them. The burn of the seat belt across her chest. The crunch and smash of glass and metal, a chorus backing to the noises her mom made when the metal bar pierced straight through her.

Harlow's heart is thrumming, her breathing shallow and raspy, her eyes barely focused on what little of the road she can see. *Not again, not again not again, Mom—*

The dull thump of bumper to bumper is unmistakable, and Harlow snaps back to the present as she whips forward in her seat. *I'm in a replay,* she thinks. The same moments over and over again, her life a series of bad choices repeated and repeated, and here she is running without truly knowing why, to a destination as yet unknown. All she can see is her and her mom that night— not just the accident, but before that too: the moment when she got Harlow out of her bed and told her it was time to go, with that fear in her eyes. The two of them on the road like so many times before, and how Harlow had wanted to ask yet again what exactly her mom was so afraid of but couldn't bring herself to do it. Hadn't she been tired? Hadn't she been so angry that this was her life? And yet here she is carrying on the old traditions when she could be the one to change things.

Harlow pulls the wheel hard to the right, setting the car into another spin that ends safely on the side of the road. She sits for a moment, watching as the gray car speeds past before turning back and coming to a stop on the side too.

Enough. She came here to find the truth, didn't she?

She watches Vincent or Oliver or whoever the fuck he is get out of his car, can feel the burn of his stare even from this distance.

If I'm going to run, let me at least know who it is that I'm running from.

She steps out of the car.

31

He's at her in seconds, looming large, and Harlow holds herself steady. Pulls up to her full height, pretending she's not afraid of this man. "I think we need to talk, you and I," he says. "Don't you?"

Harlow nods, blinking at him through the rain and fog. "Yeah," she says loudly. "First things first. You tell me who the *fuck* you really are."

He begins to laugh, taking a step back. "You can still call me Vincent," he says. "If you want."

"But your name is Oliver Prescott," Harlow says. "And you're Sloane's father."

"Yes."

Harlow is breathing heavily, grateful for the extra inches of space between them. "Tell me," she says. "Tell me what you did to my mom. To my grandmother."

"Your grandmother?" Oliver looks confused. Oliver: that's all she can see him as now. Vincent was the disguise, the front that made

Harlow give him the benefit of the doubt, and now she knows he's a liar, she can see through it all. The heavy watch that's no more than a fake. The slick smile that belongs to a con artist, not a detective. A man more used to breaking the rules than finding those who did the same. "I don't know what you—" The realization dawns, and revulsion takes over his face. "Jesus Christ, have you lost your mind? Kid, you're more stupid than I thought."

"Stupid?" Harlow bares her teeth. "I know my mom left town because she was too scared to stay, and I know my grandmother vanished one day never to be seen again. And then here you come, knowing all about me and my mom, pretending to be someone you're not so you could—" She pulls her phone out of her pocket. "You killed my grandmother. Did you kill my mom, too? Was it you, did you plan the whole thing, send the truck after us? You want to finish the trifecta, come for me now too? Fine. But I'm not going down easy." She holds her phone up now, praying he can't see the tremor in her hand that reveals all her lies. "I have Sloane on the other end of this call. She can hear everything. So when you kill me, there's going to be a witness. Your *daughter* is going to be my witness."

There's a moment where they do nothing but stare each other down, and Oliver's eyes are wide and wild, and then he lets out a feral yell and lunges at Harlow.

She's ready for it and throws herself to the left, feeling his fingers brush right by her hip. She can't let him see her phone, find out she was bluffing. She had only wanted to scare him. No: she had wanted to scare him *and* give herself a chance. See whether what he wanted to do to her was worth the risk if there was a witness to it all. *Would he still kill me knowing his own daughter could hear the whole thing?*

Landing on her knees, a jarring hit to the asphalt that sends a shock wave through her entire still-healing body, Harlow has her answer. She scrambles to her feet, but adrenaline makes her unsteady and she trips, going down again and her phone slipping out of her grasp, landing in the marshy grass at the edge of the road. Harlow is up on her hands and knees to crawl to it when a hand grips her ankle and yanks her back. Her knees go out from under her, and her hands, and her chin hits the ground, asphalt ripping at her skin. The hit turns her dizzy, but she stretches one arm out still, reaching for her phone. But then his hands are on her thighs, her waist, her shoulders, and she finds herself flipped over, back pinned to the cold road with Oliver over her. He is so close she can feel the heat of his breath on her skin, smell the stale cigarette smoke on it.

The whole thing takes less than a minute. Harlow struggles beneath the weight of him, feels the blood dripping hot from her chin. "Do it," she says through gritted teeth, a wild mix of terror and spite turning her voice harsh and hot. "Kill me like you killed Eve."

Above her Oliver's face turns red, and she feels his fingers curl tighter around her arms, digging into bone, layering new bruises over the half-faded marks already decorating her body. "I didn't kill that woman! I never even met her."

Harlow stills. She can feel the cold seeping through to her skin, and rain falls right into her eyes, blurring her already unsteady vision. "You're lying. You're a liar."

"I couldn't give a shit about Eve Kennedy," Oliver spits. "I only want what I'm owed. What your bitch mother owed me."

He lets go of Harlow suddenly, and she can feel the blood rushing back to her wrists, hands, the places on her legs where he'd pinned her with his knees. She sits up gingerly as he strides into the grass, scanning the ground. He bends and snatches her phone up, then turns to look at her, disgust evident on his face. "Here," he says. "Take this useless piece of shit and learn to lie better."

He throws the phone and it lands at Harlow's feet, the screen shattered. She's still catching her breath and trying to forget the feel of his hands on her. "What do you mean?" she says. "What my mom *owed* you?"

Oliver brushes his hands off. "A long time ago, I did her a favor," he says, looking down at her. "A very expensive favor. A favor for which she neglected to pay me. And then she skipped town, like that meant I would forget. But I don't forget people's debts, Harlow. And just because somebody dies doesn't mean their debt is cleared, either. It just means it passes to the next person."

Harlow swallows. "Me."

"You." Oliver nods. "So how about it, kid? You ready to pay your mom's debts?"

I've been doing it all my life.

Her rages rises. This, *this* is the reason she's had to pretend to be somebody she's not every day of her life? Hiding and faking identities and moving in the middle of the night all because her mom owed some washed-up piece-of-shit asshole back in her hometown? "You have got to be fucking kidding me," she says, and she starts to laugh. "Really? This is all about *money*? Oh my *god*."

"Ten grand." Oliver kicks at the ground near Harlow's hand. "And because I'm nice, I won't add on the interest. That's real generous of me, you know."

"You're out of your mind if you think I'm paying you," Harlow says. "You're out of your mind if you think I have ten grand lying around to give you." She hopes she is a better liar than he has pinned her for. The fifteen grand from the safety-deposit box is *hers.* There's no way she's going to give almost everything she has left of it—considering what she's already spent—to this fucker. That's her escape route, her get-out-of-jail-*somewhat*-free card.

Oliver crouches now, that dangerous, slippery smile back. "See, I actually don't care whether you have it or not," he says. "What matters is that you're going to get it. One way or another, Harlow, I'm going to get paid."

"You've gone this long without it," Harlow begins to say, and he's on her again before she can react, grabbing a fistful of her short hair and pulling her head back so she can't move.

"Not for lack of trying," he says, and then eyes her, eerily calm. "You know, you've changed since you were a kid, but not so much that I didn't know it was you the first time I saw you. Helps that you look just like Cora. You always were so alike, always together. Except she's dead now, so I guess it's just you, huh, kid?"

You've changed since you were a kid.

Always were so alike, always together.

It's the confirmation Harlow needed but didn't want, and it takes a second to click into place, to make her understand: Oliver knows what she looked like as a kid. Always saw her and her mom, together.

Oliver *was* the thing they were running from.

She stares at him. Hearing him talk, the confirmation that he really was chasing them and her mom wasn't making things up—it doesn't bring Harlow any kind of relief. There is just fear. A cold wave of knowing that all the times Harlow inwardly called her mom paranoid she was wrong. Of knowing that every action her mom took was actually justified, because Oliver had been right behind them, and if he was in any way responsible for what happened to Eve, then there was no telling what he could do to them. And what must that have been like for her mom, running and trying to keep a petulant kid safe while knowing somebody was tracking your every move.

"You've been following us." Harlow says it quietly, her foundations shaken. "All my life, you've been—"

Oliver releases his grip on her with a shove. "Let's not be dramatic," he says. "It hasn't been your *whole* life. I have to give it to Cora; she surprised me when she finally slipped out of my reach. I thought I had enough connections to report on her—the two of you—wherever you went, and at first I did. It wasn't hard, you know. Call in a couple favors here, get a couple tips from old friends there, and then I'd be on my way to wherever you were, but your mom, she must've had some kind of sixth sense, because she was always gone before I could catch her. And then eventually she managed to get away completely. No one knew where she was, and none of the tips I got turned out to be right. So after a few years I had no real choice but to give up. Write it off." He holds his hands out to the sky. "But then! I hear somebody's moved into the house in the woods. I hear she's some kind of distant Kennedy relative. Then I see you, and I know *exactly* who you are. I didn't need to hear you confessing all to Marcy Sheffield, but I did pick up some other things from your talk with her. That was very helpful."

Harlow blinks, stunned. "You—heard me with—"

It hits her, fast: the guy in the diner, half-asleep over a plate of food, face conveniently hidden from view as he listened in. *Oliver was there.* "You were there," she says. "At the diner."

Oliver smirks. "You think you're observant, Harlow, but you're really not. There's a lot you don't pay any attention to. And you make a lot of stupid decisions, too—like coming back to Crescent Ridge after all the trouble your mom went through to keep away. I mean—" He shrugs. "It was a stupid decision for you, at least. For me? Shit, when I first saw you I couldn't *believe* I was going to get my money back after all this time."

Harlow is still reeling from the realization that Oliver has been on her from practically day one—no, further back: those years he spent following them, tracking them down, hoping to collect on his debt. Not her whole life, he said, but it had been long enough. Long enough to leave her mom perpetually on edge, unable to tell a real threat from an imagined one. So maybe she had been paranoid, but it had not been unearned at all. "You came after us," she says, "you came after her for fucking *money*?"

"I don't forget about the debts people owe me," Oliver says. "Ever. So you're going to get me that money, clear your mom's debt, and then you can go back to your pathetic life on the run."

Harlow glares at him. "And what if I don't pay?"

Oliver taps a finger against his lips thoughtfully. "The way I see it is this. Either you pay me, clean and easy, and you can carry on doing . . . whatever it is you're doing here, asking pointless questions about a woman who's clearly dead—" He pauses, cocking his head to the side. "You get that, right? You know Eve is dead, right? People don't just disappear off to go live a happy life somewhere else. She was probably dead before the cops even heard her name." He shakes his head, like he's bringing himself back to the point. "So you either pay and keep doing that shit, or some very angry gentlemen I know will pay you, *and* the lovely Christina, a visit."

He doesn't give Harlow a chance to respond to that. He only holds up three fingers, looks at his hand and lowers one. "Two days," he says, and then smirks. "You have my number."

Oliver turns and starts back to his car, leaving Harlow lying on the road.

Before he gets there, he stops and spins around. "Harlow," he calls out. "Don't make me have to come to collect."

32

Harlow waits until Oliver and his gray car have faded away in the fog.

Then she slowly gets to her feet, brushing the dirt from her jeans and feeling gingerly around her jaw, the back of her head. She can feel the bloody scrape on her chin, speckled with tiny bits of gravel. The places where he gripped her throb, tender to the touch, and it feels like every injury from the accident is awake and screaming.

When she feels ready to move, Harlow walks over to her car and gets in. She flips the mirror down and examines the further damage to her face, wincing and sucking in a breath between her teeth as she uses a discarded shirt and a bottle of water to clean the hot wound.

When she's done, she puts the heat on full blast and sits back. *A long time ago, I did her a favor. A very expensive favor.*

All for money, she thinks. It's so pathetic, so nothing, but then, she knows, most terrible things are, at their root. What do they say—sex and money, the root of all evil? Yeah, something like that. So all those years ago Oliver Prescott, Sloane's dad, did something for her mom that she never paid for. And then her mom took off, and she had been running from him ever since.

It makes sense, Harlow supposes. In a petty, stupid way. In a way that makes Harlow want to scream and so she does just that, pressing her fists into her thighs and filling the car with a raw, feral noise, a lifetime's repressed anger turning it deep and ugly. It makes sense, and yet Harlow doesn't want to believe it because then it means her whole life has been this cycle, this repeating pattern, because of *money*.

The air blowing out of the vents finally turns hot, and Harlow shivers as she holds her hands up to feel it.

What kind of favor costs ten grand?

When Christina's name flashes up on her phone, Harlow taps at the broken screen to answer, papering over her cracks with a false-bright "Hello?"

"Hi," Christina says. "Just calling to let you know I'll be waiting out front."

The dinner reservations—*shit.* She can't go, not with Oliver's threat in her head. She can't go, because she has to leave town.

Harlow is overcome with a rush of longing for her mom, wishing she could be back performing their old two-person routine of packing up and hitting the road, the tense quiet of the car that eased the farther and farther away they got. It wasn't much, but it was some kind of security, the two of them. But her mom is dead, and what little security she had is gone.

She clutches her phone. Except there is still Christina, and maybe it's all the pain of the last two weeks wearing her down, or maybe she's weak without her mom to tell her what to do, but Harlow knows she can't leave without seeing Christina one last time.

She stares out of the windshield to the point on the road where she was laid out only minutes ago. "Okay," she says. "I'm on my way."

She steadies herself as she drives back into town. There's no need to tell Christina any of this. It will only worry her, when there's no need for her to panic. They'll go for dinner and in the morning Harlow will be gone, and Christina can go back to her wife and her kid and forget Harlow ever existed. It'll be best for both of them. Yes, she decides, that's what Christina is going to do. Go back and give her kid the life Harlow never had, and Harlow will keep on like she always has, because it's too late to stop now.

As she drives, she feels each turn like it's the last time, watching each house and then store pass like she's on a parade route of goodbyes. It's barely been a week. No longer than a vacation, really, or so Harlow would guess, having never been on a vacation herself. A holiday romance with this town, except instead of romance it has been questions and secrets and threats. She keeps thinking about what Oliver said about Eve: *You know Eve is dead, right?*

If Harlow is honest with herself, she knows that's what she should think. Eve dead by the time a day had passed, maybe less. But the part of her that knows this is the most likely thing is shouted down by the part of her that wants to believe it can't possibly be that simple. That maybe Eve is out there somewhere, living a life she likes. Or a life she can bear, at least. Maybe she lost her memory—you hear about that, right, rare cases of amnesia where people forget everything about their lives and despite all kinds of expert help can't ever recover their memories. Children forgotten, partners falling right out of their heads. Maybe that's where Eve is, out in the world with her whole life before she went missing wiped clean from her brain. That explains why she never returned to her daughters. It's the only explanation Harlow can think of. Besides the other one, that she won't let herself believe in.

When she pulls up outside the bed-and-breakfast, she arranges a controlled smile on her face and watches Christina come down the steps slowly, careful on the slick stone. "Hey," she says when Christina gets in the car.

"Hi," Christina says, and then, turning to look at Harlow, she gasps. "Harlow! What happened to your face?"

Harlow touches a hand to her chin and winces as her nails scrape the raw skin there. "Oh fuck," she says reflexively, both at the pain and at the fact that she so quickly forgot about the injury. It's her head, so blurry and filled with Oliver's threats that she momentarily forgot about her face, and how it would so easily fuck up her plan to not tell Christina anything. "I—I was walking and I tripped—"

She stops as Christina stares her down. The lie is so obvious that she's embarrassed to even try to continue. And then, to her surprise and shame, she feels her eyes filling with tears. *Don't cry,* she tells herself. *Don't cry don't cry what are you some pathetic little kid don't cry—*

The tears slip down her cheeks despite her admonishment.

"Harlow." Christina takes her hand and holds on, hard. "What's wrong?"

"I think I fucked up," Harlow says, her voice thick. "Christina, I think I really fucked up."

Christina says nothing, only stays quiet, and into the space Harlow spills everything, starting from her arrival in Crescent Ridge, fake story in hand, all the way up to her face-off with Oliver on the road moments ago that left her with every bone in her body screaming *run.*

Christina's eyes widen as Harlow talks, the color draining out of her face, leaving her ashen and biting her nails. When Harlow is finished, she stays silent still, for a minute, and then says, "How much do you need?"

Harlow looks at her aunt in surprise. "No way," she says. "Absolutely fucking not. I'm not paying him, and I'm for sure not taking your money to do it."

"Then what are you going to do?" Christina asks. "Leave? Let him chase you out of here?"

"I don't really have any other choice," Harlow says. "What, I'm going to go to the cops? And tell them what? This guy is threatening me over something he did for my dead mom before I was even born? I have no proof, and I don't exactly trust cops to get shit done. And besides, I have no idea what the *favor* he did for my mom was—what if it's something that can come back to bite me? No. It's easier for both of us if I get out of town and put as much distance between me and this place as I can. Let him try to follow me if he wants. I know how to stay hidden." One thing her mom did teach her, at least.

Christina looks like she wants to tell Harlow how terrible an idea it is, sitting there chewing her nails ragged. After a long moment of quiet she says, "Did you say his name is Oliver Prescott?"

Harlow nods. "Do—did—you know him?"

Christina takes her hand away from her mouth and wipes her fingers on her dress, pleated black-and-white silk today. "I'm trying to think," she says, "but I don't remember ever hearing his name. Maybe I'd know him if I saw him, but—you have to understand, we were so sheltered, we didn't—there's a lot of people we didn't know. Or that I didn't know, at least."

Disappointment bursts like a too-big bubble behind Harlow's ribs. "I thought maybe you might know what he did for her," she says. "Whatever was worth ten grand. I mean, it's *ten grand*." The obvious answers—pills, powders, maybe some kind of protection like a gun—don't make any sense to Harlow. Her mom favored blades as a means of self-defense, teaching Harlow how to handle a switchblade as soon as she could be trusted to use it without hurting herself. And what could her mom have done with ten grand's worth of drugs? Harlow had never seen her mom take anything more than a hit off a joint at parties, times when Harlow was supposed to be sleeping in someone's guest bedroom or sometimes in the back seat of the car. What else could her mom have possibly needed that would have cost that much money from a man like Oliver?

"I told you," Christina says. "I never knew why she left. She wrote that note and vanished. If I had known—" She sighs. "I don't know what I could have done, but I would have tried my best to help her. That's what we did. I could have figured something out maybe, or—" She pauses again and looks somewhere past Harlow. "I guess it doesn't matter now. Especially not if your mind's made up. She's gone, and you're leaving."

"Don't think I haven't noticed the irony," Harlow says with a hollow laugh.

Christina refocuses on her. "At least stay tonight," she says. "One more day. We can talk about things. Maybe we can work something out." Her face brightens. "I can talk to Mila. Maybe you can come back with me, and stay with us for a while. I'd really like you to meet her, and Otto. I really want to spend more time with you, Harlow. It doesn't seem fair that we find each other now and you're going to take off again. I don't want to miss out on more time with you. You're my *family.* That means something. We belong to each other. We take care of each other."

She stops, and Harlow is about to say *I know but this is beyond that, I can't go with you, I can't put you and your wife and your kid in danger because he will follow and it'll be way too easy to find me.*

But before she can let Christina down, her aunt closes her eyes. "I should have taken care of Cora," she says. "But I let her go. And then Clem left me too. I didn't do a good enough job when we were young. I should have protected them more."

And she sounds so exhausted, the pain right there on the surface, that Harlow can't bring herself to add to it.

So instead she says, "I'll think about it. Going with you. I'll stay tonight, and I'll think about it. Okay?"

Christina opens her eyes and when Harlow looks into them, she sees an endless reflection of herself. "Okay," Christina says.

33

Christina insists, gently, on coming back to the house with Harlow, spending the night there so that Harlow is not alone. Harlow wants to tell her *No, it's fine, I'll be fine,* like she knows she should, keeping Christina away from her and safe. But she's too tired to fight more, so all she does is nod and drives them home.

When they are back at the house it feels strange. Like Harlow has infected the air with her confession and the knowledge hanging over both of them that Oliver Prescott is out there, waiting, watching.

Harlow listens outside the living room as Christina calls her wife, hearing the way her voice changes as soon as Mila answers. She's calmer, quiet, as she tells Mila that she'll be home soon and that Harlow might be coming too, *if that's okay with you. . . . I know, she's family, but I still want to—it's our house, not just mine. . . . Of course I know that. I wanted to make sure you're okay with it first.*

Harlow feels a little sick hearing Christina talk like she's really going with her, like tomorrow or the day after, maybe, they'll be on a plane together and coming out of the airport to meet Christina's wife and son. Christina doesn't get it, Harlow knows: she's made a life for herself. She got away from Crescent Ridge in such a different way from Cora, and Harlow isn't going to do anything to jeopardize the new family Christina's made. She's beginning to think her mom was right; she can see now why she kept Harlow away from her aunts, and why she never told her about any of their history. She's still angry, still wishes her mom could have trusted her with it, but she was keeping the two of them safe, and she was trying to keep her sisters safe as well. Now Harlow has to take over. Continue making the sacrifices to keep the people she loves—is beginning to love, at least—safe.

For the rest of the night Harlow goes through the motions, helping Christina cook pasta thrown together from the ingredients Harlow bought the other day, listening as she outlines a vision of Harlow flying back home with her, making all the right noises and then clearing the dishes, standing in front of the sink washing them in hot soapy water as Christina compares ticket prices. By the time Christina goes to bed, barely able to suppress her yawns, there is a whole plan in place. Two tickets purchased on Christina's credit card for the day after next and Mila charged with making sure the guest room is ready with fresh sheets.

Harlow smiles through the guilt as Christina hugs her good night and retreats into the room that was always hers, the one with yellow wallpaper and the big window. Christina has a whole plan, but Harlow isn't going to be there for any of it.

She waits in her room, listening to make sure Christina is

asleep, that there are no sounds from the bathroom or her on the phone in her room. When she's sure, she begins the familiar old routine of packing up, except this time she has barely anything to do. She never got her clothes out of her bag, only swapped one item for another each day, so she doesn't have to go through a closet or unpack drawers. The papers—the deed to the house, the will—are folded neatly where she left them, with the money beneath that floorboard. Harlow pulls it out, then sits on the bed to count it all again. She's aware of the repeated alerts on her busted phone coming in as she flips through the cash, the intermittent light like the flashing of the strobes in one of the clubs her mom used to work in. Harlow doesn't have to look to know it's Sloane. That's the other thing about girls like Sloane: they don't like to be ignored. She's not used to it, Harlow knows, and expects a response, expects an explanation as to why Harlow was in such a rush to leave her house earlier. Girls like Sloane can't conceive of a world in which they aren't the center of everyone else's universe. Harlow wonders what she'll do when she realizes Harlow is gone for good. How long will it take her to turn from *I don't know, Ruby. Do you think something bad happened to her?* to *What a fucking bitch, she just bails without even saying goodbye, or thanks for all the shit I did for her? Fuck off, then.*

With the money counted, Harlow tucks it into her duffel and then zips it closed before lying down on the bed, fully clothed. She sets an alarm on her phone and contemplates her next name, the girl she's about to become, until she falls asleep.

34

Harlow wakes to the electronic trill of the alarm, disoriented for a second but quickly coming to, remembering what she's supposed to be doing. *Get up, leave the house, get in the car, drive away, leave Crescent Ridge and Christina and Sloane and Eve and Oliver Prescott's threats behind.*

She stops the alarm and shoves her phone in her back pocket as she gets to her feet. Her duffel is on the floor, her backpack downstairs, and she shoulders the duffel before she stops. This is the last time she's going to be here, she realizes—not just in this room, the bedroom where her mom spent her childhood, where she slept across from her little sister and dreamed about the future and hung posters of old bands on the walls, but in a space where her mom existed altogether. There is no going backward from this point. There is only forward, to towns where her mom has never been, apartments that Harlow will come home to by herself.

She allows herself to imagine, for a minute, that things will be different now. She always hated being all those made-up girls, wondered constantly what it would be like to be herself, meet a girl as Harlow, make friends as Harlow, live her life as Harlow. Now she has done that—albeit for the shortest time, albeit still hiding parts of herself—and it has been nothing like what she dreamed of. All that being herself has brought her so far is more trouble. Family who she has put in danger, secrets with no answers, a girl who enjoys stringing Harlow along. Now she knows better than to imagine that being herself is the answer to everything. She knows, too, that even though she has more questions now than answers, trying to dig into her family's history isn't going to give her what she wants. Instead of letting all that weigh her down, it's time to leave it behind with everything else. Time to leave the questions behind. Time to leave Harlow Ford behind too, shrugged off like the ill-fitting dress it always has been, another ghost of herself left to linger with the others.

Harlow takes a deep breath and one last look around the room. The blue walls, the posters, the empty frames on Clem's side. Clementine, who she will never meet, and before that would have hurt but now Harlow is too tired to feel it. She is all alone now, and it's going to be better this way. She won't put anyone else in danger. She won't disturb the past. There is no past: only forward, out of here, to disappear. To do what her mom taught her, and keep on running forever.

She looks out the window, and a flash of white catches her eye.

Harlow blinks, waiting for whatever it was to disappear, a blur in her vision, an imagined lightness in the night.

But no—there, beyond the garden wall: a blur in white, vanishing into the trees.

Harlow swallows and remembers the other day in the woods, early morning, the feeling that something was out there. The streak of white that she glimpsed between the trees, and the thought that lingered after: that it was not a some*thing*, but a some*one*, chasing behind her in the cold and white. She has tried since then to convince herself that she was wrong, that she let Sloane's haunting story overtake her, but she couldn't shake the knowledge that something was out there, and now—

Now, when she moves to the window, following the movement with her eyes, she is sure. White clothes, long brown limbs, dark hair caught in the breeze—

It's Christina.

Christina is the figure in the woods.

Harlow knows before she moves what she's going to do. Despite the smarter part of her brain arguing against it—*you are so close to getting out of here, so go, stick to the plan, leave this place*—she finds herself dropping her duffel and heading out of the bedroom. What is out there in those woods that Christina can't stay away from?

She is about to turn and walk down the stairs when she glances back and sees the door to Christina's bedroom standing ajar. Her feet lead her in that direction, across the landing and up to the door. A force drawing her there, wondering if when she steps inside she'll find something to answer the questions she's not supposed to be asking anymore.

When Harlow steps inside, all she finds is Christina.

She freezes, can actually feel the blood coursing through her veins turn cold, the sound of it loud inside her skull. There is Christina, lying in the bed, fast asleep. Beneath the covers, hair splayed out over the pillows and her lips parted as her chest softly rises and falls, rises and falls.

Harlow pushes the heels of her hands into her eyes, blurring the colors behind her eyelids. No. No, if Christina is here, sleeping, exactly where she's supposed to be, then who did Harlow see outside?

What the fuck is happening to me?

She backs into the wall and slides down it, hitting her loosely curled fists against her temples now. She could have sworn it was Christina she saw through the window, her unmistakable hair blowing in the wind, her brown skin—but it couldn't have been. Christina is right here, and Harlow opens her eyes wide to stare into the darkness, listening to the sounds of the night around her. The ghost in the woods, and the sounds she has imagined hearing, and the eyes staring at her from the darkness of the closet, a collision of night terror and overactive imagination, she thought, but now she can't stop thinking about all of it threaded together. All of it started when she arrived here, at Severn House, this place that is supposedly haunted by a woman in white, and now Harlow can't tell the real from the imagined, the paranoia from her sharp sense that something is truly wrong. "I'm losing my mind," she whispers aloud, forgetting for a moment about Christina only a few feet away from her, and then putting her hand over her mouth when Christina sighs and rolls over. *I'm losing my mind,* she thinks again, over and over, *ever since I* *got here, the dreams—the noises—*none of it can be real, Harlow knows, and yet in those moments it has all felt real, and now she is *sure* of what she saw but how can it be real when she is also *sure* that Christina is in this room with her?

Harlow gets to her feet slowly, making as little noise as possible as she slips out of the room and stands at the top of the stairs. *Go back and get your bag,* that sensible part of her says. *Get out of this place and find your sanity again,* because maybe that's what this is. The house, poisoning her mind. For the first time Harlow sees her mother in this place, with her sisters, from a different angle: three girls stuck with their mother in the depths of the woods, hidden away from the outside world. No one to talk to but each other. Nowhere to go but the surrounding woods, running through the cold, playing in the dirt. So quiet it could leave room for voices to get inside. So lonely it could leave space for something to get inside you.

Maybe those stories aren't fiction, at all, and maybe Harlow should have listened when Sloane warned her about this place. Maybe this, more than anything, was why her mom had to leave this place. Infected with fear and scribbling a note to leave in the middle of the night, so she could run far from this place and not only the man threatening her but this house and the forces inside its walls that threatened her mind.

Get your things and leave.

Harlow grips the banister and walks on tiptoe down the stairs.

Out the front door, into frozen air. She takes in a lungful, conscious of how it bites at her newly injured jaw, conscious of how her body has become some kind of war zone over the past two weeks. She never rested or recovered, not in the way she should have. Not in the way her mom would have wanted her to, after she had gotten the money and gone to the next place.

Go back and get your things and leave, now, the voice says again, and this time it's her mom speaking, words ricocheting around Harlow, whipping up through the air.

And then she hears something break the silence of the night—something real, not in her head, for as much as she can tell the two apart: the snap of wood, as if beneath a foot.

Harlow whips in the direction of the noise, to the west of the house, somewhere within the trees. "Who's out there?" Harlow calls, a yell into the absorbing wall of green. "I'm coming after you. I'm not afraid of you!"

There is no mistaking it then, the sound that follows—definite footsteps, disappearing deep into the woods.

Harlow takes one last look back at the house, full dark.

Then she turns in the direction of the noise and takes off at a run, into the depths.

Harlow is not a practiced runner, and her breath comes heavy and hard as she winds through the forest, her already sore body protesting with every poorly placed step. Yet she doesn't stop, because every so often she blinks and swears she sees that flash of white like before, and she can hear, definitely, the snap and rustle of leaves and fallen branches being crushed underfoot. The ghost escaping from her.

Harlow pushes, increasing her speed. No. There is not going to be any escape. She is going to make sure of that.

The ground is soft and loamy, perpetually watered by the rain, and Harlow stumbles a couple times but does not fall, just keeps following in the direction she's sure the ghost went in, although now she can't see anything ahead of her but the dark of crowded trees, and how far has she come? How long has it been since she heard anything?

She is running and the leaves are whispering around her and then there is rain, fresh rain, finding its way through the thick canopy and down to Harlow, cold bursts against her skin. She is running and then her foot catches on something, and before she can do anything, she is down on the ground, slamming into the earth.

Harlow lies there, the air knocked all the way out of her, and feels things go still around her. The rain drums on her back, and she lets it, keeping still until her heart has slowed some and the residual ache in her body has subsided enough for her to move.

When she can, Harlow pushes herself to her hands and knees, and sees that she is in a small clearing—maybe the same space she found herself in the other day, so early in the morning, when everything was light and the opposite of now. Above, the moon makes an effort to appear through the clouds, momentary glimpses of soft, glowing light. Harlow stands, pressing her hands against her rib cage and exhaling loudly as she looks to see what tripped her. It's not a root bursting through the ground, or a stubbornly placed rock, but a dip in the earth.

Harlow steps closer. No, not a dip: a hole. Or the beginnings of one, at least, a shallow and hastily dug scoop out of the earth.

An animal, Harlow thinks, but she's already dropping back down to her knees and reaching in to claw at the dirt herself.

Kneeling and digging with cold hands, ripping at the soft wet dirt like she is compelled, not knowing what she is searching for beneath the surface but digging digging digging until her hands are caked with dirt, ridged beneath her nails, and still Harlow keeps going, her breath coming in ragged gasps as she presses farther and farther down until—

Her fingers touch something hard. Smooth.

Harlow slows and swallows, the taste of dirt on her tongue. She knows, an elemental instinct deep down inside, even before she reaches back into the hole to rub her fingertips over the dirt, brushing it away from the surface of the object. She knows, but it does not prepare her for what she sees as the dirt comes loose and the clouds part and the moonlight shows her exactly what she has unearthed.

Teeth.

More accurately: a jaw. The teeth still embedded in the bone of the skull, what there is of it visible rising out of the ground now.

Harlow snatches her hand away and makes a noise loud and primitive enough to wake a thousand tiny creatures around her, the sudden skittering of insect and animal bodies sending a disgusted shiver up Harlow's spine, and she scrambles to her feet, backing away.

She hits a tree, or at first she thinks it is a tree, but her mind registers a second too late that instead of immovable like wood it is soft like a body, and when the dirt-covered hand clamps over her mouth, there's nothing she can do but hold still.

"Don't move," the ghost whispers into her ear. "Don't say a single word."

B E F O R E

The sisters still at the sound of the knock on the door. Clem frowns up at Cora from her position on the floor. "People?" she asks. "People out here?"

Cora glances toward the front door. The only visitors they get are the cops, when they have an update—except they haven't had an update in over a year—or reporters. The sleazy kind who want something uncensored and stolen for their blogs or whatever tabloid they can sell a story to, the kind who think nothing of traipsing out into the woods to knock on the door of the home of three girls mourning on the anniversary of their mother's disappearance.

Christina narrows her eyes. "Tell them to fuck off," she says to Cora, and Cora rolls her eyes.

"What happened to us playing the part?" she says. "The day's not over yet, remember?"

So Cora is the one who goes to the door, reaching for the

handle right as another series of raps vibrates through the wood. "Jesus, okay," she says loudly, and the temptation to follow Christina's advice is strong. She hates the vultures. As if they haven't already given enough today, with their performances at the press conference, with their candles flickering in the snow. It's not like they do that for themselves. It's certainly not like they do it for *her*.

Still, the *fuck off* hovers on her tongue as she opens the door.

And then it dies on her lips.

Cora stares at the ghost in front of her and has to grip the doorframe for support.

The ghost smiles, her pink lips stretching thin, and there is snow in her golden hair. "Surprise," says Eve. "I'm home."

35

The world shrinks to this single moment, Harlow with the feel of the ghost's cold fingers over her mouth, the taste of dirt on her lips now.

Ghosts don't have a touch, she forces herself to think. *Ghosts cannot hurt me.*

Whoever this is can *hurt me.*

It's all the thought she needs to disobey the whispered instructions, and she throws her elbow back, hitting soft flesh and hearing the pained gasp her hit elicits, and the hands that have hold of her fall away and Harlow begins to run again.

Back through the woods, retracing the winding path that led her to the skull, to the *grave*, and she wipes her hands against her damp sweatshirt as she goes, trying to get the feel of bone off her fingertips. She can hear the person following her and she wants to look back, see who is there, but she is afraid of losing her head start. She is afraid of who she will see, this person who is gaining on her now, and Harlow tries to run faster but she has already pushed herself beyond her limits tonight, nothing to do but keep trying even as she hears her pursuer getting close.

The tree line approaches so much sooner than Harlow anticipated, and she wonders how long she ran the first time, how far into the woods she actually went—did time trick her somehow, did the dark and the quiet and the poison of this place fool her?

It doesn't matter, she realizes as the trees begin to thin out but her pursuer's steps fall right behind hers. *It's too late,* Harlow realizes as she stretches toward the open, the house in view now, and she is tackled and dragged down to the ground.

Harlow thrashes, and in her mind she is confused, half in this moment and half on the side of the road with the weight of Oliver Prescott pinning her down. The weight on her now is less, though, the fingers that wrap around her wrist smaller. "Stop," her captor says. "Please, *stop* fighting me."

It's the *please* that does it. So familiar, and Harlow stills, staring up into the face of the girl above her.

Save me a slice, please.

Can you take the trash out, please?

Oh my god, Harlow, would you stop being a brat for one second, please?

Harlow looks at the girl—no, woman—who sounds so much like her mother that any other time she might have thought she was hearing her again. Another auditory hallucination. Except she knows she is not hallucinating the face looking down on hers, the deep dark eyes. Only one more person in the world who has those eyes.

"Clementine," Harlow breathes.

And somewhere behind there is the sound of the front door and then Christina, panicked, calling out. "Harlow! What's going—" A pause, and a sharp inhale. "Clem?"

36

Clementine releases her grip on Harlow's wrists and retreats, scrambling to her feet. Harlow stays on the ground, a position she has become intimately familiar with over the past twelve hours, and lets her gaze travel up Clementine, taking her in. Her hair is darker than in the picture Christina showed her, so similar to Christina's color that of course Harlow had mistaken one sister for the other in a split-second look. Any longer to look, though, and there would have been no doubt that the ghost was not Christina, because Clementine is thin, sickly-looking so, and her white slip dress, marked with dirt, hangs off her bony shoulders. Those dark eyes of hers, the eyes they all share, are wild and bright, the only part of her that truly looks alive, but in an unnerving way, a way that makes Harlow want to hide from their view.

"Clem," Christina says again, the word filled with wonder, and she crosses the front yard, steps over the broken section of the garden wall, her hands outstretched and reaching for her sister.

But she stops short of actually touching her, halting in front of Harlow on the ground. Christina twists, as if remembering that Harlow's there, and now her outstretched hand reaches toward her, instead.

But Harlow doesn't take the help. She can't, because out there in the woods there are human remains, and this is the house that Christina and Clementine and her own mother lived in while they waited for their missing mother to come home.

Oliver's words come back to her: *You know Eve is dead, right? She was probably dead before the cops even heard her name.*

"No." It comes out quiet, Harlow's voice croaky, and her face warms, embarrassed at how scared she sounds when what she wants is anger, what she wants is for Christina—and Clementine— to know exactly how incandescent she feels right now. "No," she says again, and it's better this time, loud and sharp, and Harlow pushes herself farther back from Christina as she gets to her feet. "I don't want your help, Christina. I don't want you to touch me."

"Harlow, I—" Christina shakes her head, her face the picture of worry. "What's wrong?"

"What's wrong?" Harlow tries to laugh, but she can't even force the sound out. "What's *wrong*?"

"She saw."

Clementine speaks, and her voice is so young that it sounds wrong coming out of her mouth, from a full-grown woman. Harlow didn't hear it before, the sweet tremulous tone of her voice.

She was focused on other things.

"Saw what?" Christina's saying, and she looks from Harlow to her sister and back, and Harlow isn't sure if her confusion is real or a performance, but then she looks back at Clementine and says, "What are you doing here? You look *terrible*, Clem, *Jesus*. I don't understand—"

Clementine's stained dress flutters in the wind, but she stands still, not the slightest indication that she can even feel the cold. "I couldn't stay away," she says. "You said we had to stay away, but I couldn't, I couldn't, I had to come home, I wanted to come home—"

"When?" Christina asks. "You told me you were in Europe. I called you and you told me you were there—how long have you been here?"

"A while," Clementine says, smiling. "Only a little while. All by myself but then she arrived, and you came, and I tried to keep us all safe but she saw, Chrissy. She knows."

Harlow watches the understanding wash over Christina, and then a flood of different emotions as she turns from Clementine to face her, hands clasped together. "Let me explain," she says, and the way she skips over any attempt to deny it, doesn't even *try* to convince Harlow that what she found out in the woods does not mean what she thinks it does tells her all she needs to know.

She takes a step back, and for the first time she is afraid of Christina. "Don't," Harlow says. She pulls in a ragged breath, her chest struggling beneath the weight of the moment.

All of her wondering, coming here to find out what happened to Eve, in some naive hope that it would mean closure on the fear her own mother had lived with—giving up on Eve because it seemed like everyone she spoke to was right and there was nothing more to be found, no leads to follow—convincing herself, instead, that whatever her mom had run from had been separate from Eve's disappearance—

And Eve has been dead the whole time. Hasn't she? It's her out there, isn't it? Buried in the woods that surround the house her mom grew up in. The house that Harlow has come back to, for her.

What had Cora Kennedy been running from? *The guilt,* Harlow thinks—no, knows. She knows it now. She has all the proof she needs in Christina's lack of a denial, in the wild, wide eyes of Clementine and the dirt caked under her fingernails.

Eve is dead, and you three are the ones who killed her.

She doesn't realize she has said it aloud until Clementine lets out a keening wail, a newborn wolf howling at the moon, and Christina begins to cry. "You don't understand," she says. "Please, you have to understand. It didn't happen like you think."

"No?" Harlow stares at her. "How did it happen, then?"

BEFORE

Cora can do nothing but stare at her mother, like an apparition in the dark, except Cora knows this is no vision, no image concocted by her own mind.

No. That would be too lucky.

They have been too lucky, Cora knows. She's always known it, that Eve wouldn't stay gone forever, that at some point she'd have to come back, because of course she would. She couldn't stay away and leave them alone in their happiness without her. No, Eve wouldn't be able to bear that.

"Aren't you going to let me in?" Eve says. "I've had a long drive."

There's a tightness in Cora's chest, her lungs collapsing in on themselves so that every breath she takes is too shallow, too tight, not enough oxygen reaching her. *Panic attack,* she realizes, the old familiar sensations flooding her body. It's been so long since she's had one. They used to catch her when the house had been peaceful for too long, when Eve had been playing the doting-mother role for too many consecutive weeks, and Cora could feel the tension building. Eve waiting to make her move, Cora and her sisters on edge, each wanting to not be the one who finally made her break by saying the wrong thing or walking too loudly or looking at her the wrong way.

See, there is the story they spun to the outside world, the one where they were three girls from a normal family living in a normal house, left grieving and bereft after the disappearance of their mother, praying for her return, and appealing to the public, wearing the costume of the ever-hopeful left-behinds who turned away from the theories about death, abduction, murder, and focused only on the belief that she was okay out there, somewhere, their beloved missing mother.

And then there is the truth, Cora thinks. How three girls who had been isolated from the world, raised by a woman who showed her love through punishment, through open-handed slaps and restricting food and belts lashed against their backs, had held their breath one day as that woman failed to return home. Who kept that breath held as time rolled on and she stayed away, and they knew that she had finally had enough and abandoned them because there were clothes missing from her closet, and the rings she'd kept in a dish on her nightstand ever since their father died were gone too. But they didn't tell the cops that when they reported her gone. They didn't tell them about all the times over the years when Eve had screamed at them and finished by saying *One day I'm going to leave you and let's see how well you'll do without me.* They couldn't, Christina said, as they'd all three sat huddled in Cora and Clem's bedroom, the beds pushed together in one corner. "We can't tell anyone about what she's really like," Christina said. "Because if we're wrong, and she hasn't really gone, if she decides to come back a week from now and we've gone running to the cops telling them what she does to us—how much worse do you think it's going to be when she hears that?"

Cora reached to rub at the puckered skin on her back, the scar that sat unsettled and raised against her brown skin. She could imagine only too well what Eve would do to them if she returned home to find her illusion shattered. Gone would be the rustic, homespun family in the woods, and out would come the true tale, of the woman who seemed to hate her daughters and her life and being a mother so much that Cora didn't even know why she'd done it. And besides—would anyone even believe them? They were kids, and they barely knew anybody in town, only ever going in with Eve when she allowed it, warned to be on their best behavior. Watching Eve turn on her sunny personality for these strangers, laughing and making jokes and flirting with the man outside town hall, the one who Christina whispered was the mayor. No one would believe three liars. That was what Eve had always called them, when she was accusing them of things they hadn't done, telling Cora to get down on her knees in the shattered remains of the vase she swore she hadn't knocked over, saying it so many times over and over until Cora started questioning her own mind, had she really watched the vase fall when the wind blew the back door open, or was Eve telling the truth and it was Cora's elbow that had connected with the china, sending it toppling to smash on the tile? *I can't remember,* Cora thought as the remains sliced into her knees, *I can't remember at all.*

Now, here, in the present, Cora stares at Eve and wills herself to calm down. Slow breaths, even in and out, in and out. She remembers now. She remembers everything now, the cruelty Eve put them through. The tentative hope they felt as the days passed and she still hadn't returned, always on the outside wearing their mourning faces and being the perfect girls the cops wanted. Couldn't let them know how badly they hoped for their searches of the woods to turn up nothing, for the car found left on the side of the road to bear no clues, for no one to report any sighting of their mother. If she was really doing it, Cora knew, if she had truly decided to abandon them, then there wouldn't be any sightings. No way would Eve risk being seen and someone raising the alarm, forcing her to come home to the daughters she'd abandoned.

And yet, Cora thinks. Here she is. Two full years later and she just shows up.

Two years. Two years in which they, she and Clem and Christina, have kept themselves safe and fed and loved. Two years in which Christina has worked her ass off to keep this roof over their heads, two years during which they have ventured out into the world and learned how to be functioning members of society, done all the kinds of things they were banned from when Eve was there, tasted freedom. Tasted love. Two years, and in that time Cora has come to learn she is not, as Eve always told her, weak and pathetic and stupid.

Cora feels her heart beginning to slow; the shadows at the edges of her vision recede. Only now does she have the chance to take Eve in: the knee-high boots that look like they cost more than Christina makes in a month, and a heavy black coat tied loosely around her waist, and her face healthy, flush, a brightness to her deep blue eyes. Cora takes a breath and folds her arms across her chest, leaning so she fills the doorframe, not so subtly blocking Eve from entering. "Wow," she says. "Look at you, stranger."

"Cora," Eve says, and there it is: the edge in her tone, the warning that is supposed to be enough to scare Cora back into line. It used to be enough—used to scare Cora out of saying anything she was really thinking, until all that came out of her mouth was what she knew Eve wanted to hear.

But now she is not afraid. "Eve," Cora says back. "I think you should leave."

From behind her Christina calls out, "Who is it?"

And then Clem, laughing: "Yeah, what's taking so long?"

Eve's face lights up at the sound of their voices, and Cora is halfway through turning around, stepping back inside and calling out *No, stay where you are,* but she's too late.

Christina and Clem come tumbling out of the living room, hand in hand, and Cora watches in painful slow motion as they see past her, see who is standing at the door, and the nightmare begins.

37

"She left," Christina says, and turns her face up to the sky. "She left us, and it was the happiest day of our lives."

Harlow's mind stutters. *Happiest?* "I don't understand," she says slowly. "How could you be *happy* that she was gone?"

"Because she isn't the person you imagine her to be." Clementine says it in her light, girlish voice, her eyes locked on Harlow. "And you're lucky, because you miss your mom, now that she's gone." A single tear slips down Clementine's face. "That means you loved her. That means she loved *you.* But Eve wasn't like that. She was cruel to us. She kept us locked up out here in this house, hidden away where no one could see what she did to us. Imagine that, Harlow. Imagine your mom starving you, and belittling you, and locking you out in the middle of the night in winter when you're six years old and wet the bed. Imagine living with that and how you would feel if one day you realized you were *free.*"

Clementine moves closer as she talks, light footsteps that make hardly any sound. "She's not what you imagined," Clem says, "and I'm sorry that she wasn't. But that's why we were happy when she disappeared."

She reaches Harlow, standing right in front of her and like this they are eye to eye, the same height. "That's why we hated when she came back."

Harlow recoils. When she *came back*?

No, no—she still doesn't understand. And yet she does, even though she's fighting it—watching her fantasies of the grand-mother she never knew be sliced to ribbons by the sharp truth of Christina's and Clementine's words, seeing the images she watched behind her eyelids burn out to be replaced with some-thing altogether darker and meaner. Not a quiet, soft life out among nature, a bereaved family clinging together in order to navigate life, taking homeschool lessons out into the meadows and dancing around a house filled with music and light. Instead an ominous silence, a tense atmosphere knotted with pain. She is brought out of her dazed thoughts by the feel of Clementine's hands on her cheeks, her fingers icy. "You look nothing like her," Clem whispers, and her breath is hot against Harlow's face. "Oh, I'm so glad that you look nothing like her."

Harlow keeps still, almost afraid to pull out of Clementine's hold, of what reaction that might bring. "When did she come back?" she asks, whispering in response, matching Clementine. "Where had she been? Why did she—"

"It was two years after," Christina says, and her voice seems to break the spell on Clementine, who lets Harlow go and steps backward. "To the day. Can you believe that? Of course she would time it that way. Do you know what we had spent that day doing? We had to go to a memorial, to stand there with people who had no idea about how evil she really was and listen to town officials talk about her, how we all hoped she would come home safely, how they were all praying for her return. We had to get onstage in front of cameras and reporters and say it ourselves, how much we *missed* her, how we weren't giving up on her, how we hoped that wherever she was she was safe and alive and would come back to us one day."

"And then she did," Clementine says wonderingly. "Like nothing had even happened. She acted like we were supposed to run to her. I always wonder if she thought that time away was enough for us to forget what she had done to us. Or was she that good at deluding herself, that she thought we'd welcome her home?" Clementine looks off into the distance as she speaks, as if she has forgotten Harlow and Christina are even there. "If she had left us alone, none of it would have happened. If she had just done what we'd asked—"

"You have to understand," Christina says, cutting Clementine off. She bites her lip and wraps her arms around herself, shivering. "Come on. Let's go inside—let's all go inside and get out of the cold—"

"No," Harlow says. "I want to hear it, now. What did you do to her?"

Christina opens her mouth, but nothing comes this time. She looks across at Clementine.

And Clem presses her hands together as if she's praying. "It really was an accident," she says, her big eyes faraway. "Do you believe me?"

BEFORE

—somehow they are back in the living room, but this time Eve is with them and there's no laughter, none of the lightness they felt only a short while ago. Now it is that old atmosphere Cora hates, that she has tried so hard to forget the feeling of: the sensation of being on a cliff edge, perpetually inches from doom, as Eve's voice whips at them—

"This is *my* house, you are *my* daughters, how *dare* you think you have any say in this—"

Cora can't look away from Eve, that tight face, angry patches of red on her cheeks, the terrifyingly familiar storm behind her eyes. She has the sense that she could so easily be swept up in it and drowned, all hope of life lost.

But.

Two years.

Cora finds Christina, standing behind the couch, out of the reach of Eve's grasp. She looks to Clem, her baby sister, so grown-up now, the one she's always thought had the best chance of all of them to go out in the world and live a real life, without Eve dragging her back. They always tried to protect Clem, she and Christina. Tried to make sure the brunt of Eve's anger fell on them, that they received the harshest punishments so Clem could be spared, but they didn't do a good enough job. Every time they failed, Cora felt it—the guilt of knowing she was letting her little sister down.

She's not going to let that happen again.

Two years, and in that time Cora has gotten stronger. That's the mistake Eve has made. She thought she could waltz back in to the same cowering, broken girls she left behind, but they aren't them anymore. Cora is not afraid anymore.

"It's not your house," she says, cutting Eve off in a way she would never have dared before.

Eve's mouth falls open. "I beg your pardon?"

"It's not your house," Cora says again, shrugging. "You left—sorry, you *went missing*, and there were decisions that had to be made. Someone had to be in charge. So I think you'll find that technically, if you check with the town council, Christina is actually the legal owner of this property. And so when we tell you to get out of *our* house, we mean it. It's ours, not yours. And *we* are not yours anymore either."

Eve crosses the space between them in two long strides and jabs her finger in Cora's face. "Watch yourself."

It's funny. Up close like this, it only makes the time they've been apart more evident. Eve used to tower over Cora, and now Cora is the taller one, looking down at Eve beneath her. So far beneath her.

"*You* watch it," Cora says. "You *walk out* on us and then expect us to let you back in like nothing—"

"I'm your *mother*, of course I was going to come back, I was always going to come back—"

"Oh please! You're only here because you need something—"

"I'm here because I want all of my girls to be with me—" Eve grabs for Clem then, her nails digging into Clem's arm so that she yelps. "Come here, baby. I know *you* missed me—"

"Mom!" And Clem is clawing at Eve's hand around her arm. "You're hurting me, please—"

They are all screaming over each other, Eve pulling at Clem and Cora forcing herself between the two of them, and Christina's cowering in the corner, rocking back and forth, and Cora manages to wrench Eve's hand off Clem but it only makes Eve angrier, so she turns to Cora and pushes her back, her nostrils flaring, and then Clem says, "Why can't you just leave us *alone*—"

She shoves Eve, a two-handed push with a short lifetime's worth of rage behind it, and Eve stumbles backward and it would be fine except her foot catches on the rug and she twists as she begins to fall, hands thrown out in front of her to meet the floor, but her head meets the corner of the fireplace first, a sickening thud as she smacks into it and then bounces off, to land on the floor, silent and still.

There is no more noise then. Only the silence as the three of them stare down at Eve prone on the living room floor, the blood that begins to spread across the rug, a garish red halo behind her head.

Cora looks from the body to Clem, in awe, almost. *She is so strong,* she thinks. *Maybe we didn't fail her, after all.*

Except Clem is crying already, staring at her outstretched hands. "I didn't mean it," she says, horrified. "Oh my god, I didn't mean it, I didn't mean to—"

38

Harlow stares, stunned, at Clementine. She looks so fragile, like she couldn't hurt anyone, except Harlow had felt her on top of her and felt the desperate power hidden in the frail hands. She imagines that at fifteen Clem might have been smaller, still, but healthier, too, not made of brittle bones and wasting muscle. Facing Eve down, after a lifetime of torment—*imagine your mom starving you*—and then with one explosive shove, putting an end to it, once and for all. "You did it," she says to Clem. "You killed her, then."

"It was an *accident*," Christina says sharply, as if she's said it a hundred times before. "None of us meant for it to happen."

"No, Chrissy. She's right," Clem says, and she holds her hands up in the moonlight, the clouds clearing now, and drags them through the air like some tortured, balletic expression of grief and remorse. "I killed her. I was the one who pushed her. Me. Not you, not Cora. *Me*."

Harlow sinks to a crouch, her tired legs protesting. "Tell me," she says, and glances up at Christina. "Tell me the rest."

Christina looks uncertain. "The rest?"

And Harlow nods. "Yes," she says. "Like how she ended up in fragments in the woods. Tell me what happened after that." She's not entirely sure why she's asking, when it's already clear to her: they buried her, her mom and Christina and little Clementine. They took Eve's body out of the house and carried her into the woods and dropped her into a hole that they'd dug especially for her.

But she still wants to hear Christina say it. She still wants Clem to admit to what they did. She wants to have all the answers now. "You could have gone to the cops. Right? You did it before. You told them she was missing, and you played along with that story for two whole years. But you didn't do that this time."

"We couldn't," Christina says. "How could we explain it? Sorry, but we've been pretending this whole time that we loved our mother and wanted her to come home? We knew she had abandoned us and we were thankful, actually? There's no way they would believe that her ending up dead on our living room floor was an accident."

"It was Cora who came up with it," Clem says.

Don't blame her, Harlow wants to say. *Just because she's not here to defend herself.* But she knows she's only thinking that because it's hard to believe that her mom could ever have done something like this. She wants to go back in time, to a moment where the worst thing she thought her mom could do was lie to her, or skip out on rent, or ghost a date with his credit card in her back pocket. Not bury a dead body in the woods.

She says nothing, then, waits for Clem to continue, but it's Christina who picks the story up. "We panicked," she says. "At first, we *were* going to call the cops. Or—we didn't even talk about calling them, I think it was this shared assumption, like—that's what comes next, right? The cops and EMTs and all kinds of people asking us all kinds of questions. So we panicked, but then Cora said they didn't have to know. Nobody had to know."

"She had been missing for two years," Clem says. "And Cora said—why did that have to change? If we got rid of the body, then she would stay missing. No one would ever have to know what happened."

"No one was going to be looking for her," Christina says. "Not any more than they already were, which by that point wasn't much at all. So all we had to do was put her somewhere where no one would look, and it would be like nothing happened. Like she was never even here."

"So you just . . . dug a grave and put her in there?" Harlow hears the tremor in her words. She can't tell if it is from the cold or from the shock, still trying to piece everything together, trying to understand how they could have done this dark and terrible thing. How desperate they must have been, a lifetime of terror driving them to this awful point. "Like that would make it all go away? Like you could forget it ever happened, run away from this place and never speak about her again. Right?" She shakes her head, not waiting for an answer. "No wonder Mom never told me about her. Or you, or this place. She spent her whole life trying to outrun the memory."

Because that's really what it was. Wasn't it? There was Oliver on their heels, yes, but it was more than him and his threat to call in his debt. He belonged to Crescent Ridge, and her mom was on a mission to put that place behind her. *And maybe*—things begin to weave together for Harlow, all these pieces adding up—*maybe she never even thought about the money. Maybe she was afraid of him because she thought he knew.* And if he knew and he caught her and he said out loud what they'd done, then how could her mom pretend it had never happened?

She looks back at Christina now, at Clementine. "And you both just left her to it," she says, and her heart aches on behalf of her mom. "You all left each other to handle this shit on your own. So what was the point of it all? You killed your own mother and then *abandoned* each other."

Harlow watches Christina about to speak, the way she pulls in a deep breath first, and Clem is still watching her hands in the air, and she hears the echo of her own words on the wind—*you killed your own mother and then abandoned each other.*

And then she hears a laugh, syrupy and dark, coming from the trees.

For a moment she thinks this place is playing tricks on her again, making her hear things, but then the shadows split, and a figure slithers out of the forest. Harlow takes in the tall frame, dirty-blond hair, the piercing eyes. Oliver Prescott.

And in his hand, a gun.

39

Harlow stands quickly, unsteadily, her eyes fixed on Oliver. He's at the point where the track opens out to reveal the house, emerging from the trees there, as if he walked all the way down to sit and lie in wait. *That's exactly what he did,* Harlow realizes a second later, and she swallows as she looks at the gun in his hand. Dark metal, dull and deadly. "What are you doing here?"

Oliver's laughter dies as he approaches, long, swaying steps, as if he's intoxicated. "What am I doing here?" Oliver shifts side to side as he pretends to think it over, casting his gaze to the sky. "Hmm, let's say . . . I learned my lesson the first time. I didn't want to let another Kennedy skip out on a debt. So I came out here to make sure you didn't try something stupid, like, say, taking off in the middle of the night. But!" He brandishes the gun. "Turns out lying runs in the blood in this family, right?"

He's close enough now that Harlow can smell the alcohol coming off him in waves. That's no surprise—but the state of his face is. His narrow face is swollen and deep red, bloodied around his left eye socket and up to his hairline, a split in the skin. When he talks, Harlow can see the traces of blood between his teeth. *Jesus Christ,* Harlow thinks. When he left her on the side of the road, he sure as shit didn't look like that. "Looks like someone did to you what I wanted to," Harlow says, trying to keep her voice calm. *Don't let him know you're afraid—more afraid,* she corrects.

Because the debt, the money, that was one thing. But now, Harlow knows, things are about to get a lot worse.

Oliver gestures toward his face, bloody lips spread into a wild grin. "This? Well, yeah. Turns out that two-day deadline I gave you isn't going to work. See, I've gotten myself into something of a . . . situation, and now the guys who did *this*—" He takes another step, thrusting his chin forward as if Harlow needs a better look. "They aren't going to wait for their money. So I need *my* money now. Understand?"

"It's Oliver, right?" Christina's call cuts through the moment, and Harlow moves back, putting more distance between her and Oliver and that gun dangling off his fingers.

Christina stares unblinking at Oliver. "I've heard all about you," she says. "How you think it's okay to go around threatening teenage girls. Trying to extort them. I don't know who the fuck you think you are, but I do know you're out of your fucking mind if you think you're going to get a dime out of us. So why don't you take your little Boy Scout gun and go back to whatever dive will serve you another shot of Jack. Okay?"

Oliver, though, only grins wider. "It's Christina, right?" he says, mimicking her, mocking her. "Right, right. *You* are the big sister she couldn't wait to get away from, and you—" He swings to point the barrel at Clementine. "*You* are the little sister who'd already taken off. And of course all together you were the three little girls in the wood whose mommy went missing." Oliver's smile drops. "But I guess we all know the truth now."

"You don't know anything," Harlow says quietly. Some deep-down instinct makes her say it, to try to keep the lie up. To protect her mom, even in death, and her sisters, even if in this very moment she's not sure that they deserve her protection. After what they did—

They *killed* someone. Accident or not, they were responsible for another person's death, and then they covered it up and all of that, their fucked-up actions, they shaped the course of Harlow's shitty life. She has spent her entire existence running because of this. Because of them.

Oliver swings back to her, and Harlow freezes, right in the line of fire. "Do you think I'm an idiot?" he says. "I heard everything, waiting back there. Their sad story about their mean mommy. How they bashed her head in. How they buried her out there. How *you* found the remains of Eve Kennedy tonight." He raises his voice. "What do you think the cops are going to say, when I tell them exactly where they can find that dead bitch they've been looking for for so long?"

Harlow squeezes her eyes shut and sees Oliver, booze coursing through him but still sober enough to hide, lying in wait for her to make her escape. Watching Harlow run into the woods and then come back out with Clem on her heels and then the truth, pouring out of her aunts, loud enough for Oliver to hear. Her own words—*you killed your own mother*—carrying to him crisp and clear.

Stupid, stupid, stupid. She practically handed him the leverage. And he's desperate enough to use it. It's clear from the battering he's taken that whoever he himself owes, they aren't willing to wait. And he has almost twenty years of simmering resentment ready to spill over.

She opens her eyes. "I'll tell them you're lying," she says. "I'll tell them none of it's true. They'll never believe you. You'll just be some liar looking for a quick payday."

"*You* want to talk about lies?" Oliver grins. "Maybe when I tell the cops where the body is, I'll tell them all about your fake life, too. How it all started when Cora came to me and asked me for my help getting fake papers. Birth certificate, passport, all that shit, and I got it for her." His eyes cloud over then, and when he speaks again, he sounds lost in his own bitterness. "And then she took off without paying me. I did her a *favor*, I'm the only reason she was able to get out of this place, I'm the only reason you even—"

"What do you *want*?" Christina says, drowning him out. "What's it going to take for you to leave us alone?"

Oliver rubs his fingertips together. "Price has gone up," he says. "Fifteen grand, now."

"Fifteen *thousand* dollars?" Christina says, and Harlow can hear the panic in her voice. "I don't have that."

Oliver shrugs. "Then I guess you'll have to get it somehow," he says. "I bet you have a nice house, don't you? Nice car, too."

"I can't do that," Christina says. "I have a wife, I have a—I can't just magic-up fifteen grand to give you."

"See, the thing is, there's this little something called a reward," Oliver says. "Maybe you've forgotten all about it, but I haven't. Remember? Ten thousand dollars for any information about Eve Kennedy and her whereabouts. Now, I know it was a long time ago, but I have a feeling it's the kind of shit organizations have to honor. So the way I see it is, you can give me what I want, and I'll keep your secrets. Or—I can go to the cops and get my money, and then I guess you're going to find out what jail is like."

"You can't prove it," Christina says. "They won't believe you."

"Sure they will," Oliver says, and with the hand that isn't holding the gun he reaches into his pocket and pulls out his phone, waving it. "Especially when I play them back the recording I made."

Harlow watches the color drain from Christina's face. Clem has finally let her hands fall to her side, her eyes locked on Oliver, lips parted. *Look at them,* Harlow thinks, filled with a sudden rush of dizzying panic. They don't look like cold-blooded killers. They look like what they were, back then, when it all went down: lost girls, desperate for a way out.

Suddenly Harlow feels the weight of responsibility on her, exactly like she imagines her mom felt on that night all those years ago. Being the one to make the decision. To try to make the best out of a nightmare situation.

She looks at Oliver. There he is, with the gun, loaded with the threat of death. She isn't sure that he even wants to use it or if it's there only as a warning, as insurance. But he will use what he knows, she's sure of that. The only question is whether he really recorded their conversation, or if, like Harlow earlier, he's merely bluffing.

He sees her then, glancing between the phone in his hand and him, and Oliver tips his head, still grinning like a fucking clown. *Try me,* he's telling her. *See what happens if you push me this time. I'm not some stupid kid like you.*

No. Only a stupid con artist lousy enough to get caught in a corner by his own debtors. *How did we get here?* Harlow thinks, and she imagines the domino trail, from Oliver to her to her mom, to Clementine and Christina, knocking on all the way back to Eve in the ground. It all comes back to her, doesn't it?

Harlow feels the heat of her blame beginning to shift, from her scared aunts to the woman in the ground who made them that way. *They aren't the ones I should be angry at,* she thinks. *It should be Eve.*

After all, she's part of the reason why Harlow even came to Crescent Ridge, so she could solve the mystery of her disappearance. Her mom and aunts splintered apart, had the course of their lives changed, because of her. Now Oliver knows the truth, and he's willing to use Eve to get whatever he wants.

Fifteen thousand dollars. Harlow thinks of the money tucked into her bag: she's already burned through a chunk of it, doesn't have the full amount that he wants. But he'll take however much she has, she knows, and paying Oliver off will keep Christina and Clementine safe, keep their secrets buried. And she *wants* to keep them safe, because there has been enough damage wrought by Eve's actions already.

Or maybe she wants to keep them safe because she knows it's what her mom would want her to do, and it's what she would do if it were her mom standing here tonight facing this fear.

"So," Oliver says, "what's it going to be?"

Harlow sighs, decision made. *You can have the money,* she's about to say, when she feels Clementine rush past her, a shallow cry erupting from her as she launches herself at Oliver, reaching for the gun.

"Clem!"

It's Christina who cries out, Harlow only able to watch as Clementine grapples with Oliver for the gun, a desperate struggle to wrench it from his grip—

Or so she thinks at first, but in the same split second that Clem gets her fingers around the handle of the gun, layered on top of Oliver's fingers, Harlow understands she is wrong. Clementine is not pushing the gun away, but pulling it closer—closer—fighting to get her finger on the trigger—

When the shot comes it starts a ringing in Harlow's ears, and she presses her hands to her head, trying to quiet it.

She looks up, readying herself to see Oliver in a heap, but it's Clementine who looks stunned. Clem who falls away first, with a bullet hole ripped through her dress, through her flesh.

"No—" Harlow stumbles forward, a few uncertain steps, reaching out toward Clementine, but it's done, over already.

Oliver stumbles backward too, the gun at first still in his hand and then falling to the ground when he releases it and holds his hands up, his eyes wide. "You crazy bitch," he breathes, staring at Clem as she holds a hand to her body. "You crazy fucking bitch, what the *fuck*—"

Clem sways, and Harlow wakes up suddenly, runs to her right as she drops, and even the dead weight of her is so light. "Leverage,"

Clem says, her voice hoarse. "Stay here. Wait for the cops. Find out what prison is like. Or leave, now. Leave us alone. Forever." She nods at the gun. "Your gun. Your bullets. Your prints." She coughs again. "Your choice."

Harlow can feel every shallow breath Clem takes, and she reaches down to press her hand over Clem's, applying pressure to the wound as the horrifying realization comes over her: Clem has just sacrificed herself.

Over and over. Her thoughts come fast, a rush of recognition. Over and over this family—*her* family—falls apart, in every single way possible, all in the name of sacrifice. Self-inflicted injuries that leave them fractured and fragmented, in search of a way out but where is there to go when you're operating from a place filled with such pain? So they cycle—trying to protect each other, trying to protect themselves, and only hurting more in the process. Her mom. Herself. Now Clem—

"What did you do?" she whispers, and only then does she realize she's crying. "Clementine, why did you do that?"

Clem ignores her. "So," she rasps, blood bubbling at the corners of her lips. "What's it going to be?"

There's a long, quiet moment where Harlow isn't sure what's going to happen next. Clem in her arms, and Christina somewhere behind her sobbing, and Oliver making his choice, and the noise of that gunshot echoing loud and heavy above it all.

Harlow sees his eyes dart toward the gun. Without thinking, she lets Clem drop to the earth and throws herself forward, hand outstretched toward the gun. She hears Clem's words—*your bullets, your prints*—and in the second before she makes contact, she pulls her fingers back into her sweater sleeves and picks the gun up that way, the fabric the only thing touching the metal and plastic grip. She rises slowly, the gun trained on Oliver, and all she can think is how comical this moment is, that she's holding a gun and pointing it at someone, and laughter bubbles up inside her.

She suppresses it, swallowing it, pulling herself to her full height as she stares Oliver down. "Come on," she says, and repeats his words back to him like Clem had. "What's it going to be?"

Oliver's eyes narrow. "Twisted," he says. "This entire family is twisted."

Then without another word, he turns and runs. Away from the house, onto the dirt track, until he is out of sight.

Gone.

40

"Clem!"

Christina rushes to Clem's side, kneeling and pulling her sister's head into her lap, her hand pressing against the gunshot wound. "Clem," she says again, her voice thick. "Why did you do that?"

Harlow crouches slowly and gently sets the gun down on the ground, as if it might go off again of its own will. That's what people always say, isn't it, in cop shows and true crime documentaries and whenever else. *Then the gun just . . . went off. It was an accident.*

Harlow crawls away from the gun, to Clementine's side. Her already filthy dress is stained dark red now, no matter how hard Christina presses on the wound, how much Harlow tried to keep the blood from pouring out. *Except this was no accident,* Harlow thinks. The gun didn't *go off*, no: Clementine pulled the trigger, on purpose, and it wasn't Oliver Prescott that she was aiming for.

"Don't worry," Harlow says, to both Clementine and Christina, but mostly to Clem, her eyes flickering in and out of focus. With one hand she reaches up and wipes the blood from Clem's chin, flinching at the icy chill of her skin, and with the other she pulls her fractured phone out of her jeans. "Everything's going to be okay, all right? You're going to be okay." She has to be okay. Harlow is not going to let Clementine sacrifice herself like this, give up her whole life because of some asshole who Harlow brought into their world. She is not going to let Clementine die before she even has a chance to know her. "It's going to be okay," she says as she dials 911 carefully, trying not to slice her fingertips on the shattered glass, and puts the phone to her ear. When the operator answers, Harlow finds herself shaking. "Yes, we need an ambulance at—"

Clementine rears up, knocking the phone out of Harlow's grasp. "No," she says, "no, no, *nononono*—" over and over until it's one long moan.

"Clem." Christina looks up at Harlow, and there's pure terror in her eyes. She looks back at Clementine. "We have to get you help. You're hurt. It's *bad*. But we're going to get help and—"

"*No,*" Clem says again, so vehement, and she's panting with the effort. "My fault, all my fault, I never . . . I pushed her and it's all broken, I broke it all . . . let me go, let me die, please, Chrissy, let me go . . ."

Her words pierce deep into the soft, bruised flesh of Harlow's heart. Clementine, lying there with her head in Christina's lap, emaciated, in her stained dress—Harlow thought she was a ghost, hadn't she? She looks already half-gone, somewhere between this world and whatever comes next.

"... wanna be with Cora," Clem's saying now, and her eyes close but she continues to babble, stream of a fractured consciousness. "... let me see her, Chrissy, say sorry ... all my fault always ..."

Christina curls over her sister, their long dark hair pooling together around Clementine's face. "Don't say that," Christina says, and she's crying so hard the words barely get out. "Clem, I love you, okay? It's all going to be okay."

Harlow's phone is on the ground with the screen still alight. She reaches to pick it up, and it feels like she's moving in slow motion, her hand pushing against something thick and solid, but she gets the phone and lifts it to her ear, to hear the operator saying, "We have your location. If you can hear me, help is on the way. Hold still."

Harlow lets the phone drop herself this time, and she puts her hand over Christina's like before, the two of them trying their hardest to keep Clem from bleeding out.

Somewhere in the far distance, sirens begin.

41

The sun is coming up on the morning Harlow returns to Severn House.

It has been a week. A week of surgeries to save Clem's life, of waiting for her to wake up, of Christina crying when Clementine finally opened her eyes and said hello.

A week of dealing with the cops, of Harlow telling them that no, she didn't see who it was who had shot Clem—she had been inside the house when she heard the gun go off, and by the time she ran outside, there was nobody to be seen, *isn't that right, Christina?* A week of the cops treating the house like a crime scene but finding nothing, only the gun with Oliver Prescott's fingerprints, and tire tracks on the dirt road that didn't belong to Harlow's car. *No,* Harlow said, *I don't know why anyone would want to hurt Clementine. I just met her. Yes, she's my aunt—yes, Eve Kennedy. My grandmother.*

A week of the whole truth of who Harlow was making its way

around town, along with the events of that night and the old morbid fascination being awoken anew.

A week of Harlow holding her breath and praying that the cops didn't look too closely around the house, ask to search her car where they might find her bag hidden beneath the passenger seat, cash and fake IDs inside, or make the connection between her and the accident thousands of miles away, her mom's body sitting in the cold drawer of the faraway morgue.

A week of hoping that the cops didn't venture too far into the woods, to stumble across the place where Eve's remains lay.

(A week of Harlow trying hard not to think about the hours when Christina slipped out of the hospital and then returned later, to whisper *It's taken care of*, with traces of dirt under her nails and the kind of distant, empty look a person gets when they do something like reburying the remains of their dead mother.)

Harlow sighs as she steps over the threshold, feeling Christina close behind her. Now they're back and Clem is getting better and the police presence has disappeared, the county sheriff telling them both that they have alerts out for Clementine's attacker and not to worry, they know how stressful it all is, *especially with your family's past situation, but leave it with us—we* will *catch him.*

"Do you think they will?" Clem asked, sitting up in her hospital bed, already looking so much healthier despite the fact that she had undergone a life-threatening injury and several surgeries in the past week. "Will they find him? Because if they do—"

"He's long gone, if he knows what's good for him," Harlow said. "Somehow I think being charged with attempted murder is not an enticing offer."

Christina, on the other side of the bed, holding Clem's hand: "But he still knows," she said. "He still has the recording."

Harlow tried not to think about that. They could hurt him, but he could hit back equally as hard. The only hope they had was that there was too much else for him to risk coming back— the people he owed, whatever other seedy shit he had been up to. "Mutually assured destruction," Harlow said. "That's all we have."

We. They are a *we* now, Harlow's uncertainty over what her aunts—her mom—had done in the past overshadowed by the dread she felt holding Clementine, the fear of another dead body, and then the relief that she is still here. Then there are the things Christina told her, in quiet, stilted whispers while Clem was unconscious. Things she had never told anybody, she said, not even her wife, about growing up with Eve. Things Harlow has to try not to think about because they turn her stomach. Things that make her mom's edginess, her aversion to being touched, her colder edge, make all too much sense.

She has been putting other things together now too, slowly and surely. Separating out what was real from what her mom's paranoia had conjured. So the day Harlow always remembered when her mom grabbed her from the school playground during lunch and they were on the road less than an hour later because *someone was watching, I felt it*—real. Thinking that her boss was reporting back on her to somebody when Harlow was thirteen— not real. The driver of the truck that killed her being some kind of contractor, aiming for them on purpose—not real.

Still so much to sift through, but it's a start, at least.

Now she and Christina are back from the hospital, the house

returned to them, and as Harlow makes her way upstairs she can feel the difference in the air. No more secrets hidden in the walls, no more strange sounds in the night, and no more ghosts to haunt her. Now she knows what—who—it was all along.

She bypasses her mom's old bedroom and goes to the one she has only stepped foot in once, on that first day here. Eve's room.

Inside it is just like it was on that first day, quiet and still. But now Harlow opens the closet and looks for the panel in the back—the one that, when she pushes it with her fingertips, springs open to reveal a staircase behind it.

"The attic," Clementine said a few days after everything, when she was finally lucid enough to explain. "I've been living in the attic."

She had been spiraling for a while, it transpired. Keeping up appearances for Christina, feeding her stories of nights out with new friends in distant cities, dinners at hidden-away restaurants, decorating the apartment she came back to when her jobs were over. Except she had quit that flight attendant job almost a year ago and scraped by on savings until she lost her apartment nine months later. Then she bounced from couch to couch of old friends, until even they said she couldn't stay anymore, because they weren't really friends anymore either—not since Clem had begun closing herself off from everyone in her life, the years of guilt eating away at her until there was virtually nothing left. "I dream about her all the time," Clem said, looking far away. "That moment. The sound she made when her head hit the fireplace. When she hit the floor."

She had nowhere else to go, she said, and shook her head when Christina said, "You could have come to me. You know you can always come to me. Who else understands what we went through? I'm always here for you, Clem."

"You *don't* understand," Clem said, and here she sounded broken beyond repair, despite all the stitches and staples keeping her together. "You aren't the one responsible for her death. It was me. *I'm* the one who pushed her. You don't ever have to bear that, okay, Chrissy? It's my fault she's dead. It's my fault that Cora's gone—"

Harlow took that as her cue to take Clem's other hand in her own, lacing her fingers through those of the woman who was both a stranger, yet completely known to her. That guilt, the feeling that everything comes down to you, and you alone must carry the weight of that forever—*if I had been driving,* Harlow sometimes thought, about the accident. If she had gotten ready to leave a minute or two faster, or slower, even, so that they would have been crossing that intersection at a different point in time. If she had been a better daughter and somehow fought to save her mom's life in that moment, instead of watching her take her last breath and then abandoning her.

Except none of those things were her fault, not really, and that's what she told Clem, too. "It was an accident," she said. "It's not your fault that my mom died. It's not my fault either. I don't even know if it's the fault of the driver of that truck, or if it was Mom—whichever way, it wasn't a deliberate decision on either of their parts. There was nothing anyone could have done." *There was nothing I could do,* she tells herself, wondering if she'll believe it this time.

"But she wouldn't have been on the run if it wasn't for me,"

Clem said. "So she never would have been there in the first place. Do you see? It all comes back to me."

So she had nowhere else to go, in her own mind, and Clementine did what so many people do: she returned to the scene of the crime.

Standing at the foot of the concealed stairs, Harlow peers up into the gloom. She hears Christina's footsteps on the floorboards, and then her voice as she says, "I can't believe I never knew these were here."

"It makes sense," Harlow says, watching dust motes spiral in the air. "To me, at least. If there's one thing everybody in this family has in common, it's that we are very good at keeping secrets." A secret staircase, to a secret room—a corner of the dusty attic Harlow had stuck her head into when she first arrived, looking at the bones of the roof and insulation covered in an inch-thick layer of dust and insect remains. A secret room built in one corner of that space, bordering the attic Eve told her daughters was off-limits, and that if they ever tried to go up there—through the access panel in the far corner of Christina's bedroom, the one Harlow had used—they were sure to fall through and break every bone in their bodies.

"Still," Christina says, and she sounds young suddenly, as if she has been thrown back to the girl she was when she lived here under Eve's rule. "Even after she had left us, we never found them. We never came in here and explored. Only Clem was brave enough to do it, finally."

Harlow imagines Clementine creeping through the house

alone in the dark, her mind barely holding on, and what she must have thought when she opened the closet full of her mother's old clothes to find the back panel halfway open, revealing a glimpse of the stairs. A perfect place for a guilty conscience to hide itself away. To hide herself away.

Harlow starts up the stairs, Christina behind her. The temperature drops as they ascend, and when Harlow steps out into the room, she shivers. Clementine hadn't brought much with her, that is clear enough. On the floor there is a sleeping bag, unfurled to cover the bare floorboards, and a blanket thrown on top of it. A small cushion, one that matches the set downstairs, sits near the farthest wall, clearly serving as her pillow. To the left is a neat carry-on bag in royal blue, and Harlow imagines this is what Clem used when she was working, envisions a different, brighter kind of Clem striding through the terminals in her heels and uniform, red lipstick on a wide smile. Now it sits open with clothes spilling out of the top, impractical slip dresses and lingerie, thin tights with runs visible even from this distance. To the right Harlow sees where the sour smell is coming from—discarded food remains, the blackened, rotting peels of bananas, an open jar of peanut butter with ants crawling around the rim. There are empty beef jerky wrappers too, and dark, sticky stains on the floor that might be coffee or might be soy sauce, and the cracked remnants of a coffee mug.

"Jesus," Christina says, and she kicks at the corner of Clementine's makeshift bed. "To think she was up here, all this time."

Clem, up here. Clem, the one actually responsible for getting the power turned back on—not Harlow somehow, like Christina had assumed, and not Christina keeping it on all those years for their mother, like Harlow had thought before she knew all the truth.

Harlow walks over the blankets and crouches at the carry-on bag, lifting a pair of tights from the top. She can hear a note of disdain in Christina's voice, like even though she knows Clem is sick and this is all the result of a severe PTSD spiral, she still can't quite believe her sister was willing to live like this. But Harlow can only see how hard she was trying. Some part of Clementine brought her here, and some part of her kept going, feeding herself enough to stay alive, knowing she needed to keep herself warm at night. *It's not perfect,* she wants to tell Christina, *but she's fucking traumatized. What more do you want from her?*

She tosses the tights onto the makeshift bed. Another reason she decided to keep the secret of what really happened to Eve, and who she really was. To tell the truth would mean damning Clem to a punishment for an act that not only did she not mean, but that Harlow isn't sure wasn't warranted. You subject someone to enough pressure, and one day they're likely to snap. You raise your children in cruelty, and one day they're going to repay the favor.

The ringing of Christina's phone interrupts Harlow's thoughts, and she glances over her shoulder.

"It's Mila," Christina says, flipping her curls from one side of her head to the other. "I'll take it downstairs."

"Okay," Harlow says, and turns back to Clem's worldly possessions as she hears Christina take the stairs and her voice greeting her wife, warm and wistful.

She sifts through the clothes, quickly realizing that Clementine packed as if she were going on a tropical vacation, not going to spend the winter in the Washington woods. Those slip dresses, a single pair of jeans, one thin sweater wrapped around something hard and square.

Harlow frowns, unrolling the sweater carefully until a small, lacquered jewelry box comes loose. She catches it and runs her fingers over the warm wood, wondering what treasures are inside, what Clem deemed special enough to bring with her even in her unstable mindset.

When Harlow opens it, she is met with a mess of tangled chains, gold and silver necklaces knotted together, a few earrings trapped in their net. She lifts them up and contemplates untangling them for a second, but then what is beneath catches her attention and she sets the necklaces on the floor, smiling. On the bottom of the jewelry box are photos, and unlike when Harlow found the same thing in her mom's safety-deposit box, this time she doesn't have to guess at who the girls in the images are.

She lifts them out and holds them by the edges, slowly flipping through them in the quiet of the room. Clementine at around fifteen, sixteen maybe, posing to show off a sparkling stone in her navel, a matching glimmering grin on her face. Christina suntanned and smiling behind heart-shaped sunglasses, a clear cup of bright blue icy slush in one hand. Cora on the very same couch that Harlow has sat on downstairs, her mouth halfway through a word and a hand outstretched toward the camera as if telling whichever sister was taking the picture to *stop, god, enough already!*

Harlow's cheeks ache from smiling as she catches glimpses

of their lives, these moments seemingly all in the years between Eve's disappearance and her death, that brief period of time where the girls were free to do as they pleased. Making their own way in the world, experiencing life without their mother's tyrannical rule. She can almost hear their laughter, looking at them in matching pajamas and rainbow socks. Can sense the lightness, seeing them walking hand in hand through the summer woods. Can feel the sun on her own skin as she finds herself looking at a familiar image, Christina and Cora and Clem at the lake, wading in the shallow water. Tears roll down her face and she laughs, breathless, realizing that Clem and her mom have hung on to the same moment even through all their years apart. "Look at you," she says softly, touching a finger to the younger version of her mom, no sign of stress on her bright face, not yet weighed down by darkness. Before fear and paranoia took over, when she was wild and free. Her mom must have pulled her picture from this set, Harlow realizes as she shuffles through a whole series of the girls playing around in the water, sprawled out on the pebble shore, eating burned-to-a-crisp marshmallows. And then again, back in the water, arranged in the same pose as they are in the photo Harlow has: her mom in the middle in cutoffs and a bikini top, Christina on the left in a short white dress, Clem on the right with purple flowers in her hair. And—

Harlow stills, and the imagined heat of the sun on her face disappears, so that she is left in the freezing cold of the attic. Because there is another person in this picture. Or not a person, but—

In her mom's arms, a tiny, mewling thing that Harlow recognizes as surely as if it is herself.

Cora is holding a baby, dimpled legs and chubby arms, dark hair and deep, dark eyes staring at the camera.

Harlow's lips part as she touches the baby's face this time. As she touches her own face.

"What?"

She turns the photo over slowly. Sees the writing on the back.

Cora, Christina, Clementine, and Harlow.

Behind her she senses rather than hears Christina coming back up the stairs. "Hey," Christina says. "What did you find?"

And Harlow turns around slowly, holding the photo up. "What is this?" she says, and she watches the color drain from Christina's face. "I said, *what is this?*"

42

The silence is loud enough to start Harlow's ears ringing.

She's holding the photo up and Christina's just staring at it and Harlow is trying desperately to understand what this means, because it makes no sense.

Why—*how*—is she in this photo? She doesn't belong there. She wasn't born then, she didn't come along until after her mom had fled this place, this house, until she had left her sisters behind— except there she is, with the three of them, defying her own logic of her life.

She can't take her eyes off Christina. Christina, who said she hadn't even known Harlow existed before Harlow picked up the phone and called her. *Did you forget?* she wants to ask. *Did you somehow completely erase all memory of my existence from your brain, because here I am, right beside you. How do you explain that?*

Maybe there is an explanation, Harlow thinks, her mind run- ning through the math, trying to calculate things: maybe this was—no, but then how could—so maybe her mom was the one who—

Harlow shakes her head to quiet the noise, her fingers folding the edges of the photo. "Please," she says to Christina, and she hadn't meant to sound so uncertain, so like she is begging, but all she wants is to understand. "I don't get it. Tell me. Tell me what this means."

Cristina sighs. Mournful. Exhausted. Her eyes are cloudy and her voice soft when she says, "We never wanted you to know. You never needed to know."

Harlow's heartbeat drums in her throat. "Know what?"

Christina sinks to the floor, hands on her knees, so she is level with Harlow. "That night," she says. "When Eve came back." She swallows and looks away. "She didn't come alone."

BEFORE

Cora stares at the ghost in front of her and has to grip the door-frame for support.

The ghost smiles, her pink lips stretching thin, and there is snow in her golden hair. "Surprise," says Eve. "I'm home."

Cora can do nothing but stare at her mother, like an apparition in the dark, except Cora knows this is no vision, no image concocted by her own mind.

No. That would be too lucky.

They have been too lucky, Cora knows. She's always known it, that Eve wouldn't stay gone forever, that at some point she'd have to come back, because of course she would. She couldn't stay away and leave them alone in their happiness without her. No, Eve wouldn't be able to bear that.

"Aren't you going to let me in?" Eve says. "I've had a long drive."

• • • •

Cora feels her heart beginning to slow; the shadows at the edges of her vision recede. Only now does she have the chance to take Eve in: the knee-high boots that look like they cost more than Christina makes in a month, and a heavy black coat tied loosely around her waist, and her face healthy, flush, a brightness to her deep blue eyes. Cora takes a breath and folds her arms across her chest, leaning so she fills the doorframe, not so subtly blocking Eve from entering. "Wow," she says. "Look at you, stranger."

"Cora," Eve says, and there it is: the edge in her tone, the warning that is supposed to be enough to scare Cora back into line. It used to be enough—used to scare Cora out of saying anything she was really thinking, until all that came out of her mouth was what she knew Eve wanted to hear.

But now she is not afraid. "Eve," Cora says back. "I think you should leave."

From behind her Christina calls out, "Who is it?"

And then Clem, laughing: "Yeah, what's taking so long?"

Eve's face lights up at the sound of their voices, and Cora is halfway through turning around, stepping back inside and calling out *No, stay where you are,* but she's too late.

Christina and Clem come tumbling out of the living room, hand in hand, and Cora watches in painful slow motion as they see past her, see who is standing at the door.

"Mom?"

Christina is the one who says it, sounding only faintly surprised, as if she, too, knew that Eve wouldn't stay away. Wouldn't leave them alone like she should.

"Chrissy," Eve says brightly. "Clem! Oh, I've missed you so much."

Cora stays firm in the doorway. No. This cannot happen. Eve cannot come back into this house, back into their lives, like nothing at all is wrong. *You left us,* she wants to say. *You abandoned us, and we were happy! So go, back to wherever it is you've been these last two years, and leave us be. We are so much better off without you.*

"I think you should leave," Cora repeats, speaking the words slowly and clearly. *Get out.* "What are you even doing here? Jesus, Mom, it's been two years. Why have you come back now?"

Eve's smile is conspiratorial, and she tugs at the belt around her coat until it falls loose. "Girls. I want you to meet someone."

Eve peels her coat open, and there, peeking out from between the lapels, Cora sees it. Soft downy hair and hands balled into tiny fists, resting on their mother's chest. A small and delicate bundle strapped to Eve with creamy white fabric. "Baby girl," Eve says, rubbing her knuckle against the baby's plump cheek, "these are your sisters. Girls—" She looks up, smiling. "Meet your new sister. Harlow."

43

"Eve . . . Eve is my mother?"

As soon as the words are out of her mouth Harlow feels the flood of bitter saliva, like she's about to throw up. She presses both hands over her mouth, willing the sensation away. Willing what Christina just told her to be a lie.

But Christina is deadly serious, so quiet and curled inward, as if to protect herself against a volley of blows that isn't coming. "I'm so sorry this is how you found out," she says, and then again: "You were never supposed to know."

"I still don't understand," Harlow says. "I wasn't born until after—" Wait. What had Oliver Prescott said? *Cora came to me and asked me for my help getting fake papers. Birth certificate, passport, all that shit.* And *I'm the only reason she was able to get out of this place, I'm the only reason you even—*

She closes her eyes, suddenly understanding how that sentence ends, what it means. *I'm the only reason you even exist.* A fake birth certificate, with a fake birth date and a fake name, too. Harlow Ford, not Kennedy. "That's what he meant," she says, looking at Christina again. "Oliver. That's the favor he did for my mom. He got papers that made it look like I was born some time when I wasn't. That made it look like my mom *was* my mom. Didn't he?"

Christina nods wordlessly.

"Why?" Harlow claws at her cheeks. "What happened, that night? I want the real truth this time, Christina. I want to know everything."

Wind whistles through the roof, louder up there than in the rest of the house. Christina presses her hands together and doesn't look at Harlow as she talks. "It's like I told you before. Eve showed up, two years to the day after she vanished. Except she wasn't on her own. She brought you with her. She told us she needed to come home, so we could all be a family, so she could have all her girls together. But we didn't want her to come home, and we *really* didn't want her to have another daughter to hurt. We didn't want her to hurt *you*," Christina says. "I mean, it was like a nightmare. When she opened up her coat and there was this tiny little thing inside—*you* inside—it was the most afraid I've ever been, because all I could see was her—your—future playing out in front of me, and I knew exactly what it was going to be. The yelling and the punishments, scars on your perfect skin, a life of abuse that would leave you changed forever—my whole life, everything we had experienced, but when it happened to us there was nothing we could do to change it. When it was us that she was terrorizing, we were too young to understand what was happening to us, and too young to do anything. But we were older, that night, and we'd spent all that time without her in our lives and we were better, in a lot of ways. Tougher." Christina does meet Harlow's gaze now, and she is fiery. "I saw you, tiny, innocent you, and I knew in that moment there was no way were letting Eve stay, but there was no way we were letting her leave with you, either."

Harlow holds a hand to her throat, the thrum of her pulse. "The argument," she says. "It was about—"

"Yes," Christina says. "You."

BEFORE

They are all screaming over each other, Eve pulling at Clem, and Cora forcing herself between the two of them, and Christina cowering in the corner, their brand-new baby sister who they will *not* let Eve take in her arms, rocking back and forth as the baby wails, and Cora manages to wrench Eve's hand off Clem but it only makes Eve angrier, so she turns to Cora and pushes her back, her nostrils flaring, and then Clem says, "Why can't you just leave us *alone*—"

She shoves Eve, a two-handed push with a short lifetime's worth of rage behind it, and Eve stumbles backward and it would be fine except her foot catches on the rug and she twists as she begins to fall, hands thrown out in front of her to meet the floor, but her head meets the corner of the fireplace first, a sickening thud as she smacks into it and then bounces off, to land on the floor, silent and still.

There is no more noise then. Even the baby finally soothes

into quiet as Christina keeps on rocking her, back and forth, back and forth. Only the silence as the three of them stare down at Eve prone on the living room floor, the blood that begins to spread across the rug, a garish red halo behind her head.

Cora looks from the body to Clem, in awe, almost. *She is so strong,* she thinks. *Maybe we didn't fail her, after all.*

Except Clem is crying already, staring at her outstretched hands. "I didn't mean it," she says, horrified. "Oh my god, I didn't mean it, I didn't mean to—"

Cora moves first, crouching and putting her fingers to Eve's neck. *Is that a pulse?* She moves her fingers around, unsure. But Eve's eyes are closed, her face slack, and her chest doesn't seem to be moving.

And the circle of blood around her head only gets bigger, falling into the cracks of the floorboards and traveling along, like it's found a new vein. No pulse, no breathing, and a head injury—

"I think—"

Clem moans. "Don't say it, don't say she's dead, oh my god, Cora—"

Cora stands and faces them. "I can't find a pulse." Cora reaches for Clem's outstretched hands and takes them in her own, squeezing tight. "We couldn't let her stay, and she wasn't going to leave without her."

"It was an accident," Christina says, sounding only a little hysterical. The baby—*Harlow,* Cora thinks, *her name is Harlow*—writhes against Christina's chest. "Maybe she's not—Cora, come here. I'll check again. She can't be dead, like—she just hit her head. That's it."

It's like they're in some twisted black comedy, a body on the floor and the three of them calculating exactly *how* dead their mother is. But Cora goes over anyway, and Christina hands her the baby.

Everything recedes the moment Harlow is in her arms. Cora has never even held a baby before, not really—she was two when Clem was born, barely cognizant. Now there is this tiny, hot little creature in her arms, and it's not *somebody*, it's her *sister*, and she's staring up at Cora with the same big, brown eyes they all have, as if she's saying *Yes, it's me, I'm one of you, hello.*

"Hi," she whispers, bouncing the baby the way Christina was doing, the way she seemed to like. "Look! You're home now. You like that? You wanna live with your sisters?"

Christina wrings her hands over Eve's body. "I can't find a pulse either," she says. "Shit, this is bad. What do we do? Call 911?"

Cora's bouncing the baby and Harlow smiles, a gummy happy grin that sets Cora's heart on fire. No. They are not letting their sister end up in foster care or with some well-meaning evangelical Christians who need a brown baby to add to their collection or whatever. They are not going to let Clem get in trouble for protecting herself, for protecting all of them. And they are not going to call 911.

She turns to her sisters, their newest member still happy in her arms. "No," Cora says. "I have a better plan."

44

Harlow stares at the tiny photograph version of herself. "Is that it?" she says. "Is that everything?"

"Yes," Christina says, and then she winces. "Wait, shit. No. I told you your mom left first. That she wrote a note and took off."

Harlow is too shell-shocked to be surprised by anything else. "That was a lie, too," she says, but it's not a question.

"Clem was the one who ran," Christina says. "She left us first. She was okay for a while but she hated being in the house, thinking about what had happened. I thought once she was out of here she'd be okay. She was okay, for a long time—she's traveled so far, farther than me or your mom ever got. But I guess there are some things you can't outrun."

"So when did Mom leave?" Mom. Sister. *My mom is really my sister,* she thinks. *Cora, my sister. Eve, my mother.* Except of course Cora was always, will always, be her mom—the one who raised her, who kept her safe in her own flawed way, was there for every busted knee and period-stain emergency and the late night *Mom? I'm a lesbian* pronouncement three years ago. Who loved her enough to make sure she didn't have to endure the same pain she had. Who loved her even if she couldn't always show it, was consumed by other things. Fear. Guilt. The memory of the body buried in the cold dirt and the threat that one day it would catch up to her, that someday Eve would be found in the woods and it would all be over.

Eve.

She is nothing, Harlow thinks, and maybe if she tells herself that enough, she'll believe it, one day. Won't be thinking about the blood running in her veins, how half her DNA comes from a woman who chose cruelty over love, and the other half still comes from a stranger she has no idea about.

All of a sudden she remembers the way Clem caressed her face on that night they came crashing out of the woods and said *You look nothing like her. Oh, I'm so glad that you look nothing like her.* In the moment she had pushed past it, chalked it up to Clem's shaky state of mind, but now it falls into place: it wasn't Cora who Clem was talking about. It was Eve.

"When did my mom leave?" Harlow asks again, a hand snaking up her neck to tug on her short curls. "How come it was her that took me, and not you?"

Now Christina smiles, the slightest rise of her lips. "She loved you," Christina says. "She loved you so much, and you loved her so much—you would smile as soon as you heard her voice. You two were attached as soon as you got here. It only made sense that she would be the one to raise you. And it had to be that you were her daughter, not our sister, because no one could ever know that Eve came back. We didn't ever want you to know about her either. And we knew you couldn't stay here. People would ask too many questions. So we made a plan for Cora to leave, and to take you with her, and we'd see how it went. We put the house in her name, so if there was ever a problem, she'd have that to fall back on. A safety net for you, in a way." She pauses, quiet. "I didn't know about the shit with Oliver until now. I mean, I knew she got your new birth certificate, but I didn't know who she went to or how much it cost. She told me she'd handled it, and I believed her. Then she left, and it was just me here, and she checked in pretty regularly at first, but then I started to hear from her less and less, and then before I realized, it had been something like six months, and I couldn't get in touch with her at all. Then I get this message from her saying you're safe, you're both doing okay, and not to worry. That I should go off and live my own life now. That I deserved to do that." She holds her hands up. "And that was it."

That was it.

Harlow wonders where they were when her mom wrote and sent that last message. Who they were pretending to be when she wrote to tell her sister goodbye, basically. "Didn't you worry?" she asks. "Didn't you try to find her?" *To find us,* she means.

"Of course I worried," Christina says, "but also—I finally left here. Moved away, started working my first big-girl job, got a place to live that I could decorate however I wanted and no one could tell me no. I met friends, I fell in love for the first time, had my heart broken for the first time . . . I started to see why Clem had run, why Cora distanced herself. It was so much easier to forget everything about our lives here when I was away. I didn't have to be the Christina who did such terrible things, had such awful secrets. I got to be free."

Harlow looks at the photograph of the four of them, four sisters, where it has fallen on the floor. She smooths her fingers over the creases, trying to press it out back to how it was before. *They look so happy,* she thinks; you would never even know all that they were hiding deep inside. You would never know that in only a few months they would be fractured, splintered across the country, the world. "I was wrong," Harlow says quietly.

Christina leans over. "What?"

"Before, when I first found out about . . . all of this," Harlow says, drawing a spiral in the air. "When I found out you and Clem existed, and about Eve and how she was missing, I thought that must be why my mom ran. I thought you had all run, and then you came here and told me about your life, Clem flying around the world, and I thought I was wrong. You two were living perfectly happy lives in a way that me and my mom weren't. But I was wrong. Or, I was right the first time," she says, and then rubs at her eyes, tired despite the morning hour. "I don't know. I don't know anything anymore, this is all so—" She gulps at the cold air, and it stings as it enters her lungs. "It's a lot." Too much, maybe.

But then Christina takes Harlow's chin gently, turning her to face the light. "I know one thing, and I need to make sure you know it too," she says fiercely. "Your mom loved you. She was nowhere fucking *near* perfect, but everything she did, she did because she loved you."

"I know," Harlow says, and she lets Christina pull her into an embrace, wrapping her arms so tight around her aunt—her *sister,* now she has two sisters, what the *fuck*—and allows herself to collapse into the kind of heartbroken weeping that leaves a body wracked, aching, wrung out and empty. "I know."

When Harlow arrived here in Crescent Ridge, Sloane told her the house was haunted. Harlow let herself give in to that in some ways, turning the sounds of Clem in this attic above her into a ghost, imagining voices and smells that were no more than memories, really. Of course there was no ghost in the woods. This house, this place, she knows now, is not haunted.

But we are. She and Christina and Clementine, her mom, too, chased by the ghosts of secrets better left buried. Chased by fears kept too close to the heart. *We are haunted,* Harlow thinks, and there are shadows of all the girls she's ever been beating on her rib cage, desperate to get out, and there are the lies she has told and the ones she will go on to tell, truths she will die without letting slip. You don't live a life like that without paying for it in some way.

Harlow can feel Christina's heartbeat, slower than her own, and on her fingers she still feels the cold wet dirt of that night. The chill of the bone against her fingertips. The remains of Eve, the woman who brought her into this world, hidden deep in the ground.

A month ago Harlow didn't even know that Eve existed, and now she is going to carry her around for the rest of her life. Haunted not by fantastical ghosts and creatures in the night, but by her own blood, by the very fabric of her own being. *I am my own ghost,* Harlow thinks, and outside the trees whisper their agreement, and again:

I am my own ghost.

45

ONE MONTH LATER

Harlow waits outside the coroner's office, watching through the window as fat white clouds drift across a perfectly clear blue sky. The kind of weather that, from looking, seems like a scorching summer day, until you step into the winter chill and remember where you are.

She had to hold her breath as she drove back within the town limits, the sign welcoming her to Madigan blurring by and retreating into the distance in the rearview. Couldn't put it off any longer, and now that she has nothing left in Crescent Ridge, she has finally returned.

The door to the office opens, startling Harlow out of her cloud watching. "Ms. Ford?" The coroner is young, pretty, freckles dotting her amber skin and a raft of rainbow pins decorating her ID badge. A pretty girl, except Harlow finds she doesn't have the same desperate reaction to every one she sees now. She's been trying, recently, to fantasize a little less. Live in reality and let the unknown remain exactly that, instead of filling in every gap with a series of constructed daydreams. Pretty girls are still nice to look at, but Harlow doesn't have to imagine their entire lives, map herself onto a projection of them. They're just trying to live. Harlow thinks she might start doing the same.

She gets to her feet. "Yes," she says, "that's me. Harlow Ford."

She follows the coroner into the viewing room. This is all a technicality, really: the police know who they have in the morgue, but still they need a relative to identify her, to check every box. Her mom was brought to the hospital once she was cut out of the wreckage, a liaison officer told her, and pronounced dead upon arrival. The driver of the eighteen-wheeler had a shattered collarbone and a mild concussion but otherwise walked away unharmed. And it turns out that neither of them were to blame for the collision: blame the electrical fault instead, which set the lights on the wrong cues and resulted in too many greens all at the same time. The driver would still like to apologize, the liaison officer said, but Harlow turned it down. *Tell him I understand,* she said. *It wasn't his fault. He doesn't need to be absolved by me.* True, yes, but also she still has to be careful. So far the cops don't seem to suspect that she was anywhere near the accident that night, that there was anybody else in the car, and Harlow wants to keep it that way. She doesn't even know how she would begin to explain fleeing the scene, abandoning her mom dead in the middle of the street. Not in any way that anybody besides her and her mom, maybe her newfound sisters, would understand.

When the coroner pulls the sheet back, Harlow nods once. "Yes," she says. "That's her. That's my mom."

The coroner marks something on a tablet and says, "I'll give you a minute with her, if you'd like," and Harlow nods again, so the coroner leaves, and then they are alone.

Just Harlow and her mom.

Harlow sighs, slowly. "Hi, Mom." She has never really believed what people say about dead bodies looking peaceful, but now that she is faced with her mom's corpse, she has to admit she was wrong. They've done a good job making her look clean and unblemished, as if she slipped away while she was sleeping rather than being torn apart by metal. Although she is mostly covered by a stiff blue sheet—maybe beneath that, Harlow thinks, she would see the real damage. Better that it's like this, her mom with her eyes closed and the slightest shadow of bruising on her jaw, her long curls fanned out around her head, her brown skin sickly but smooth. Harlow touches her own jaw, the place where Oliver Prescott slammed her face into the ground. It's almost healed now, but there's still a mark left. Scars she is going to wear forever, on her skin—her jaw, her head—and under it—her ribs, her brain. Her heart.

Harlow runs a hand through her hair, which has grown just long enough for her to be able to do that now, and she's not sure if she's going to cut it back to how it was before or keep growing it out so she can eventually match Clem and Christina. She looks around and spots a chair, which she drags over to sit beside her mom. "Hi," she says again once she's sitting down. "Sorry I took so long to come and get you. Although—you were the one who told me to run and never look back, so I guess me coming back for you is probably more than you expected. So actually, you're welcome,

I guess." She laughs, and it should sound wrong in this grim place, but instead it bounces off the cold, gleaming surfaces and refracts into a thousand tiny notes. "I kind of fucked up, Mom. I didn't do what you told me. I did the exact opposite of what you told me, really, going to Crescent Ridge. But you fucked up too. I mean, you made some *wild* choices in your life. Including somehow stealing an entire year of my life, so that I had to find out I'm eighteen, not seventeen, and I still don't know when you managed to do that. I can't believe I've been a legal fucking adult for an entire *year* without knowing. But I don't blame you." She pauses, pinching the skin on the back of her left hand. "No. That's a lie. I do blame you. Jesus, I'm still so fucking mad at you, you know? I'm so *mad*, Mom, like all the time. If you had just told me the truth I wouldn't have done any of this. But you could never let me *in* and now it's too late. But you could have trusted me. Maybe I could have carried some of the weight for you. Then maybe we wouldn't be here. So was it worth it? You kept the truth about my life secret from me like you wanted, but it ended up killing you, and I found everything out anyway. So was it really worth it, in the end?"

Harlow swipes at her nose and clears her throat. "I know you were doing your best. I don't know what I would have done if I were in your position. Probably run too, but I couldn't have taken somebody else's kid with me—I'm too selfish for that," she says. "I'm done with that place now, though. I don't know what I'm going to do with the house—wait, let's hold on that for a second. I own a *house*, Mom. I inherited an entire *house* from you. After all those apartments, you finally got me a house! Not the dollhouse I wanted when I was seven, but close enough, I guess. Anyway.

I don't know what I'm doing with it, but I don't need to be there. I've gotten everything out of that town and that place."

Without trying, she pictures Sloane. Maybe the only thing she sometimes thinks is left for her there, except even they are done; she knows that. They have to be done, because of the way things were left. A couple days after Harlow finally learned the entire truth and was on her way to visit Clem in the hospital, she drove up the dirt road only to find Sloane's car waiting at the other end. When Sloane stepped out of the car, she held her hands up like she was surrendering. "You didn't leave me any choice," she called out, her words penetrating the protective shield of Harlow's car. "What else was I supposed to do?"

So Harlow got out of her car too. Sloane wasn't lying: Harlow had ignored every call and text and any chance of a possible inter-action with her since the night of the shooting. What was she ever going to say? *Yeah, I lied about who I really am, and then your dad was blackmailing me and my sisters because they killed Eve, and Clementine forced your dad into shooting her because she wanted to die and she wanted to force him to leave us alone, and I have no idea where your dad is now, but wherever he is, I don't think he's ever planning on coming back*—no. No fucking way Sloane needed to know any of that.

But there she was, leaning against the hood of her car, as mag-netic as ever, and this was the real reason Harlow had been avoid-ing her. She couldn't trust herself not to let the truth slip out, if she was face-to-face with this girl. Like all reason fell out of her mind when she was within Sloane's atmosphere, being swallowed up by those stormy eyes and electric sense of her. "Sorry," Harlow said. "It's been a crazy week."

"Tell me about it," Sloane said. "First it turns out you aren't exactly who you said you were, and now my dad isn't just a deadbeat, but also a wanted felon accused of attempted murder. Just a *stellar* week for me, too." Then she softened, guilt bright on her face. "I'm sorry. About Clementine. I have no idea why he would—" She stopped. "She's going to be okay, though. Right? That's what I heard."

Harlow nodded. Keep it simple, short answers, nothing more than the absolute basics. "She'll be home soon," she said. "They fixed her up pretty good."

Sloane twisted her fingers together. "I just don't get it," she said. "I mean—your aunt showing up here, and my dad—I never thought he would do some shit like that. I'm not stupid, I knew he always had some kind of shit going on, but—I figured small time. Fraud, robberies, maybe drugs, but trying to kill someone?"

Simple. Short. Basic. "I don't get it either," Harlow said. "I guess the only way to know would be to ask him. And I don't think that's going to happen."

Sloane watched her, uncertainty in her gaze. "So it had nothing to do with whatever was going on with you that day?" she asked.

"What do you mean?"

"At my house. When you saw him there, you completely changed. You basically ran out of there as fast as you could." Sloane raised her eyebrows. "Come on, Harlow. Tell me what it was."

"I don't really remember," Harlow lied. "That day, I mean. It's all kind of a blur now."

"Harlow."

"What?" Harlow shrugged, pretending her adrenaline wasn't

spiking. "I swear to you, it had nothing to do with your dad. How could it? That was the first time I met him. Up until then, he was just the guy you mentioned once or twice. And now he's the guy who tried to kill Clementine."

It was cruel, she knew, but at least that part was also the truth. The way they'd twisted it to be, anyway. Sloane shifted uncomfortably. "Did you see him? That night?"

Harlow shook her head, tired of the effort of playing it all down now. "No," she said. "I heard the noise, and I ran outside, and Clem was lying on the ground. Like I said, it's all kind of a blur." She opens the car door. "And now I really have to go. Visiting hours are only between ten and twelve."

"Harlow, wait—"

But she didn't wait. Only got in the car and drove on, past Sloane standing there, blond hair whipping in the wind. *Pretty girls want the truth,* she thought to herself. *Sorry, Sloane.*

Harlow comes back to the present, her mom's unmoving form on the table in front of her, the stringent smell of whatever cleaning fluids they use down here. "So, yeah. Done with Crescent Ridge, done with Severn House. And done, I think, with the old way of doing things, Mom. You taught me really well, but I'm so tired of running. Besides, I'm not sure what there is to run from anymore. Now I know everything. What you went through. What you had to do. And what Clem did for all of us." She nods. "I mean, was it the *best* decision-making on her part? No, but it worked. And we're going to get her help. Me and Christina. I'm going to go stay with her for a while. I think I might go back to school and try to finish out the rest of the year in one place. Can you even fucking imagine?" She laughs again. "I guess we'll see how it all works out. Me with the family I always wondered about. Them with the sister they killed to protect." She's quiet for a moment, sitting in the everlasting silence with her mom, so like the quiet they used to share on those late-night car rides. The sound of the road and music playing soft.

"Oh." Harlow sits up and pulls the souvenir from her back pocket. "I can't believe I almost forgot to tell you. I met Ruby." Harlow looks at the postcard, running her fingers over the web of drawings. It took her way too long, really, to understand why her mom had kept the postcard—not as a memory of a place, but of a girl. Her only girl, who left her a black kiss that her mom could carry forever. "I really liked her," Harlow says. "I could tell how much she loved you, still. And you kept this from her, for all those years." She presses her thumb against the lipstick print, like she can feel Ruby's energy through the faded outline. "I'll keep it safe for you."

She glances up at the clock on the wall, conscious that the coroner will probably walk back in any moment. "I have to go now," she says. "I'll tell Christina and Clem that you said good-bye." Then Harlow leans over and places a kiss on her mom's cold, waxy cheek. A touch in death that she never could have given her in life. "Bye, Mom. I love you. Thank you for everything you did for me."

This time when she leaves her mom behind, it feels less like an abandoning and more like the only kind of ending they were ever going to have. One sacrifice after another, for all those years.

When Harlow walks out into the cold, clear day, she closes her eyes and turns her face up to the sun.

BEFORE

Cora can feel the sweat trickling down her spine as she and Christina carry Eve's body through the woods. She's wrapped up in a sheet, along with a shovel and the only pair of gloves Cora could find beneath the sink, neon-pink rubber.

They left Clem at the house, because someone needed to watch the baby, although in the state Clem had worked herself into, Cora doubted she would be any use in an emergency. *Better than she would be doing this,* Christina said.

It takes them what feels like forever to find the right place, a small clearing where they can dig without getting stopped by the gnarled roots of trees. They take it in turns to dig, the earth tough from the near freeze of the night. It takes even longer to carve a deep enough space in the ground, and when they're done, Cora's arms are screaming from the effort. She steps back and throws down the shovel, breathing heavy. "Okay," she says. "Ready."

They pick up either end of the sheet. Cora counts, and on

three, they swing it into the grave and let go, the weight of Eve's limp body dragging the sheet down, and she lands with a thud on the hard-packed soil. *She looks like a doll,* Cora thinks idly, like one of the toys they were never allowed to have, splayed out at odd angles on a backdrop of shiny golden hair.

"Okay," she breathes. "Give me the—"

She's interrupted by the sound of Christina retching and looks over to see her sister spitting stringy, pale vomit onto the forest floor. "I can't," Christina says through a sob.

Cora moves to her and strokes her hair as Christina brings up whatever's left in her stomach. "Are you done?" she says gently, after thirty seconds pass with no more noise.

Christina nods but doesn't look up. "I can't do it," she whispers. "Cora, I can't—"

"Okay." Cora helps her sister to her feet. "It's okay, Chrissy," she says, even though she never calls her that, only Clem does. "I got this."

Christina stares at her with watery eyes. "You do?"

Cora nods. "Go back to the house," she says. "Take care of Clem. Take care of the baby. I'll see you back there."

She waits until Christina has vanished back in the direction of the house and picks up the shovel. *Do it quickly,* she tells herself. *Don't look at her. Just do it.*

She follows her own instructions, listening to instead of watching the first scoop of dirt fall onto Eve's body. Lift, turn, fall. Lift, turn, fall. It's repetitive, meditative even. As long as she doesn't look down at the body.

But then curiosity gets the better of her, and Cora looks down at her mother as she drops another shovelful of dirt onto her, and what she sees makes her stumble and almost fall into the grave herself.

Down there, beneath a thin dusting of dirt, Eve's eyes are open.

They stare up at Cora, unblinking, and for a second Cora thinks maybe this is fine, maybe this is something that happens to dead bodies; after all, hasn't she seen in shows and movies how people close the eyelids so softly? Maybe this is the opposite of that, somehow.

Except then, as Cora watches, Eve blinks.

And her mouth moves.

"Help me."

The dirt drifts off her lips as the words rasp their way out and up to Cora's ears, and there is a long, silent moment where Cora can only stare in shock at the sight below her.

Eve, head sticky with blood, pale as the moon itself, moving. Talking, breathing.

Not dead.

A series of possibilities flickers through Cora's mind like a film-strip: She could jump down now and help Eve up out of the hole. She could run back to the house calling for her sisters, to let them know Eve is still alive and Clem doesn't have to bear the responsibility of their mother's death. They could get her to a hospital and let the doctors stitch her up, piece together whatever else might be broken. They wouldn't have to be the girls who killed their own mother. They wouldn't have to be the girls who buried her in the woods.

But all of that is followed immediately by the rest of what Cora knows will be true: they won't get away with this. It's not the cops she's afraid of, but Eve. There's no way she'll let them forget what they did to her, as accidental as it was. And then—she'll never leave them, she'll never leave Harlow, they'll be back to the same argument that precipitated her almost death in the first place. *And then what?* Cora thinks, watching Eve as she continues to mewl down there, begging Cora for help. *She takes that baby and she does to her exactly what she did to us. She takes that baby and tells her she's ugly, she's worthless, she's stupid stupid stupid, she hits that baby with a belt until the skin rips and that baby is left with a scar to remind her for the rest of her life how unloved she is.*

I can't let her do that. I can't let her come back here and choke the life out of us again. I can't, I can't, I won't.

Down in the hole Eve summons all her strength and pulls an arm free of the dirt, reaching up to the sky. To her daughter watching. "Cora," she says, a thin plea. "Help me."

Without Eve, they can be free. That's the way it has to be, Cora decides. This is how it has to end.

She picks the shovel back up and begins piling the dirt down on top of her mother. It falls into Eve's cloudy eyes, fills her open mouth. She is alive but too weak to fight what is coming for her.

Cora piles dirt into the grave until she can no longer see any part of Eve. Until she can no longer hear her cries for help.

When she is done, she turns her back on her mother's final resting place and leaves her behind.

ACKNOWLEDGMENTS

My biggest thanks to the following:

Suzie Townsend, Sophia Ramos, and everyone at New Leaf.

Kate Prosswimmer, Nicole Fiorica, Morgan Maple, Lindsey Ferris, and everyone at McElderry Books.

Ella Whiddett, Molly Holt, Emma Quick, Emma Matthewson, Tia Albert, and everyone at Hot Key Books.

Elena Garnu, for the beautiful cover art.

Maggie Horne, Rory Power, and Janet McNally.

My family.